BOOKS BY VINCENT "CHIP" LOCOCO

TEMPESTA'S DREAM

A Story of Love, Friendship, and Opera

THE BELLAFORTUNA SERIES

A SONG FOR BELLAFORTUNA - **Book 1**

SAVING THE MUSIC - **Book 2**

SICILIAN MELODY - **Book 3**

THE DEVIL'S JAZZ

The Haunted Chronicles of the Axman of New Orleans

NOTE TO READER

Although this is a novel, the story is based on the true crimes of The Axman of New Orleans, one of America's first serial killers, who targeted the Sicilian immigrant community of the Crescent City spanning the years of 1910-1919.

The murderer chose to spell his name as "Axman" instead of the conventional "Axeman." Consequently, this distinct spelling of the killer's identity is used throughout the novel.

The letter written by the Axman to the *Times-Picayune* is reproduced exactly as it appeared in the published letter dated March 16, 1919.

In the novel, Henry's Bar, a New Orleans institution for over 100 years, is featured. Originally known as Crone's Bar during the story's timeframe, I opted for the present name, Henry's Bar, to pay homage to the bar's connection to the Krewe of Thoth, a Mardi Gras organization of which I am a member. The krewe continues the tradition of stopping along the route on Thoth Sunday to toast to the bar's role in its creation.

THE DEVIL'S JAZZ

THE HAUNTED CHRONICLES OF THE AXMAN OF NEW ORLEANS

VINCENT B. "CHIP" LOCOCO

Cefalutana Press

Monument to the Immigrant - commissioned by The Italian American Marching Club of New Orleans, sculpted by Franco Alessandrini, erected in March 1995 along the banks of the Mississippi River.

CONTENTS

Rejoice at the death and cry at the birth: New Orleans sticks close to the Scriptures.

— JELLY ROLL MORTON

THE DEVIL'S JAZZ

1

RETIREMENT

New Orleans was in his soul. The city's rhythm of life pulsed through his veins like the syncopated notes of jazz music that spilled from the many dimly lit bars. Despite having seen the seedy underbelly of the city, he still could overlook it all and find her hidden charms – the magic that danced through the alleys and whispered along the cobbled streets of the French Quarter.

Even after all these years, he remained entranced by the captivating landscapes of the Crescent City. From the majestic oaks of City Park, which stood like ancient guardians, to the eternal embrace of the mighty Mississippi River, New Orleans beckoned like a siren, her call irresistible and seductive. But it was truly in the people where he found his inspiration to look past her flaws and still call this city home.

Giancarlo Rabito had arrived in New Orleans from Sicily many years ago and was now one of the top police detectives on the New Orleans Police Force. He was also the leading expert on the Black Hand, a loosely knit extortionist group of Sicilian-Americans who at one time had preyed unfettered on their fellow Sicilian immigrants. Connected to the *Mafia*, the Black Hand's reign of terror had finally come to an end, with many crediting Giancarlo, the de facto "Italian Expert" on the police force, for the result. With his growing reputation, he had received many offers to leave New Orleans and bring his expertise to other cities, like New York, Boston, or Chicago. But Giancarlo rejected them all. He knew better than most that once New Orleans took hold, she never let go.

It was on a cold December afternoon when Giancarlo lingered outside the imposing Criminal Court building that housed the police headquarters on the corner of Saratoga Street and Tulane Avenue. Pulling up the collar of his trademark trench coat to ward off the chill, Giancarlo couldn't shake the somber feeling that engulfed his entire essence.

Christmas was only four days away, but Giancarlo was not in the Christmas spirit. Just a week ago, the New Orleans Police Chief, James Reynolds, a man he considered a friend and ally, had been senselessly shot and killed in his own office by another officer suffering from a mental illness. The news left Giancarlo reeling with a mixture of shock, sorrow, and disbelief.

For a Catholic city like New Orleans, what should have been a joyous and festive time was already tempered in late 1917 by the ongoing war in Europe. Chief Reynolds' death only added to the bleak atmosphere that seemed to hang in the air.

Giancarlo stood before the courthouse, feeling the weight of anticipation settle on his shoulders like a heavy cloak. He had considered every possible alternative, but none offered a viable solution. His mind, a swirling sea of memories, replayed past cases, reliving encounters with victims and criminals alike. Among the haunting recollections, the spectre of the Cleaver loomed large, a killer who had terrorized Sicilian immigrants in attacks many years ago.

Giancarlo had led the investigation, yet the elusive identity of the culprit remained forever shrouded in mystery. With the Cleaver's sudden disappearance six years ago, the killer had eluded justice, casting a long shadow on Giancarlo's career and soul, leaving an indelible mark on his journey in law enforcement.

With a determined gait, he ascended the stairs of the courthouse, each one marking a step closer to a decision he wished he didn't have to make. As he reached the summit, he paused, as his hand reflexively clutched his chest, the pain serving as an unwelcome confirmation that his decision was the right one.

Entering the building, Giancarlo removed his Fedora hat and proceeded down the hallway toward the office of the newly appointed police Chief, Frank T. Mooney. Mooney was no cop, but he had been tapped by his good friend, Mayor Martin Behrman, as the man chosen to replace Reynolds. The skepticism surrounding Mooney's appointment lingered like a ghost in the hallways; a railroad man stepping into a world of crime and justice. The announcement had been met with raised eyebrows from both citizens and the press. Even within the police department there were murmurs of doubt due to Mooney's lack of prior police experience, questioning his suitability for the role.

Giancarlo intentionally avoided making eye contact with

his fellow detectives and policemen along the hallways in an effort to keep the purpose of his visit strictly to himself. None of his colleagues were privy to the reason behind his meeting, and he was not inclined to engage in discussions about it with anyone.

Giancarlo hesitated for a moment at the threshold of the Chief's office door, which was slightly ajar. He took a deep breath, gathering his thoughts and composing himself before entering.

The desk in the middle of the room stood bare, amid unpacked boxes and the lingering scent of fresh paint. The bullet holes in the walls from the shooting of Chief Reynolds were no longer visible. Seated behind the desk was the new police Chief, Frank Mooney.

Chief Mooney looked up, his gaze meeting Giancarlo's with a mix of curiosity and perhaps a trace of self-doubt. He rose, extending his hand in a welcoming gesture, and remarked, "They said you wanted to speak with me. How can I help the Italian Expert on my police force?"

Giancarlo shook Chief Mooney's hand firmly and responded, "I hope you're settling into your new job." Despite his proficiency in English after decades living in New Orleans, Giancarlo's words still carried a distinct Sicilian accent.

"It's daunting, but I'm managing. I have big shoes to fill." Chief Mooney paused, before adding, "I'm sorry for the loss of your friend. I know you were close to Chief Reynolds."

"He will be missed by many," Giancarlo responded with solemn dignity.

"Well, I will do my best to fill the void his death has left on this department. However, I'm sure you have heard the whispers, and they are true. I ran railroad companies. I have never been a cop. And yet, Mayor Behrman has asked me to serve the citizens of this city. I agreed to answer that call, all the while knowing that I will need to rely on people like yourself for help, you long-time members of the Department."

Giancarlo took another deep breath before replying, "That's why I am here, and why I wanted to speak with you." Giancarlo's voice resonated with an unwavering resolve, yet his eyes betrayed a profound sadness, burdened by the weight of his decision.

Deliberately, he reached into the pocket of his trench coat and took out his badge. His gaze lingered on the emblem of his duty; the silent testament of years spent in service. Without a word, he placed the badge on the Chief's desk, the metallic thud echoing around the room.

Surprised and uncertain, Mooney inquired, "What are you doing?"

"The time has come for me to retire."

"Retire? Why? How old are you?"

"I'm 53, Chief." Giancarlo then raised his hand to his chest and continued, "I visited the Police Benevolent Association's doctor. He thinks it's best. The very day that Chief Reynolds was killed, the doctor gave me my prognosis."

Chief Mooney laid both of his hands on his desk as he slumped forward. "I know we don't know each other very well yet, but I've already been told of your unbelievable work as the 'Italian Expert.' Your commitment and success in that work have not gone unnoticed. I was counting on that work continuing."

"I would if I could, but I know this is the right decision.

My mind is made up. My heart condition will not allow me to work anymore."

"Does the doctor think you will get better?"

"No, Chief. I'm on a road with no return."

Chief Mooney lowered his head at Giancarlo's words. Meanwhile, Giancarlo pulled back his trench coat, revealing his service revolver. As he was reaching to unholster it, presumably to turn it over, Chief Mooney looked up and intervened, saying, "No, Giancarlo. Keep it. You earned it."

"*Ah, Grazie,*" he responded before catching himself, a subtle reminder that his Sicilian roots still sneaked their way into his speech every now and then. Quickly, he amended, "I mean, thank you, Chief."

Chief Mooney extended his hand toward Giancarlo. "I would have liked to work with you."

"Good luck, Chief."

"Luck? I think I will need more than luck."

Giancarlo offered a reassuring smile, giving the Chief's hand a final firm shake. "Well, if you or the department ever need an old detective's advice, you know where to find me."

Chief Mooney returned the smile with a nod of appreciation.

With that, Giancarlo turned and departed from the office, closing the door behind him. It was a symbolic end to a chapter of his life dedicated to justice and duty.

As he left the building and stepped into the cool embrace of the early evening, his thoughts suddenly circled back to the Cleaver, that elusive phantom who had escaped his clutches. Giancarlo had sworn to protect and serve the citizens of New Orleans. But his failure to bring the killer to justice was like a stain on his career he could not wash away.

And now with his retirement looming, it seemed as if his legacy was marred, incomplete, like an unfinished symphony, fully aware that now the final note would most likely never be written.

The retired detective glanced back at the imposing courthouse, a fortress of justice that seemed like a mere illusion in the face of the early evening light. Giancarlo turned and began walking away, a man on the precipice of an unresolved past and an uncertain future.

2

A VISION IN LITTLE PALERMO

A short time later, Giancarlo walked down Royal Street in the French Quarter, surrounded by festively adorned shops prepared for Christmas. Elegant wrought iron balconies whispered tales of the city's old Spanish influences. Gas lamps flickered, casting dancing shadows on the buildings. Familiar faces waved from windows, reciprocating Giancarlo's nod and pinch of his fedora. The most cherished aspects of his career were the connections he had forged in this community, and he was keenly aware that these would be the things he'd miss the most in retirement.

Giancarlo stopped at the intersection of Conti Street to let a mule-pulled carriage pass. The clip-clop sound, as the mule's hooves hit the cobblestone street, echoed against the close-knit buildings of the Quarter, providing an almost mesmerizing effect on Giancarlo, transporting him to another time. The allure of the Quarter, where echoes of the past intertwined with the present, tugged at him as usual.

Resuming his walk, he crossed Pirates Alley and continued down Royal Street, entering the area once occupied by Creoles but now bustling with many Sicilian immigrant families who called this part of the Quarter home. Vendors haggled in the Sicilian dialect of Italian, and children laughed and played in the streets, adding their own music to the symphony of life in the Quarter.

The Sicilian-New Orleans connection began in the 1830s with Sicilian merchants establishing a citrus trade into America via the Mississippi River. Starting in 1880, around 300,000 Sicilians arrived in another wave of immigration in response to Louisiana farmers seeking sugarcane field workers after the Civil War. While some worked in fields, many settled in the deteriorating, abandoned Creole homes in the Quarter. The influx of Sicilian immigrants was so substantial that this part of the Quarter quickly earned the moniker "Little Palermo."

Facing challenges like language barriers, low-paying jobs, prejudice, and violence, Sicilian immigrants found solace in this community. They worked alongside Black families, which brought them even more ridicule from white Americans. The dream of a better life in America clashed with the harsh reality of prejudice and hard labor they encountered upon arrival.

Giancarlo strolled through the weathered streets toward his apartment, nestled in an area where the resilient Sicilian spirit endured—in its food, music, and fellowship. A deep sense of pride welled up in him as he admired the diverse businesses lining the streets, the vibrant scenes never failing to inspire him. He passed produce stands overflowing with their colorful array of fruits and vegetables showcasing the bounties of Louisiana soil and the tradition of Sicilian farming. Olive oil import businesses beckoned with reminders of the sun-drenched Mediterranean, their bottles lining the windows like golden treasures. Scattered macaroni factories, where skilled hands crafted the finest pasta, added to the old world feel of the neighborhood. Aromas of Sicilian cuisines wafted from open restaurant doors, teasing Giancarlo with authentic flavors and creating an immersive experience in the heart of the thriving community.

Yet, the heart and soul of Little Palermo resided in its corner groceries, found on nearly every street. These havens, offering Sicilian ingredients and delicacies were more than places to shop; they served as anchors, firmly rooting the community in its cultural roots. Within their walls, conversations flowed like a gentle stream, people exchanging stories as precious currency. Usually guided by the shopkeeper, each anecdote contributed to the collective narrative of the Sicilian experience in America.

Over the years, there had been a changing dynamic in Little Palermo as Sicilians began to move out of the Quarter into different sections of the city, such as the Bywater, the Marigny, the Carrollton area, and even across the Mississippi River to the town of Gretna on the Westbank, with each neighborhood establishing their own grocery stores. Yet for now, in 1917, the heart of Little Palermo remained lively and beating, with the vast majority of Sicilians still residing and working in that part of the city.

Giancarlo reached his apartment in the heart of Little Palermo. It was on the second floor above Giorlando's Grocery, a store owned by Augustino Giorlando and his wife

Maria. Giancarlo noticed Augustino, a fellow Sicilian immigrant, standing outside his small grocery store, puffing on a cigar. The grocer had arrived in the city years ago with dreams of a better life, opening the small grocery soon after his arrival. Augustino became a fixture, a beloved figure in the neighborhood, who knew all his patrons by name and could anticipate their needs. As Giancarlo approached, Augustino inquired, "How are you this fine evening?"

"I'm well, Augustino. On my way to eat dinner in my apartment before heading to the French Opera House."

"Verdi's *Aida* tonight, I heard."

"Yes. I can't wait to see it." Giancarlo paused and then said, "Augustino, you and Maria have been so kind to me, from when I first moved in so many years ago now. I wanted to let you both know that I turned in my badge today. I'm officially retired."

"Oh no. Retired? You will be missed, especially by all of us Sicilians. You were an honest cop, unlike some. You always looked out for us. Always."

"I tried."

"Tried? You kept the Black Hand at bay as best you could. You also investigated the attacks on those Sicilians back in '10 and '11. There are some who think the attacker knew you were onto him, and that you were close to arresting him for his terrible deeds. They think that's why he disappeared and has not been heard from these past six years."

Giancarlo's expression changed at the mention of those attacks; the very same attacks he had thought about earlier that afternoon outside the courthouse. He shrugged his shoulders. "I never could discover who he was."

"The Cleaver," said Augustino.

"Yes, the Cleaver. That was the name the press gave him because of the weapon he used: meat cleavers."

Augustino raised his finger, and pointed it toward himself. "There are some, and I guess you could say I'm in that number, who believe that he was not a man at all but a phantom. An instrument of the devil himself."

Giancarlo smiled. "New Orleans is filled with stories of ghosts and the supernatural. But in my business, there are no ghosts or boogeymen. The murderer is just as real as the murdered. He is flesh and blood, just like us."

"Think what you want, but I believe the Cleaver was a phantom. And that is why he has never been found. But he's gone now, thank the Lord. Hasn't killed since Joe Davi in '11. Gruesome scenes back then. That was a terrifying time."

Images of the grisly aftermath of the last heinous crime committed by the Cleaver flashed through Giancarlo's mind. Blood everywhere. Blood on the walls. Joe Davi's once-white bedsheets drenched in blood. Giancarlo was a young detective back then, young and in good health. He investigated that murder along with the two earlier attacks, which he also believed to were the work of the Cleaver. The one unifying thread among all three episodes was that the victims were all grocery owners of Sicilian descent. None of the attacks happened in Little Palermo but the connection had still been obvious.

But that was years ago. And the Cleaver and the fear he brought to the Sicilian community had disappeared. He had vanished, vanished like a phantom, as Augustino had said.

Augustino interrupted Giancarlo's thoughts. "I'm so sorry to hear the news of your retirement. What's your plan now?"

"First? I plan to talk to you about lowering my rent," Giancarlo said, smiling broadly.

"We will see what we can do," his landlord responded before adding, "And then what?"

"Maybe write a book about my time as a detective on the New Orleans Police Force. People may find my stories interesting."

"Oh yes, lots of intrigue, I bet. The Sherlock Holmes of New Orleans."

Giancarlo laughed.

"Well, enjoy the opera. Nice way to celebrate the night of your retirement."

"It is."

"Soon, let's have dinner with Sebastian Mandina and Charlie Cortimiglia. Charlie's wife, Rosie, just had a baby girl. He could use a night out."

"Oh, Rosie had the baby—a girl. Dinner would be a wonderful idea."

"And we will raise a glass to your retirement."

"*Grazie. Arrivederci*, Augustino."

Giancarlo walked to a small door that faced Governor Nicholls Street. A long stairwell led to the second floor where the door to his apartment was located down a small hallway. The Cleaver from earlier was still on his mind. He felt his chest tighten as he remembered interviewing the victims of the first attacks. They had survived, but their wounds were terrible to behold. And then the bloodied scene from the Davi home flashed again before his eyes, the only fatality of the Cleaver.

As Giancarlo ascended the creaking stairs, an eerie premonition crept over him. The dimly lit stairwell seemed to whisper forebodings, casting shadows on the walls that danced liked elusive spirits. The horrific scenes of the Davi bedroom would not leave his mind. The tightness in his chest took his breath away.

Midway along the stairs, he paused, sucking more and more air into his lungs to help him proceed. After a moment, he started trudging up the stairs again until he reached the top. Closing his eyes, he clutched his chest as he bent over, catching his breath.

When he opened his eyes at the top of the stairs, he suddenly became aware of a sinuous shadow that flickered on the ground beneath him, like a serpent slithering through the darkness. As he lifted his head, a shadowy figure stood above him, more of a spirit than a man. The figure's shape undulated and twisted like smoke and mist. A shiver ran down Giancarlo's spine, as a wave of coldness washed over him.

The apparition held something in his raised right hand high above his head. Giancarlo's heart pounded in his chest, as he blinked his eyes, trying to focus on the item the figure held. It was then that he could make out the object. It was a gleaming meat cleaver.

Instinctively, he raised his arm in defense and lowered his head, bracing himself for the fatal blow that he was sure would come. But no strike fell. Instead, when Giancarlo dared to look up again, he found himself alone in the hallway. The figure had vanished without a trace.

A wave of dizziness washed over him, his chest constricted with fear and disbelief. The apparition's image lingered in his mind, refusing to fade away.

Clutching his chest tighter, Giancarlo's strength failed him, and he collapsed to the floor, darkness enveloping his senses as he succumbed to unconsciousness, the world around him fading into blackness.

3

THE CLEAVER

*M*oments later, Giancarlo's eyes flashed open. With trepidation, he gazed around his surroundings, but there was no sign of the figure or his gleaming meat cleaver. Giancarlo's body relaxed as his chest pain subsided, but his fear remained.

As he remained sprawled across the floor, each crime scene unfolded vividly in his thoughts, like a festering wound that refused to heal. His mind continued to replay the ghastly scenes he had witnessed while investigating the Cleaver's crimes. Bloody images flashed behind his eyes in a frenzied loop. The faces of each victim haunted him. He could almost hear their voices, see their pleading eyes, and feel their fear.

Giancarlo had spent countless hours back then pouring over evidence, trying to piece together the puzzle that was the Cleaver case to discover the madman's identity. He had studied his patterns and methods, hoping to find a breakthrough that would end the Cleaver's reign of terror. He recalled the sleepless nights, his weary eyes burning from hours spent pouring over case files and chasing leads that always led to dead ends.

But the Cleaver had remained elusive. And now, with his retirement, Giancarlo couldn't help but feel a sense of defeat. The Cleaver's trail of pain and suffering would forever go unpunished. It would haunt him for the rest of his life.

Giancarlo closed his eyes, allowing the tide of recollections to wash over him. The hallway around him faded away, as his mind became filled with memories. With a heavy sigh, he thought back and remembered each and every one of the Cleaver's attacks.

Victim 1 – August Crutti

The first known attack of the Cleaver had happened on Saturday, August 13, 1910 at 3 a.m. August and Harriet Crutti, both children of Sicilian immigrants, owned a grocery store and saloon at the corner of Royal and Lesseps Streets in the area of town known as the Bywater. Their home, where they lived with their two boys, was part of the same building where their business was located, as was customary in the area and the Quarter. The establishment had only been open for a month at the time of the incident.

Something awoke Harriet in the earliest hours of the morning. As she rolled over in bed, she was shocked to find a shadowy figure standing over her, lifting the mosquito netting around the bed in one hand and holding a bloody meat cleaver in the other. She sat up in bed trying to find her husband. Her eyes locked on August lying in a pool of blood on the floor.

Thinking her husband was dead, she said, "You've killed him."

"Give me the money," the shadowy figure growled.

Harriet pulled a small box from under her pillow. She opened it and handed the cash to the man.

He quickly looked at the money before asking, "Is that all you got? I want all of it."

"I swear, that's all I have," she lied.

The man turned to leave. However, as he glanced at the table in the corner, his gaze fell upon the birdcage that housed the Crutti's mockingbird. He grabbed the birdcage and left.

After the man had left, August suddenly moaned on the floor, prompting Harriet to leap from her bed and rush to aid her ailing husband. Her screams would awaken her neighbors who came to assist.

Outside, in the darkness of the night, the perpetrator's grip on the meat cleaver relaxed, and he let it fall from his fingers. With the birdcage still in his hand, he leapt over a fence in the back of the property and continued walking.

Half a block away, he found respite on the stoop of a home, according to a witness who saw a man with a birdcage. The gentle strains of the jazz tune, *Make that Trombone Laugh,* slipped softly from his lips. As he settled on the stoop, he reached into his pocket and pulled out the cash the woman had handed to him. He counted it, all $8.00.

His attention then turned to the birdcage. He slowly opened the door, the hinges creaking softly. The captive bird quickly hopped through the open door, and then with an elegant flutter of its wings, soared into the night sky. The man then stood up and disappeared into the darkness, all the while humming his jazz song.

When the police arrived on the scene later that morning, August Crutti had already been brought to Charity Hospital where the injuries to his head and face were found to be non-life threatening.

The man in charge of investigating the crime was James Reynolds, then Chief of Detectives. Reynolds was a friendly man liked by everyone on the force.

Reynolds brought his young protégé, Giancarlo Rabito, to assist with the Crutti investigation. Reynolds had been instrumental in getting Giancarlo a job in the police department, and eventually helping him to be promoted to detective within just a few years. Giancarlo interviewed Harriet Crutti, who had remained at the home while her husband was at the hospital. After conducting his interview, Giancarlo walked the entire property and was able to reconstruct the events as best he could.

He possessed an uncanny, almost intuitive talent for such tasks, and his ability to articulate and share his hypotheses with others was even more impressive. Police investigations relied on the detective's intuition and gut feelings, as forensics were a new and untested science.

Giancarlo stood in the room where the attack had happened. James Reynolds was seated in a chair, while three other detectives stood off to the side. Giancarlo proceeded to outline his hypotheses.

The man had forced open the kitchen door of the home using a railroad shoe pin. He had removed his shoes prior to entering the home, most likely to avoid making unwanted sounds on the wooden floor. Based on the description provided by Mrs. Crutti, the attacker was believed to be a white male in his mid-thirties, about five feet six inches tall, heavy and with no beard. He had dark hair, tucked under a black derby hat that he was wearing. He wore a workman's shirt and dark pants. He spoke unaccented English.

With that information, Reynolds proceeded to look for the culprit. Days later, he charged John Flannery, a cocaine addict of diminutive stature in his early twenties, with the attack on Mr. Crutti. Giancarlo argued with his friend, Reynolds, and the District Attorney, Benjamin Didier, that they had the wrong man. He did not match the description of the Crutti attacker. But he had recently been arrested for breaking into another grocery store using a railroad shoe pin, and so Reynolds and Didier were convinced that they had their man.

Flannery was ultimately declared mentally unfit to stand trial. He remained in prison awaiting his transfer to a mental hospital. The Crutti case was closed. August Crutti was reunited with his relieved wife after his wounds healed, and the once-lost mockingbird miraculously returned, perching itself on the Crutti's roof after a few days. The Crutti crime was listed as a simple burglary and assault.

Something inside Giancarlo remained unsettled. But as the days passed, Giancarlo slowly began to forget about the Crutti case, for the time being.

Victims 2 and 3 – Conchetta and Joseph Rissetto

The second known attack of the Cleaver happened just a little over a month later, on Saturday, September 20, 1910, at 1:45 a.m. Joseph and Conchetta Rissetto owned a grocery store at the corner of Tonti Street and London Avenue. They were both children of Sicilian immigrants who moved to New Orleans and had married seventeen years earlier. Their grocery store had a pool hall and saloon that were both very popular with the local Black community with whom the Italians shared the neighborhood.

The couple was asleep in their bed. A dark figure slithered into their room. Conchetta was struck first. The swing broke her cheekbone. A surge of agonizing pain tore through her, as her eyes flew open, glittering in terror. The next swing came across her delicate neck. That stirred her husband sleeping next to her. Just as Joseph awoke, he was struck twice in the face by the assailant, who then quickly fled. He dropped his weapon in the front yard, and then vanished, hopping over a fence in the front yard.

Despite bleeding profusely from his wounds, Joseph grabbed his revolver from his nightstand, walked to the porch, and fired it in the night air. Neighbors ran to the home and found the bloody scene. They rushed the couple to Charity Hospital, where doctors worked feverishly to save them. They both survived, although the injuries left Joseph disfigured and blind in one eye, while Conchetta was paralyzed on one side of her face for the rest of her life.

Detective Reynolds was back on the scene, along with Giancarlo, who, in the dead of night, was roaming the yard with a flashlight in his hand looking for clues. The whole time, Giancarlo kept thinking of the Crutti case, and he could not stop comparing the two.

A few hours later, all of the detectives were back inside the home as Giancarlo reconstructed the scene for them. Reporters stood outside, anxious for news. Giancarlo started out by pointing out that nothing had been stolen. No money had even been taken from the cash register in the grocery. The footprints outside where the intruder had entered showed he had removed his shoes before climbing through an unlatched window in the kitchen. The weapon was a meat cleaver. It was later discovered that the meat cleaver had been stolen from a butcher stall several weeks ago. Mrs. Rissetto was able to provide a concise description of the attacker, which closely matched the description given by Mrs. Crutti.

With John Flannery sitting in jail awaiting his move to the mental institution, Giancarlo fought the desire to scream out to his boss, "See, I told you, you had the wrong man!" But instead, he kept quiet. He thought it was unnecessary to rub the error in the face of his mentor, who had been so instrumental in getting him where he was today.

And yet, despite the evidence, when Reynolds left that meeting, he announced to the reporters outside the home that the crime was a result of a burglary gone bad. While Reynolds was speaking to the press, Giancarlo stood off to the side. He was convinced the attacks on August Crutti and the Rissettos were committed by the same person. As to the motive, he had no answer.

The newspaper headlines over the next few days began to cause panic in the city. They referred to the unknown assailant as *The Meat Cleaver Fiend.*

Although Reynolds was as yet unconvinced of the connection between the attacks, he did allow that Flannery was likely not the attacker of August Crutti. Within days of the second attack, the charges against Flannery were dropped.

Among the press and the police, there was much debate.

Was the attack on the Rissettos a burglary? Were the attacks on the Rissettos carried out by the same man who had attacked August Crutti?

Some of the papers noted that both families were of Sicilian descent. They begin to wonder if it was the result of a vendetta, an attack by the Black Hand? This hypothesis soon took hold.

The grocery owners sprinkled throughout Little Palermo slept uneasily at night. The entire city was on edge. But the weeks passed, and no other attacks happened. The calendar turned to 1911, and the tensions of the citizens finally relaxed.

In February, 1911, James Reynolds was promoted to Police Chief. Giancarlo was happy for him but hated to have him leave his position as Chief of Detectives. George Bombay, a long-time detective, who despised the Sicilian community, was promoted to Chief of Detectives, and was now Giancarlo's boss.

Victims 4 and 5 – Mary and Joe Davi

The third attack of the Cleaver happened on Tuesday, June 27, 1911 at 1:30 a.m. Joseph and Mary Davi owned a grocery store on the corner of Arts and Galvez Streets. The grocery had an attached saloon and the Davis's lived above their businesses. They both had arrived in the city as children, immigrating from Sicily. The two had married just five months earlier. They loved each other and relished being married, as they put their hearts and souls into the business.

Something awoke Mary that night. She looked around the room and saw a dark figure standing nearby. She tried to wake her husband.

The man in the room gruffly asked, "Where is your money?"

Mary was unable to respond because of her fear. The man then suddenly grabbed a porcelain jug off the nightstand and, through the mosquito netting, smashed it against Mary's head. She fell back onto the bed, unconscious. At that point, Joe Davi stirred in the bed.

The man raised his meat cleaver and brutally beat Joe Davi to death, crushing his skull with blow after blow beating the poor man's brains out. Joe Davi's blood soaked the sheets and pillows on the bed, and splattered up the walls inside the bedroom. The brutal force of the blows collapsed the leg of the bed on Joe's side.

Once finished, the figure stood breathlessly over the results of his horrendous deed, holding the bloody meat cleaver in his hand. Mary had just come to and was laying perfectly still. While humming the popular jazz tune, *Chinatown, My Chinatown,* he vanished out of the building.

With Chief Reynolds out of town on business, the man in charge of the investigation was the Chief of Detectives, George Bombay. He was the first to arrive at the home. The gruesome scene inside the bedroom shocked even the long-time detective. Most murders in the city were the result of passionate outbursts, either in barroom brawls or domestic fights, or a vendetta hit by the Black Hand. But outright murder with no known motive was unknown for this city.

Giancarlo arrived on scene about a half an hour later. When he first entered the bedroom, his stomach turned, and his face went ashen white. He had never seen such a scene as that before him. Finally gathering himself, he went about his job of reconstructing the events as best he could.

Later, he made his report to George Bombay. The intruder had used a railroad shoe pin to pry open a window and enter the building. Nothing had been stolen from the residence, and no money taken from the business. As for his interview of Mary Davi, all she could report was that the intruder was a white male, around 5'8 or 5'10, heavy build, who wore a workman's shirt and dark pants, and who spoke unaccented English. She also believed he did not have shoes on.

Giancarlo was convinced that the Cleaver was the culprit. He was back, but this time he had brought death to a citizen of Giancarlo's beloved city. He told Detective Bombay his theory.

Detective Bombay gave no response to Giancarlo and left the premises immediately. Detective Bombay did not buy in. He firmly believed the attack was a hit by the Black Hand. He proceeded to telegram Chief Reynolds, alerting him to the death of Joe Davi and sharing his belief that the Black Hand was behind the attack. To his credit, Chief Reynolds began to wonder if indeed all of the attacks were connected to one man.

When Giancarlo left the crime scene early that morning, a reporter caught up to him. It was Giancarlo's first public comment on any of the attacks. He simply said, "There is no apparent motive here."

However, off the record, he told the reporter why he believed all of the attacks had been perpetrated by the same individual. Giancarlo felt it was his duty to let the citizens know what they were facing, since it was clear Bombay and the others would not make the connection.

With the information supplied by Giancarlo, the reporter's story that afternoon emerged under the headline in the newspaper, proclaiming *FIENDISH CLEAVER ABROAD AGAIN*. While not explicitly naming Giancarlo, the accompanying article reported the connections Giancarlo had drawn between all the attacks.

The Sicilian community was ratcheted with fear. People dreaded the nighttime and most slept uneasily. Chief Reynolds made a few arrests of suspects, but none of them turned out to be connected to the crime, typically proven in a matter of days.

Everyone waited for the next attack. But it never came. Most of the non-Italian citizens were convinced that the Cleaver was a member of the Black Hand. That was the answer non-Italians *wanted* to believe. Some on the police force agreed. Other people, including those inside the Sicilian community, had begun whispering that the Cleaver was the boogeyman of their nightmares.

Giancarlo knew that the Cleaver was not connected to the Black Hand. His gut told him this was no *Mafia* hit. This was something that the city had never seen before. A cold, blooded killer. Someway and somehow, Giancarlo would find him, if it was the last thing he did.

It was after the Davi murder that Giancarlo began nightly patrols of various sections of the city, focusing particularly on the Sicilian owned grocery stores nestled on dimly lit streets, ever with a watchful eye, looking out for any sign of the Cleaver. But he never saw a thing, and there were no further attacks. The Cleaver had vanished.

As the years passed, people began to put the terrible events behind them as the Cleaver stories became nothing more than legend and neighborhood lore. He became a bedtime story told by parents to frighten naughty children.

The Cleaver was gone.

GIANCARLO SAT UP IN THE HALLWAY OUTSIDE HIS APARTMENT. The pain inside his chest had finally relented, yet the memories of the Cleaver attacks left him feeling ill at ease. Sweat beaded around his temples, as he tried to push the Cleaver attacks and the scenes of the Davi murder back into the recesses of his mind. It was a futile effort. Resigned to the fact that he could not shake those dark memories, he rose from the floor and made his way into his apartment.

A short time later, he was seated at his modest kitchen table, eating a tomato sandwich with a glass of red wine. He ate quickly, as he still wanted to attend the opera.

He finished eating and then walked out of his apartment on the way to the Opera House just a few blocks away.

4

THE FRENCH OPERA HOUSE

owering over the city on the corner of Toulouse and Bourbon Streets, with its gleaming white façade, sat the majestic and elegant French Opera House. Designed by renowned architect James Gallier Jr., it was completed in 1859. The 80-foot-tall structure stood as both a testament to and the pinnacle of high society in New Orleans.

The fact that New Orleans would have such a world-class opera house did not come as a surprise. Long before New York became the American capital of opera, New Orleans held that place of honor.

Opera in the city dated back to 1796. Many French and Italian operas had their American premieres in New Orleans, such as *Mignon* by Ambroise Thomas, *Le Cid* by Jules Massenet, *Samson et Dalila* by Camille Saint-Saëns, *Adriana Lecouvreur* by Francesco Cilea.

The opera house was the vision of one man, Charles Boudousquié, who had been the director of the opera company at the Théâtre d'Orléans. When Boudousquié got into a dispute with the new owners of the Orléans, he became determined to build a grand new house for French opera. The glorious French Opera House was the result.

Built in Italianate style, the house became the center of social activity in New Orleans. It hosted not only operas but also vaudeville acts, debuts, benefits, receptions, concerts, and even Mardi Gras balls for decades.

By 1917, the opera house had fallen onto hard times. The War raging in Europe had taken its toll on attendance. There was also a new competing sound in the city. Jazz had entered the scene and there was a clash between the old and the new.

On February 26, 1917, the Original Dixieland Jazz Band, led by a Sicilian immigrant named Nick LaRocca, released the world's first jazz record for the Victor Talking Machine Company. It introduced New Orleans jazz to the world. The record's two songs were *Livery Stable Blues* and *Dixie Jazz Band One Step*.

Jazz most likely originated in the Voodoo rituals of Congo Square before the Civil War. However, it was in the brothels, saloons, and dancehalls of Storyville that the true jazz sound developed—and where the genre acquired its name.

Storyville, renowned as the city's red-light district, owed its name to Sidney Story, the city leader who authored legislation legalizing prostitution in the area. Legend suggests that the jasmine-scented perfumes worn by the girls inspired the nickname "jazz." Jelly Roll Morton pounded out his tunes on pianos all over Storyville, while a young, up-and-coming trumpeter began making a name for himself, playing nightly. His name was Louis Armstrong.

But in 1917, Storyville was shut down by reformers

seeking to reshape the city's landscape. However, despite their best efforts to suppress jazz, it endured and even thrived, emerging as a rival to opera for cultural dominance.

The question of whether the city could support both jazz and opera was on the minds of many. Because of its financial crisis, the French Opera House had changed hands and was now owned by Tulane University, who engaged the French tenor Agustarello Affre to run things. There was a newfound belief that it would thrive under this new leadership and that opera would continue to be the beacon of high society in New Orleans.

GIANCARLO ARRIVED AT THE OPERA HOUSE JUST AS THE LAST OF the attendees pulled into the carriage lane on Bourbon Street. The women exited their carriages in splendid gowns, with the men accompanying them in full dress, complete with top hats. Giancarlo looked in awe at their appearance and felt slightly embarrassed when he looked down at his brown, tweed suit with a darker brown tie.

He proceeded beneath a balcony where a few patrons stood, taking in the views of the street scene on Bourbon Street. He continued through an open-air arcade and to the front door, showing his ticket to the attendant. He then walked into the beautiful lobby.

There were just a few patrons in the lobby, as most were already seated. He checked his pocket watch and saw it was close to starting time for the performance. Trying to avoid breathlessness, he slowly went up the stunning staircase, which had been built by some of the best artisans in the city.

He passed the second floor where off to the right stood the club room, a den for the very wealthy, which was empty now as the opera was about to start. Giancarlo continued slowly to the third floor.

He walked through a curtain and into the theater. He found his seat that was conveniently on the aisle close to where he had entered. A woman in a beautiful, lace purple dress was seated next to him. He recognized her immediately, but she was first to greet him.

"Detective Rabito, glad to see you at the opera," she said, as Giancarlo sat down.

Giancarlo was immediately taken by her looks, as Caroline Saxon was a woman of immense, regal beauty. Her diamond necklace lay just above the low neckline of her dress, adding an extra element of glamor to her appearance. Now, before the death of her husband, Caroline Saxon would have been seated on the first floor. But now, everyone knew that money was tight for the widow. Her move to the third tier was evidence of this fall from grace.

Giancarlo responded, "Good evening, Mrs. Saxon. I love Verdi and can't wait to see *Aida*."

Mrs. Saxon smiled, yet her eyes betrayed a hint of sadness. "You always loved the arts," she said softly. "I remember meeting you and your lovely wife for the first time during the intermission of *Manon*, so many years ago now. She was such a beautiful, kind woman. I miss her so."

Her words evoked a feeling of longing and sadness in him. "Yes, she was truly a remarkable woman," he replied. "I'm sorry for your loss as well."

Recognizing the shared grief between them, she smiled again, while Giancarlo's gaze drifted towards the vast expanse of the elliptical auditorium. He was always in awe of the architectural beauty of the place. The stage, situated on a curved apron, commanded the attention of the crowd. In front of the stage was the orchestra pit, its musicians poised to breathe life into Verdi's music.

His gaze then shifted toward the parquette, which was the seating area closest to the stage. Encircling the parquette were four tiers of seating. The first two tiers contained stalls and boxes. The third tier held seats that provided cheap tickets for white patrons. Non-whites were only allowed in the fourth tier of seating.

Mrs. Saxon tapped his arm. "Did you get a program?"

"No. I forgot. I was trying to get to my seat in time."

"I have two. My friend is not coming. Here you go," she said, handing him the program. On the cover were the words,

French Opera House, 1917-1918 Season.

But it was the picture on the program that quickly caught his attention. There was a drawing of a chorus girl, a radiant and graceful young woman adorned in dancer's attire. She struck a captivating pose, captured mid-arabesque ouverte. Holding the program tight, he found himself transfixed by the image.

Mrs. Saxon noticed his intense reaction and asked, "Are you alright? It's as if you have seen a ghost."

Giancarlo loosened his grip and laid the program on his lap. He turned toward Mrs. Saxon and replied, "I have."

The conductor entered the pit right at that point, and the audience erupted in applause. Then the Prelude of *Aida* began. Giancarlo tried to get lost in the music, but now and then, his eyes would glance down toward the picture of the woman on the program. Her name was Marguerite. The drawing of her was as a much younger woman from when Giancarlo knew her. Her death had been the first investigation Giancarlo had ever handled as a young detective.

First, the apparition of the Cleaver in his home earlier tonight and now the face of Marguerite. He had to wonder if this would be how he would spend the rest of his days in retirement, haunted by old ghosts. He guessed maybe that was why so many of those who had retired before him spent their days drowning in cocktail glasses, a mechanism to forget and dismiss from their mind all that they had born witness to. Things that people were not supposed to see. Policemen see the same crime scenes, but the detectives relive every grim detail repeatedly in their minds as they try to ascertain what had occurred. Giancarlo had seen a lot as a detective, and it had all started with the story of Marguerite.

While *Aida's* music swelled during the Triumphal March, Giancarlo's thoughts brought him back to that first investigation.

MARGUERITE WAS BORN MAGGIE O'DONNELL IN THE CITY OF New Orleans. She was the youngest of twelve children born to Irish immigrants and the only one of the O'Donnell girls to inherit her mother's beauty. At eighteen, she married Octave Sauvé. They were happy. Then the Civil War erupted, and her husband left to fight. Her five brothers and four of her sisters' husbands all died in the War. Octave survived and returned, broke and broken. He was bitter and began to treat Maggie terribly. Unbeknownst to him, she began working as a chorus girl at the French Opera House, changing her name to Marguerite.

Back then, Marguerite was a beautiful girl with a gorgeous voice. She loved being a part of the theater world. She was not sad when a few years later, her husband died of yellow fever; But then the disease wiped out the rest of her family. Alone, she continued working at the opera, a place she loved with all of her heart.

As she aged and her beauty diminished, the opera company slowly cast her less and less. Although still attractive, the exquisite looks of her youth had vanished. Her once flowing black hair was now almost entirely white, which she kept neatly fashioned in a tight bun.

It was at this time that she met Monsieur de Boisblanc, a wealthy gentleman. They married, and then soon thereafter her elderly new husband died, leaving her a sizable sum of money.

With her career as a chorus girl ending, she used her money to open a pastry shop called *Les Camelias*, located near her beloved opera house. Now, not knowing anything about being a pastry chef, she used her money to take a trip to Paris, where she lured the young protégé of a famous baker in Paris to return with her to New Orleans. The twenty-one-year-old Pierre des Grieux quickly showcased his talent at the little pastry shop, which became the favorite after-show spot of the patrons of the French Opera House.

Then, an unexpected love also blossomed between the young chef and the aging Marguerite. His lovemaking made her feel young again, as he used sexual techniques he had learned in the brothels of Paris. He called her, *La Primavera*, an Italian word meaning Spring. After they made love, he would always produce a red rose, that he would lay between her breasts while they lay naked on the bed.

But, just as Marguerite was hoping for a marriage proposal, her young chef's eyes looked elsewhere. Lisette Carre, a young soprano at the opera house, caught his attention when she entered the pastry shop one afternoon. It was after a rehearsal of Bizet's *Carmen*. That encounter resulted in the two meeting in his apartment later that night, where they made love for the first time. A friend of Marguerite's saw the lovers leave the apartment later, kissing before they parted. The friend told Marguerite about the encounter.

Over the next few weeks, Marguerite followed Pierre. She sat outside his apartment door on three occasions, listening to the sounds of lovemaking within. The fervent moans of pleasure coming from Lisette not only served to deepen Marguerite's feelings of sadness and resentment but made her depressed and angry.

This is where Giancarlo, a newly appointed detective, enters this sordid tale.

Pierre and Lisette were both found dead in his apartment one morning in 1902. They were lying nude in bed together, wrapped in an embrace. A single, red rose lay across his chest. Giancarlo arrived on the scene and was told by the investigating policemen that the two had died from a gas leak.

However, some of the neighbors were beside themselves as they reported that they had seen a witch, and that the witch had killed the couple. They described a pale woman, garbed in a long white dress in tatters, which draped loosely around her form. Her long, white hair hung down by her back, in a disheveled manner.

However, the most shocking part of her appearance were her eyes. They were described as a piercing, intense shade of red, glowing with an unnatural luminescence. This detail made it clear she was not of this world, fueling the belief that she was not of the realm of the living.

They even said who it was: the owner of *Les Camelias*, Marguerite.

Giancarlo proceeded to Marguerite's apartment, but she was not home. He called upon her landlord who let him in. On her nightstand, next to the drawing of her as a young woman, the same drawing which now graced the program for the current opera season, was where Giancarlo found the note, later to be identified as her suicide note. In that note, she swore vengeance against Pierre, his lover, and anyone else who caused her harm, for eternity. Giancarlo quickly went downstairs to the pastry shop, but it was closed. Another detective came running down the street. Giancarlo's presence was needed at the opera house.

A chill washed over him when he walked into the dimly lit auditorium, the sight before him providing the true meaning of the note he had found. There, suspended from the catwalk high above the stage, hung Marguerite's lifeless body, swaying gently in the stillness of the theater. She had levied the harshest of punishments against herself for her crimes. The opera stage, once a gleaming symbol of her artistry and beauty, now bore witness to her violent end. It was a tragedy that would make Puccini weep.

The Police Chief's conclusions, based on Giancarlo's

report, were soon known throughout the Quarter. Marguerite had murdered Pierre and Lisette by turning on the gas inside the apartment, and then she'd gone to the opera house where she hung herself.

But those who reported seeing the apparition were convinced she had hung herself first and that her ghost had killed her lover and rival. And indeed, after these tragic events, people claimed to see a woman in a long white, tattered dress, with piercing red eyes, walking between the opera house and the apartment where the murder had happened. At other times, people reported seeing her peering out from the windows of the theater. Some even said they could hear the sounds of a woman wailing when they passed by late at night.

People began to call her the "Witch of the French Opera House." Giancarlo scoffed at the notion, and repeated his mantra: the murderer is just as real as the murdered.

As the first act of *Aida* came to a close, Giancarlo crumbled the program up in his hands. First the image of the Cleaver earlier that evening and now the memories stirred by the picture of Marguerite. He was overwhelmed. He told Mrs. Saxon that he was not feeling well, and with a polite smile, he left his seat and made his way towards the exit.

He walked out the front door of the theater on Bourbon Street. The opera house's grand façade was bathed in the soft, romantic glow of the gas lamps. Giancarlo paused, taking a moment to gather his thoughts. He was so much looking forward to the intermission, a time he cherished for discussing the performance with fellow opera aficionados out in the opulent lobby. Intermissions at the French Opera House confirmed what he knew. Opera and the opera house were a world unto themselves. Where people of all walks of life came together to share in the magic, the music, and the drama.

As he reluctantly turned away from the front doors, and began walking down Bourbon Street, he couldn't help but cast a wistful glance upward to the windows on the second floor. He could see patrons engaged in animated conversations. Their voices floated down to him, discussions of the opera's storyline and of the singers punctuated by occasional laughter.

It was in the second set of windows when he first saw her. Peering out from the window, he noticed a young, beautiful woman in a white dress. Her black hair gracefully fell around her shoulders like a waterfall. Her enchanting presence drew him in. Their gazes met, and for a moment, time seemed suspended as an inexplicable connection sparked between them.

But then suddenly, and without warning, the fabric of her dress unraveled, as it changed into tatters, her dark hair lengthened and turned ghostly white, like a spectral veil. As she leaned forward against the glass, her eyes flashed red and bore into the depths of Giancarlo's soul.

He recoiled in terror. Stumbling backward, he tumbled off the edge of the curb. Catching himself before falling, he dared to steal another glance at the window. To his shock, the image had reverted to the serene vision of the dark-haired beauty, clad in her untattered white dress, with her shoulder length black hair.

He rubbed his temples. Marguerite? Unthinkable. He was glad to be going home. His mind was playing tricks on him. His imagination was running rampant. Ghosts? Never. The murderer was always just as real as the murdered. Always.

Giancarlo proceeded down Royal Street toward his apartment. He felt for his badge in his pocket, which brought forth a chuckle. It would take a while to break that habit.

Once at his apartment, he got undressed, and climbed into bed. Tomorrow would begin his official retirement. He did not want to think about anything related to his work as a detective.

He prayed for a peaceful night.

5

THE RETURN

ust as Giancarlo finally fell asleep in his apartment, a few miles away, Epifanio and Anna Andollina were saying goodnight to their five daughters. Their two sons were already asleep in one of the other bedrooms, while their infant daughter was in her crib in the bedroom the couple shared. The Andollinas sat in their cramped living room, talking until past midnight, enjoying a few moments of each other's company away from their typically busy day. They then proceeded to the bedroom, undressed, and quietly climbed into bed under the mosquito netting. Without waking their daughter, they made love.

The Andollinas were Sicilian immigrants to the Crescent City. For the past five years, they had run a grocery and saloon on the corner of Apple and Dante Streets in the Carrollton area of the city. Their business thrived in the neighborhood. The couple and their children lived in the same building as their business. They fell asleep holding hands.

AROUND 3 A.M., A FIGURE DRESSED IN BLACK APPROACHED THE Andollinas' grocery store at 1803 Apple Street. There was a brisk breeze that chilly night. The moon peered over a passing cloud, bathing the entire area in a murky glow.

Christmas was coming, but evil was here.

A dog barked down the block, and the man stopped and turned, looking down the street. Empty and quiet. He smiled and continued on his path of terror.

He went to the side of the building where the family lived. He peered in one window, then the next. He finally came to the second to last window and looked in. The man saw a baby crib on one side of the room and two people sleeping in the large bed on the other. He had found what he was looking for.

He crept to the back of the home and approached a door. He sat down next to the door and pulled a chisel from his pants pocket. He then reached into his waistband and produced a small axe. He listened for a sound, any sound, but heard nothing. He then placed the chisel on the bottom left door panel, and with the back end of his axe, he began to chisel away at that wood. While he did so, he gently hummed the jazz tune *Darktown Strutters Ball*, a new song released on record by the Original Dixieland Jazz Band.

Within minutes he had finished his job and removed the panel, placing it against the side of the house. He removed his shoes and put them next to the panel. He then went to his knees and peered into the home through the newly opened hole in the door. Within moments, he was inside the kitchen. He closed his eyes and took a deep breath, savoring the moment of anticipation for what he had come to do. Placing the axe back in his waistband, he pulled a revolver from one of the pockets of his dark pants.

Knowing where the couple's bedroom was, he wasted no time and went directly to it. Their infant daughter was asleep in the crib. He approached the husband's side of the bed. With the revolver in one hand, he reached into his waistband and pulled out the small axe.

The dog from down the block barked again, causing Anna to stir. She rolled over in the bed, and with her eyes half open, looked over at her sleeping husband. It was then that she noticed the dark figure standing over her husband. Before she could do anything, the man pointed the revolver directly at her and said in a hushed undertone, "Shut up."

Frozen with fear, Anna said nothing but watched in silent horror as the man raised the axe and then swung it downward across the top of her husband's head. Epifanio awoke with the first blow. He pulled the bedsheets above his head in an almost comical attempt to protect himself. Anna watched in shocked silence as the shadowy figure brutally struck the hapless man four more times with quick strikes. Blood soaked the bedsheets as Epifanio lay still.

The intruder then quickly turned and began to walk from the room. It was at this point that Anna let out the first of her many blood-curdling screams, waking everyone in the home.

Their eldest daughter opened her bedroom door and

quickly went to her parent's bedroom. She did not see the man just steps away down the hallway, standing in front of her brothers' bedroom door.

When she entered her parent's bedroom, she immediately saw the blood-soaked sheets and the look of terror on her mother's face. She ran over to the crib and quickly picked up the child, just as her mother hurriedly got out of bed and met her by the crib.

Meanwhile, the man opened the sons' bedroom door. John and Salvatore had just been awoken by their mother's screams when the man entered their bedroom. The intruder flipped the axe around in his hand and hit fourteen-year-old John in the head with the blunt end of it. The young boy collapsed to the floor. Salvatore stood in the middle of the room, unable to move, as now his mother's voice could be heard, yelling to all of her children to flee the house and get help for their father.

With John holding his head in a fetal position on the floor, the man turned toward Salvatore. He grabbed the end of his revolver and struck the boy with the butt of his gun. He then walked out of the room and back toward the kitchen. He dropped his axe on the kitchen floor, and then vanished into the darkness of the night.

Anna entered her sons' room and screamed more when she saw their injuries. She helped them up and ran out the front door into the street, where her other children were already standing.

"Help us," Anna yelled. "Somebody help us. Call an ambulance. Please."

Two neighbors came sprinting out of their homes to

answer Anna's pleas. Soon, an ambulance was taking Epifanio Andollina to Charity Hospital. Detective Arthur Marullo, who had just been appointed by Chief Mooney to replace Giancarlo Rabito as the Italian Expert, was on the scene within the hour, trying to gather information and determine what had happened at the Andollina home.

By the next morning, the Italian Expert Marullo and the Chief of Detectives George Bombay were having a meeting inside the Andollina home with Chief Mooney. The Andollina attack was one of Mooney's first cases since being appointed Chief by Mayor Behrman.

Had James Reynolds been alive, or if Giancarlo Rabito had not retired the day before the Andollina attack, perhaps the connections between the Cleaver attacks and this one would have been made. As it happened, neither Mooney nor Marullo had been on the police force during the Cleaver attacks some six years ago. George Bombay had been, but he remained convinced the same person was not involved in each of those attacks, and instead was the responsibility of the Black Hand, who he believed had never truly disappeared, but rather had been laying low these past few years.

Except for George Bombay, the consensus among the other investigators was that this was a burglary that went bad. Epifanio Andollina and his boys survived the attacks. When Detective Bombay interviewed the Andollinas, both he and his wife denied receiving threatening letters from the Black Hand, and they knew of no one who had a beef with them. Bombay did not believe them and was adamant to the other investigators and Chief Mooney that the Black Hand was behind the attack.

A little while later, Chief Mooney stood alone in the backyard of the property, his gaze fixed on the backdoor. How the perpetrator got in was a mystery. The door had been locked from the inside, and only a small child could have fit through the open panel that he saw there. But that was not the only thing Mooney was contemplating. He had a problem on his hands: not only was he dealing with an attack on one of his citizens, but his lead detective on the case was placing the blame on the Black Hand.

With the success of the Sicilian working class in New Orleans, the Black Hand's presence in the city had emerged years ago as a means for powerful men to shake down the business owners or enforce strict penalties for not obeying requests for money. A letter would be sent to the business owner, demanding money. On that letter would be a drawing of a black hand as a type of signature, and thus the nickname was given to this extortionist enterprise. Kidnapping, murder, arson, and dynamite were all tools used by this malevolent organization, which had its roots in the old world but had found a place in the new world easily enough. The fact that the police department had a detective identified as "the Italian Expert" showed that they were well aware of the problem.

But by 1917, it was thought that the Black Hand had finally been eliminated. The police had declared victory years ago, in fact. Mooney hoped his detective was wrong, and for now, he publicly took the same position as his other investigators that this was just a burglary that had turned violent.

The attack on the Andollinas got no mention in the press, which was a welcome break for the rookie police chief. Most of the citizens of New Orleans did not hear of the attack, including the just retired detective, Giancarlo Rabito.

6

PICCOLINA RABITO

Giancarlo had slept well. No more apparitions. No more thoughts of cases from the past. Once awake and dressed, he went downstairs to the Giorlando grocery where he bought a coffee and a newspaper. He then walked over to Jackson Square, where he sat on a bench, sipping his coffee, reading the paper, and taking in the sights.

Amidst the historical charm of Jackson Square, Giancarlo found a moment of solace immersing himself in the architectural beauty of the city. Founded by the French in 1718 on lands originally inhabited by the Chitimacha Tribe, it had a fraught colonial history. It was taken over by the Spanish, returned back to the French, and then sold to America. New Orleans boasted a unique architectural richness that reflected her varied influences. The city's buildings, a blend of French, Spanish, and American, stood as living testaments to its diverse past, creating an atmosphere that resonated with the echoes of centuries gone by.

Nestled in the center of the French Quarter, Jackson Square, originally designed as a military parade ground, remained unchanged after all these years. The Square was surrounded by wrought iron fences. Walkways and benches dotted the square. Outside the fences, on both the east and west sides of Jackson Square were the Pontalba apartments. They were matching red-brick, one-block-long, four-story buildings built between 1849–1851 by the Baroness Micaela Almonester Pontalba. On the north side were three of the most historic buildings in the city, the Cabildo on the left, where the Louisiana Purchase was signed, and the Presbytère on the right. Centered between the two was St. Louis Cathedral, the seat of the Roman Catholic Archdiocese of New Orleans and dedicated to King Louis IX of France.

The statue of Andrew Jackson, the savior of New Orleans during the War of 1812, sat atop his horse in the middle of the Square, tipping his hat toward the Pontalba Apartments across the way. Legend says that was in recognition of the secret affair the General had with Baroness Pontalba.

Off to Giancarlo's left, a father was seated on the ground, rolling a ball back and forth with his young daughter. The girl's mother stood off to the side, her long black hair framing her beautiful face. Giancarlo had noticed the woman when he first sat down. She closely resembled his wife, the love of his life, Piccolina.

Watching the tender scene of the family, Giancarlo couldn't help but reflect on his own life's journey and the circumstances that led him to this bustling city. Memories flooded back, unveiling a poignant tale of resilience and hope.

Born in Monreale, Sicily in 1864, Giancarlo's early life was marked by tragedy. When Giancarlo was just fourteen, his father fell victim to the ruthless grip of the Sicilian *Mafia*. Two years later, Giancarlo was left orphaned when his mother succumbed to her broken heart. He moved in with an uncle and stopped going to school. He made every effort to find work and earn money. He moved from one odd job to another. However, work became scarce as the conditions in Sicily worsened. The drought on the island further exacerbated the situation, affecting the food supply, and for the first time, Giancarlo experienced the sharp pain of hunger.

Advertisements displayed around Monreale promised work and a better life in the sugarcane fields of Louisiana. So, at the age of eighteen, and driven by a relentless spirit to make a way for himself, Giancarlo took a momentous step. With the support of his uncle, Giancarlo purchased his $40 ticket and made a life-changing decision to journey across the Atlantic, seeking a fresh start in America.

It was a Sunday in March 1882 when Giancarlo stood on the Palermo dock waiting to board the *Darlington*, a vessel destined for New Orleans. Joining him were 1,300 other Sicilian individuals, including men, women, and children, lined up to board. Like Giancarlo, they believed that America provided an opportunity that Sicily did not. Poverty, crime, corruption, and drought on the island had taken their toll, and these Sicilians were willing to make the long, arduous trip across the Atlantic to the Port of New Orleans. It was there where they would start a new life, a better life. Or so they hoped. They held a genuine belief that they were coming to a place where the streets were lined with gold and where they could achieve what they called, *il sogno Americano*…The American Dream.

The voyage from Palermo to New Orleans spanned 29 days, a tumultuous passage made survivable thanks to camaraderie among fellow immigrants in the ship's dimly lit confines. They had all saved what money they could for this supreme event, the journey to the new world. Rare moments on the deck provided a respite from the perpetual nausea, revealing a sea of diverse faces, each carrying dreams and aspirations of a new life.

Hearing the common plans for family reunions awaiting them in New Orleans, Giancarlo grappled with the reality that he would arrive alone in this new place. He would be a solitary figure in a foreign land where everything down to the language would be unfamiliar, except for a few phrases he had learned while on the ship.

After many weeks at sea, the ship navigated its way up from the mouth of the Mississippi River and anchored in quarantine near Jesuit Bend. Unlike Ellis Island in New York, New Orleans had no immigration station. So, the immigrants were required to stay on the ship midstream before they were admitted to the United States. The inspectors rowed out each day on skiffs, and all inspections of each and every immigrant took place on the ship. This process would last many days, an agonizingly long time for the immigrants eager to disembark.

On the morning of April 12, 1882, with the inspections finally complete, those below deck were instructed to ready themselves for their arrival in New Orleans. Packing their few belongings, the immigrants anxiously and quietly awaited what lay ahead, a mix of nerves and excitement coursing through each of them.

The hushed atmosphere was soon disrupted by distant cheers from the crew, heralding the approach of New Orleans. Giancarlo, along with the other immigrants, hurriedly ascended to the deck, their collective anticipation palpable.

Giancarlo stood pressed to the handrail on the side of the ship, his gaze fixed on the majestic St. Louis Cathedral and its crosses, reaching towards the heavens. In that moment, a silent prayer escaped his lips, a plea for protection to both God and the parents he had lost.

As the ship docked at the Governor Nicholls Street Wharf, the bustling port came alive with the cheers and tears of families awaiting their loved ones, waving to each other between the ship and the dock. In that moment, Giancarlo felt more alone than ever before. He would be stepping onto unfamiliar soil with no familiar faces awaiting him.

As Giancarlo stood in line to disembark, he held a small bag containing all his possessions. Observing others leaving the boat, he witnessed emotional reunions and embraces, some even bending down to kiss the ground as they stepped off the boat. When Giancarlo finally descended the gangway, he found himself in the midst of chaos. The exuberant hugs and kisses of reuniting families sharply contrasted with the immigrants who had no one to welcome them, prompting in Giancarlo a profound reflection on the choices that led him to this moment.

His moment of reflection passed as he stepped off the ship. Giancarlo dropped to his knees and kissed the ground, relieved to feel the American soil beneath his feet. He had made it, and though uncertain about the path ahead, he was determined to forge his way in this new land.

Not certain of his next move, Giancarlo's attention was drawn to the commanding voices of non-Italian men issuing instructions from the back of wagons, summoning laborers for work in the sugarcane fields of Louisiana.

"Looking for work, Dagoe? Climb aboard!" hollered a robust man, signaling towards the rear of his wagon. Simultaneously, another voice rang out, standing next to another wagon. "Steady hands, strong backs! The sugarcane fields need you!" A third man, waving his hands high above his head, declared loudly, "I'm in need of strong men. I pay well." Another man roared his instructions, his impatience cutting through the air like a whip. "Don't stand there like a fool, you bunch of Dagoes. Get on this wagon. I have no time for lollygaggers."

The collective calls formed a chorus in the air, each offer presenting a potential pathway to a new beginning for Giancarlo. Giancarlo, buoyed by hope at the prospect of work and a better life, dashed towards one of the wagons, eager to grasp the opportunity before him. Adjacent to the wagon, a young Black man, a few years older than Giancarlo, was intervening on behalf of an older immigrant who was being denied entry due to his age.

Locking eyes with Giancarlo, the Black man pointed at the wagon and cautioned, "Don't."

Surprised, Giancarlo echoed, "Don't," his enthusiasm momentarily subdued by the unexpected advice.

"No. You don't want to work the fields. Take it from me. I worked in the fields. Never again."

"*Scusi. Non capisce,*" Giancarlo responded apologetically, expressing his lack of understanding.

The Black young man sighed. Through a blend of Italian and English words, accompanied by gestures and nods, a mutual comprehension developed, as Giancarlo came to understand that he was being advised to not get on the wagon. The young man then pointed to Giancarlo. "You. Follow me. You work?"

"Work. *Si.*"

"Good. Come."

As the two turned and walked away from the wagon, Giancarlo extended his hand. "*Mi chiamo, Giancarlo.*"

"William. My name is William."

The two shook hands as they walked away from the dock, forming an unlikely yet immediate connection.

ALTHOUGH GIANCARLO CAME TO LOUISIANA TO WORK IN THE sugarcane fields, he ultimately remained in the city of New Orleans. William took him to a man named Franco "Frank" Mastracchio, an immigrant to New Orleans from Noto, Sicily. At William's behest, Frank offered Giancarlo a job on the bustling New Orleans riverfront. Giancarlo's responsibilities included unloading goods from ships arriving from various ports around the world. Frank also arranged for Giancarlo to live in a tenement building with other workers. William worked for Frank as well, so Giancarlo continued to see him often. Over time, their interactions evolved into a genuine friendship as they faced the challenges and embraced the opportunities presented by their shared experiences living in New Orleans.

With a job and a place to live, Giancarlo knew his decision to come to New Orleans had been a wise one, yet even he was surprised by the hatred and prejudice shown to him and the other Sicilian immigrants in the city. He and his compatriots were looked down upon by most of the other white citizens in the city. An article in the *Mascot* newspaper mused, *"If given our choice between the Negro or the Dago, we are inclined to believe that we would take the wooly son of Africa in preference to the greasy, filthy son of Italy…The Dagoes are a curse to New Orleans."*

With such sentiment, it's no wonder the Sicilians clung together in enclaves like Little Palermo, which provided them a place where they could live, pray, work, and hopefully thrive, all the while trying desperately to keep alive their Sicilian culture that was so important to them.

Giancarlo developed a deep admiration for Frank Mastracchio, recognizing him as both a benevolent individual and a savvy entrepreneur. Frank had a kind disposition and was keen on ensuring his workers assimilated into their new city. Motivated by this vision, he actively supported and guided the workers in acquiring proficiency in English. Giancarlo, demonstrating remarkable adaptability, swiftly mastered the language under Frank's encouraging guidance.

It was around this time when Giancarlo first laid his eyes on Frank's eighteen-year-old daughter, Piccolina Mastracchio. What began as a friendship gradually blossomed into a deep and genuine love between the two.

As their relationship evolved, so did Giancarlo's professional trajectory. He ascended to the role of a clerk in

Frank's business, a position that not only brought increased responsibilities but also a higher income. With this financial stability, Giancarlo reached a point where he could finally afford to rent his own small apartment, the one above Giorlando's Grocery, marking a significant step toward independence and the building of a life for himself and, hopefully, Piccolina.

At the age of twenty-four, Giancarlo sought Frank's permission to marry his daughter. With Frank's blessing, the couple celebrated their union the following year at St. Mary's Italian Church, situated beside the historic Ursuline Convent. This church held a central role as the lifeblood of the Sicilian community in the heart of Little Palermo. It became the backdrop for the beginning of their shared journey as husband and wife.

However, joy gave way to sorrow as tragedy struck just a year after their wedding. William, by now a loyal friend, fell victim to a wrongful shooting, and the police showed little interest in solving the crime. Moreover, the ominous shadow of the Black Hand loomed large over the lives of all Sicilian immigrants trying to make their way in New Orleans. Piccolina's father met a grisly end at their hands, having valiantly refused their impossible demands for payment.

Determined not to let the deaths of William and his father-in-law be in vain, Giancarlo began to discuss with his wife the possibility of becoming a policeman. She was supportive, but the Hennessey Affair derailed his plans in the short term.

At that time, David Hennessey was the beloved Police Chief in New Orleans. He had been sworn in as Chief in 1888 and had dedicated himself to combatting crime and corruption. He had been involved in resolving the dispute between two groups of rival Italian immigrant families, the Matrangas and the Provenzanos, who were well known on the docks of New Orleans. In 1890, Hennessey was shot and killed. Before dying, when asked by one of his associates who had done the deed, he allegedly replied, "Dagoes."

Over 100 suspects of Sicilian descent were swiftly rounded up and arrested. A restless crowd gathered outside the police station as the prisoners were loaded into mule-drawn prison wagons destined for Orleans Parish Prison without evidence of crime or the hint of a fair trial. The crowd, fueled by anger and prejudice, chanted "who killa da chief" and screamed obscenities, creating an atmosphere of hostility and tension in the city.

Eventually the number of suspects was reduced to 19, with nine of them going to trial. Ultimately none of the nine suspects were found guilty of murdering Chief Hennessey, yet their ordeal was far from over. They were still held in jail on propped up, unrelated charges.

The subsequent day witnessed a horrifying turn of events as a mob of over 10,000 people, including individuals from the privileged elite of the city, among them, a future Mayor of New Orleans and a future Governor of Louisiana, answered the call to meet by the Henry Clay statue on Canal Street. Passionate speeches whipped up the crowd to a frenzy. The speakers conveyed their belief that the jury was bribed and spoke of the rise of the *Mafia* in New Orleans. They called for vengeance. With the crowd chanting, "We want the Dagoes," they marched to the prison where a chosen small "execution group" violently stormed the jail.

They shot the nine Sicilian prisoners and then dragged them, along with an additional two Sicilian prisoners, outside the jail. With some of the prisoners still alive, the mob hung all of the men from lampposts. Their lifeless bodies were then used as target practice, as the crowd cheered. This would go down in infamy as the largest mass lynching in American history.

The National media was supportive of the actions of the lynch mob, calling the killing justified. Future president Theodore Roosevelt wrote that the killing "was rather a good thing."

The affair even had international repercussions. The Italian government recalled its ambassador to the United States and demanded that the American government compensate the lynched men's families, which was done to cool the tensions between the two countries.

Tensions between Sicilians and the rest of New Orleans society were high after those events. In the aftermath, the Sicilian community in New Orleans experienced a period marked by fear and sorrow. So many of their fellow citizens had taken part in the storming of the jail that the grand jury looking into punishment for the lynching concluded that there were simply too many people involved to hold anyone accountable. While it was true that the Sicilians arriving in New Orleans had always faced hatred and prejudice, the widespread vengeance showcased during the Hennessey affair only intensified their sense of alienation. This resulted in a shared sense of being ostracized by the very city that they had chosen as their home.

Despite the challenging circumstances, Giancarlo remained determined to contribute positively to society. It was something instilled in him by his father, to not just complain about life's circumstances, but to do something to improve your situation. However, he understood that pursuing his dream of becoming a policeman would have to be postponed. The absence of Italians on the police force, coupled with the slim chances of their inclusion following the Hennessey affair, meant that Giancarlo would have to patiently await an opportunity to pursue his aspirations.

Other events in his life solidified the decision not to pursue the career change. Two months after the Hennessey Affair, the couple received the news of Piccolina's pregnancy. With the impending arrival of their child, the couple enthusiastically started making plans and preparations for the upcoming birth. For nine months, Giancarlo and Piccolina lived in a state of pure bliss.

But then, the worst tragedy of all. Piccolina and their child, a daughter, both died during childbirth.

What followed was a dark time for Giancarlo. But as his grief finally relinquished its control, and in a bid to fulfill their shared dream, he mustered his courage, walked into a police station and discussed with a young police officer his desire to join the force. That young officer was James Reynolds.

Reynolds found something compelling in the young Sicilian and became his advocate. He passionately lobbied his superiors to hire Giancarlo, and they eventually agreed.

The year was 1895. Giancarlo had come to the city of New Orleans some 13 years ago. Over these years, he had experienced the loss of his friend, his father-in-law, his wife, and now his child. Yet, the burning desire to make his way in life persisted. He accepted that every achievement would be tinged with the sorrow that had become an indelible part of his journey. Putting on his police uniform that first day was a poignant achievement after all of the hardships he had overcome, and it became his sole purpose in life.

GIANCARLO CONTINUED STARING AT THE YOUNG MOTHER IN Jackson Square who was busy watching her husband and daughter playing together. He missed Piccolina so much. He swore he would never be with another woman after her death. He had lived up to the vow. When the doctor had informed him of his heart condition and that death by a heart attack could happen at any moment, all he thought about inside the physician's office was the opportunity to finally be reunited with his love and his daughter.

As the bell tower of St. Louis Cathedral chimed the hour, Giancarlo looked around the Square at the people beginning their day, heading to their places of work or down to the French Market to buy their groceries.

His job as a police detective had kept him busy every day. He spent his time gathering facts, and interviewing victims and witnesses. But now, all of a sudden, that was all over. He had worked long enough to have earned a nice pension. It would allow him to live comfortably, even providing him excess for tickets to the opera, which he planned to attend frequently.

He looked at his coffee cup on the bench beside his newspaper. So, this was retirement, he thought. How boring. He decided then and there that he would follow through and begin writing his book.

Giancarlo stood up from the bench, tucking his newspaper under his arm. Holding his coffee cup, he began walking back to his apartment, thinking the whole time that writing a book could give him something to do. He left Jackson Square and walked up Royal Street toward his apartment.

Day one of his retirement, and he was already ready to return to work.

7

THE STRUGGLING WRITER

Upon his return to his apartment that morning, Giancarlo sat at the table in his living room, staring at the blank page before him. His mind a whirlwind of thoughts and ideas. He had never attempted to write a book before, and the enormity of the task ahead weighed heavily on him. Hours slipped by as he pondered over what to write, but by that night, not a single word had made its way onto the page.

As he rose from his chair, he fought the sense of frustration that had permeated his entire being. With determination and resolve, he told himself that tomorrow would be different. Tomorrow, the words would flow effortlessly. With a heavy sigh, he walked away from the table, leaving the empty pages behind. Perhaps a good night's rest would clear his mind and ignite his creativity.

However, Giancarlo's plans were abruptly derailed by unexpected news he received the very next morning. Walking into Augustino's to get his morning paper, his landlord's somber expression caught Giancarlo off guard.

"Did you hear the news?" Augustino's voice was heavy with sadness as he handed Giancarlo a newspaper.

Giancarlo's heart sank as he read the headline announcing the passing of Mother Cabrini in Chicago. He instinctively made the sign of the cross, and then brought his thumb up to his lips and kissed it.

Giancarlo's voice was soft, tinged with sorrow. "She was one of the kindest souls I ever met. I vividly remember her walking the streets of Little Palermo with her sisters back when she lived in our city."

Augustino rubbed his chin absentmindedly. "She would come to my store," he said, his voice tinged with both fondness and a hint of amusement, "and with those crystal clear blue eyes of hers staring at me," he glanced upward, mimicking the action with his own eyes, "would ask me for donations. I could never refuse her."

Giancarlo tucked the newspaper under his arm. "She came to our city after the Hennessey affair for the simple purpose of caring for the forgotten souls. She dedicated her life to caring for the Sicilian community. As a young cop, I brought many children over to her orphanage on Esplanade Avenue who were then alone in the world due to the death of their parents from yellow fever. She and her sisters always welcomed them and provided them sanctuary and love. How sad this news is to me. Her nuns, who are still carrying on her mission here must be devastated. Thanks for letting me know," he said, then paused and added, "First Chief Reynolds and now Mother Cabrini. This is not a joyous Christmas."

A moment of silence passed between the two, before Augustino asked, "Can I get you anything else from my store?"

"No, just the paper, Augustino." He handed him the money and then added, "Going back upstairs to work on my book."

"How's it going?"

"It's not."

With that, Giancarlo retreated to his apartment, where his struggles continued with the writing of his book. His mind remained clouded with memories of Chief Reynolds and Mother Cabrini, as well as the haunting visions of the Cleaver and Marguerite. The words eluded him, lost amidst the swirl of emotions that gripped his heart.

By that afternoon, his modest living room was filled with crumpled pages of paper, his writing marked by numerous stops and starts. Once the floor was littered with the remnants of his creative struggle, he found himself on the brink of abandoning his endeavor.

At that moment, a recollection of his conversation with Augustino, the evening of his retirement, stirred in his mind. His landlord had playfully dubbed him "The Sherlock Holmes of New Orleans." An idea began to form about how he would narrate his stories. He envisioned adopting Sir Arthur Conan Doyle's technique to craft his tales.

Doyle, the revered creator of the beloved Sherlock Holmes tales, used each short story to tell the tale of a singular case solved by the brilliant detective. That's how Giancarlo would write his book. Each chapter in his book would unveil one New Orleans crime story, intertwined with Giancarlo's own experiences as he tried to solve the case. But rather than embarking on a personal memoir, he would write his stories in the style of a novel, immersing his readers into a world of mystery and intrigue. Although based on facts and real cases, they would be told fictionally. His first story was the simple tale of Giuseppe di Carlo.

In 1903, Giuseppe, the owner of a produce company, started receiving threatening letters demanding money or else see his business burned to the ground. Giancarlo was a newly minted detective back then. What made the case so interesting was that, through his hard work, Giancarlo had been able to penetrate the inner workings of the Black Hand, which would be instrumental in his handling of other cases as the years progressed. He thought the story of Giuseppe di Carlo was a perfect beginning to his tales of New Orleans crimes.

As he picked up his pen, now clear on how these stories would unfold, the words flowed easily, bringing his novel to life. Although writing was an arduous task, he quickly became enamored with the creative process and the solace it brought to him. He felt a surge of inspiration as he surrendered himself to the flow of his storytelling.

Over the next few days, except for Christmas day, when his heart ailment flared up and he remained in bed, every day was spent working on his novel. He became immersed in his writing. The world outside faded into the background. His vision was ever before him: to infuse each and every story with a sense of intrigue, suspense, and tension.

He finished his first chapter about Giuseppe di Carlo and turned his attention to the fateful tale of Ignazio Costanza, the owner of a very successful produce stand that sold Limoncello direct from Sicily. This case showed the true terror that the Black Hand brought to the working populace of the Sicilian community. The Black Hand initially approached Ignazio demanding small sums of money for their "protection." As the demands escalated and Ignazio staunchly refused to comply with their exorbitant demands, the Black Hand lost their patience. A stick of dynamite planted in his Decatur Street store not only spelled the end of Ignazio's business but also claimed his life. Giancarlo, through great investigative work, was able to ultimately track down the killers and bring them to justice. However, this act of justice also marked Giancarlo as the prime adversary in the eyes of the ruthless Black Hand, and brought his name front and center to one of the leading heads of the *Mafia* in New Orleans: Charles Matranga, who had brought his branch of the *Mafia* direct from Monreale, the same town in Sicily that Giancarlo was from.

As Giancarlo delved into the chilling accounts of the Black Hand's terror, one story led seamlessly to the next. Giancarlo's confidence in his ability to write grew with each new paragraph. Although his stories concerned horrific crimes, Giancarlo savored every moment of growth, discovery, and self-expression that unfolded with each new page.

8

SPIRITS

wo nights before the new year, Giancarlo went to dinner with his landlord, Augustino, and two other friends, Sebastian Mandina, owner of a grocery store and pool hall on Canal Street, and Charlie Cortimiglia, whose grocery store was located on the west bank of the Mississippi River, in the little town called Gretna. The friends met at Tujague's, the second oldest restaurant in New Orleans, located on Decatur Street.

As they sat down, the three friends knew they were about to indulge in a culinary experience steeped in tradition. The evening commenced with the customary start for every patron at Tujague's - appetizers of shrimp remoulade and the restaurant's most famous dish, boiled beef brisket. The unique touch to Tujague's brisket was a red sauce generously placed on top. This sauce was a special creation of the restaurant's madam, Clemence Castet. The sauce consisted of a bold combination of horseradish and fiery Creole mustard, adding a spicy kick to the brisket.

Next came their main courses: speckled trout for each with a succulent meunière sauce. As the friends enjoyed their dinner in this historic establishment, they weren't just enjoying a meal. They were immersed in the rich culinary traditions and unique flavors that define New Orleans.

After dinner, and while waiting for their dessert, Sebastian asked Giancarlo, "How's retirement?"

"Boring," quickly retorted Giancarlo.

"He's working on a book," Augustino said. "A book about the crimes he's investigated."

Giancarlo interjected, "A novel. A novel based on my life as a detective."

Charlie replied, "A novel? A novel written by the best cop this place has ever produced. It should be a wonderful read."

Giancarlo laughed. "Oh please, Charlie. You embarrass me."

Charlie raised his finger and said, "Augustino and Sebastian know this just as much as me. Your role in the Italian community was so much more than preventing and investigating crimes. You went out of your way to help us ordinary citizens. You even helped rivals become friends. You know what I am referring to, right Giancarlo?"

"Yes, Charlie, your neighbors over in Gretna."

"Iorlando and Frank Jordano," replied Charlie. "As you know, I live in Jefferson Parish, which was out of your jurisdiction. Iorlando has a competing grocery right by mine. At first, we did not get along. As a matter of fact, I would say we were rivals, and it got heated between us. You spent many a weekend over in Gretna, during your off time, I might add, working the issues out between me and the Jordanos. With your help, we now consider each other friends. The battle between us is over. Frank comes over often now to hold our new baby."

Giancarlo smiled. "I'm glad I could help."

Sebastian sighed. "In your retirement, you will be missed."

Augustino clarified, "You are already missed."

He then raised the wine glass sitting in front of him. Charlie did the same, followed by Sebastian and Giancarlo.

Augustino then toasted his friend, saying, "I hope your health returns."

"*Grazie*," replied Giancarlo, before turning toward the two other men, saying, "You think he's being kind, but he just doesn't want to lose my rent."

Charlie and Sebastian laughed.

Then Charlie said, "Get well, my friend. Get well."

Giancarlo nodded his head. "And good luck with your newborn."

"Yes, we named her Mary. She looks just like her mother."

Sebastian chuckled and said, "That's great news. I was concerned she would look like you."

They all laughed.

Giancarlo added, "Congratulations to you both."

The waiter walked up to the table with their desserts, and their attention turned to the magical creations in front of them.

THAT SUNDAY MORNING, JUST LIKE COUNTLESS MORNINGS before, Giancarlo left his apartment and headed to St. Mary's Italian Church for the 9 a.m. Mass. Upon entering the intimate church, he was welcomed by the familiar fragrance of incense and the gentle glow of candlelight. Positioned in the back corner was a remarkable *Pietà* portraying the mournful scene of Mary cradling the lifeless, crucified body of her son Jesus, her beautiful face wretched with indescribable grief.

The morning sunlight streamed through the stained-glass windows, casting vibrant patterns onto the well-used wooden pews and the statues of Catholic Saints that adorned either side of the church. The polished marble aisle, worn by generations of faithful footsteps, guided the collective gaze of the congregation toward the elaborate altar and sanctuary. The combination of white marble and gold embellishments bestowed an atmosphere of grandeur and solemnity upon the sacred space. Perched high above the doors of the ornate, golden tabernacle stood two angels adorned in colorful robes, brandishing trumpets that seemingly heralded the presence of something holy, beckoning worshippers to rise above the ordinary and forge a connection with the divine.

St. Mary's Italian Church, with its rich history and connection to the adjacent Ursuline Convent, held a special place in the hearts of the New Orleans Sicilian community. Giancarlo often marveled at the endurance of the Ursuline Convent, the oldest building in the Mississippi Valley, which had survived the two devastating fires that had swept through New Orleans in the late 18th century.

The Ursuline nuns who initially occupied the Convent dedicated their lives to caring for the poor and educating young girls. Over time, the nuns moved uptown, leaving the Archdiocese in charge of the historic property. The adjacent chapel, once part of the Convent, found new purpose as it was donated to the Italian community by the archbishop.

St. Mary's Italian became a spiritual haven for the Sicilian residents of Little Palermo. The weekly Mass, conducted in Latin, added a sense of tradition and continuity, while the sermons in Italian provided a connection to the cultural roots of the congregation.

As Giancarlo took his seat in the church, he felt a deep sense of belonging and reverence. St. Mary's Italian Church not only served as a place of worship but also stood as a testament to the resilience of faith and community in the face of challenges. The sacred rituals performed within its walls connected the past to the present, traditions that had withstood the test of time.

Giancarlo sat in his usual pew near the front. Waiting for Mass to start, he prayed for God to heal him. The flare-up of his heart had scared him on Christmas Day, and for the first time, he truly believed that death was coming for him. The once promising prospect of reuniting with his wife in heaven had now given way to fear of death's looming presence. He realized he was not done with life just yet.

After Mass, as was his custom, he first walked to Ruffino's Bakery on St. Philip Street. Upon entering the small establishment, he was greeted by the enticing aroma of baked bread. On the counter, warm Italian loaves were stacked one upon another, their golden crusts hinting at the rich flavors within. The shop owner Giuseppe Ruffino was an immigrant from Cinisi, Sicily. He carefully chose a loaf, taking great pride in his craft, and handed it to Giancarlo with a smile.

With the warm bread cradled in his hands, Giancarlo exchanged a few pleasantries with Giuseppe, inquiring about his family and the latest news from the neighborhood before bidding him farewell.

Giancarlo left the bakery and headed to Brocato's. Established in 1905 by Angelo Brocato, a Sicilian immigrant from Cefalù, the pastry and gelato store exuded an irresistible charm. Inside, the enticing display cases brimmed with delicious treats from Granita al limone (Lemon Ice) and gelato, Torroncino and Spumoni, Napoleons and Biscotti, and of course, cannoli. For all of the Sicilian immigrants in the city, walking into Brocato's was like stepping back in time. It resembled the pastry shops from the towns and villages they had emigrated from. It provided an opportunity to reminisce about their former homes and the family members who had remained back in Sicily.

Giancarlo ordered his usual, a cappuccino and glass filled with Lemon Ice. He then walked over to one of the inviting tables, dropping his jacket and hat on one of the chairs. He placed the bread he had acquired from Ruffino's on the table. He sat down, breaking off a piece of the still warm bread, and dipped it into his glass brimming with refreshing Lemon Ice. The crisp texture of the bread melded with the icy sweetness, offering a harmonious blend of flavors. He then retrieved a few sheets of paper from the pocket of his trench coat. He began reading the last few paragraphs he had penned the night before, the beginning of the sordid and heart-wrenching tale of the kidnapping of a child, an eight-year old boy named Walter Lamana.

Walter was the child of Pietro and Carolina Lamana, well known owners of a funeral home in the city. The Black Hand had employed the sinister tactic of child abduction to instill the most profound dread in those they sought to dominate. Back in 1907, the Lamana story held the full attention of the citizens of New Orleans, and Giancarlo aimed to transport his readers to a time when the Lamana story dominated conversations, and swept the people of New Orleans up in feelings of curiosity, fear, and a longing for justice. Giancarlo's mind reflected back to the tension that gripped the entire city, and he was determined to try and recreate that tension through his words.

There, amidst the aroma of coffee and the smell of the freshly baked pastries, Giancarlo continued his writing journey. The words danced across the page, as the atmosphere of Brocato's provided a perfect source of nostalgia and inspiration.

As the last remnants of bread and Lemon Ice vanished and Giancarlo's coffee cup emptied, his focused work was interrupted when Salvatore D'Antoni pulled out one of the other chairs and sat at his table.

"*Buongiorno*, Detective Rabito."

Giancarlo looked up from his paper. Although their acquaintance spanned many years giving way to a genuine fondness, there were moments when Salvatore's exuberance for the supernatural tested Giancarlo's patience. He hoped his face didn't reveal how much he was not in the mood to hear another round of Salvatore's never-ending stories.

Giancarlo replied with a forced smile, "*Buongiorno*, Salvatore. Please, just Giancarlo. As I'm sure you have heard, I'm retired."

"I've heard. It's a sad time for all of us. And I mean that. It is a joke to call Detective Marullo 'the Italian Expert.' That name should have been retired with you. I fear with you gone now, the Black Hand may come out of the shadows again."

"He's a very competent detective. He will keep them at bay. I truly believe that."

Salvatore looked down at the papers on the table and asked, "What are you working on. Your memoirs?"

"Something like that. A story, based on my work as a detective."

"Ghost stories?"

Giancarlo quickly responded, "No," hoping that would end the conversation, but it did not.

Salvatore said in reply, "Ghosts are real, my friend. You should know. You investigated Marguerite's death. She is still around. The Witch of the Opera House. I have proof."

Giancarlo placed his elbow on the table and laid his chin into his hand, wanting to return to his writing, but Salvatore continued, unperturbed.

"Two nights ago, I was at Lafitte's Blacksmith Shop. Their Sazerac is a dream. Can't have just one, you know."

"I'm sure," Giancarlo replied.

"I was there with Antonio Costa, the landlord of the apartment where Marguerite killed Pierre and his lover."

"I know Antonio well."

"While having our drinks, he told me that his new tenants had fled from the building. They were renting the very same apartment where the murders had occurred. Those, of course, are not the first tenants to flee that building. Antonio says the young woman who was living there with her husband swears she saw her. She saw the Witch of the Opera House with her own eyes. The sighting happened as the couple was making love. As I told you before, based on other stories I have heard, the witch does not like when a woman has pleasure in that place. She makes her appearance, and let's just say their pleasure ends. The couple packed their belongings and fled the apartment vowing never to return, exactly as others have done in the past. When Antonio went into the room to clear out the couple's belongings, he found a single rose lying on the bed."

"Salvatore, Antonio does nothing to repair his apartments. They are in horrendous shape. What better way to get out of your lease than to say the place is haunted?"

"Hmmm, Detective. You of all people should know the role the spirits play in our city. So many unsolved crimes. You and your cohorts in the police department should have spent time studying the spirit world and the Casket Girls."

"Salvatore, I know all about the people who believe in such nonsense. They are confident the spirits were introduced into our city by the Casket Girls, those ladies who were sent over from France to find husbands in the new colony."

"Indeed, *mio amico*. They carried all of their belongings in little wooden chests that resembled small caskets. Those who could find no husbands eventually resided at the Ursuline Convent. But those caskets held more than their belongings."

"I know what people believe."

"It's the truth, Detective. Those Casket Girls unleashed the spirits who have been haunting our city ever since. And New Orleans *is* a haunted place. It's a perfect place for spirits to survive. Here you will find not only ghosts, but Voodoo, dark magic, and a long history of death from disease and other horrific ends. These are things in which the spirit world thrives. After all, we live with the dead buried above ground here in our city, unlike anywhere else in America. We are surrounded by spirits. Delphine LaLaurie's Mansion, Pirates Alley, Old Absinthe House, and St. Louis Cemetery #1, to name just a few. All are alive with spirits. All haunted. If you would come to understand this, then you would come to realize that Marguerite is still here. Something has her trapped in our world. That is why she has been seen throughout the Quarter, around the Opera House, in the location where her pastry shop used to be, her apartment, and in the apartment of her lover. The place where the murders occurred."

"Trapped?" Giancarlo asked somewhat aggravated. "Trapped like the pirate, Jean Lafitte, looking for his treasure, whom you have *also* said you have seen in the past? Did you see him that night when you were with Antonio Costa at the Blacksmith Shop drinking your Sazerac?"

"One day you will see a spirit. One day you will see something or someone from your past, and then you will understand. Marguerite is still here."

"You believe what you want to believe, and I'll believe what I want to believe." Quickly realizing that his words may have come across as too harsh, Giancarlo added, "But I will still respect your feelings and beliefs."

Salvatore stood up. He extended his hand to Giancarlo. "Congratulations on your retirement. Too bad, as you could go investigate what happened over at that apartment and speak to the woman who saw the witch."

"Too bad," replied Giancarlo, as Salvatore walked away.

Giancarlo returned to his novel, delving more into the story of Walter Lamana. While retelling this grim tale, Giancarlo remembered his role as detective on the case and the desperate search for the missing child that had consumed the entire city. Amid the collective efforts to locate the boy, it was Giancarlo who made the chilling discovery of Walter Lamana's lifeless body hidden amidst the swamps of St. Rose, Louisiana.

Walter had met a tragic end, having been strangled to death, shrouded in a blanket, and abandoned in the desolate swamp, now drenched with the brackish water. Giancarlo recounted the instincts that led him to check the swamp and, with a heavy heart, described the ghastly scene he stumbled upon. As he gingerly unwrapped the body from the waterlogged blanket, he made the gruesome realization that the boy's head had become detached from his body due to the severe neck injury sustained during strangulation. Giancarlo found the severed head a short distance away from the rest of the body, adding a chilling layer of horror to the already macabre tale. The scene was as fresh in his mind as it was so many years ago.

In the subsequent pages, Giancarlo penned a concise account of his investigative efforts and shared his theories regarding those responsible for the gruesome abduction and murder. He meticulously detailed the arrest and prosecution of certain members of the Black Hand, shedding light on the justice served in their cases. Giancarlo even ventured into the realm of speculation, mentioning another figure whom he suspected of involvement but who mysteriously vanished before he could be apprehended. This enigmatic individual was Joseph "Doc" Mumfre, a multifaceted character who served both as a pharmacist and a ruthless enforcer within the *Mafia* hierarchy of New Orleans.

As Giancarlo finished the last paragraph, he returned the pages to the pocket of his trench coat, as he unsuccessfully tried to put the scenes from the swamp out of his memory. He distracted himself with thoughts of his next story.

His conversation with Salvatore came to mind. Giancarlo decided then that the next story he would tell in his novel after the Lamana murder would be Marguerite's. He would put to bed once and for all the rumors. Her ghost did not kill Pierre and his lover. She had done it. She had done it and then killed herself rather than face the consequences for her actions.

He picked up his jacket and, placing his Fedora on his head, he left Brocato's. On his way home, he wanted to stop at the French Market to buy some tomatoes, which he would eat later for lunch.

Giancarlo turned down St. Peter Street to make his way to the French Market. There was a chill in the air late that morning, and Giancarlo adjusted his trench coat to provide more warmth. The memory of the St. Rose swamp was front of mind after his afternoon reliving the tragedy.

Suddenly, out of the corner of his eye, he caught sight of a small, shrouded figure seated in a doorframe, concealed within a blanket. Something about the image unsettled him, drawing his attention towards the figure, like a moth drawn to a flickering flame.

The mysterious figure, almost beckoning him closer, stretched out a frail hand as Giancarlo cautiously approached. A sinking feeling gnawed at Giancarlo, but his curiosity got the better of him. He looked toward the outstretched arm's direction, and his gaze fixated on what lay before him.

To his horror, the blanket unraveled, unveiling the grotesque and nightmarish sight of Walter Lamana's severed head, positioned grotesquely on the figure's lap. The lifeless eyes of the young boy bore into Giancarlo's soul.

A surge of horror coursed through Giancarlo's veins, causing him to recoil in shock. His eyes squeezed shut. When they opened again, the figure and the horrifying apparition had vanished.

Giancarlo rubbed his temples and sighed heavily. He would have to come to grips with his own spirits, spirits from past cases playing tricks on his mind. They were not real, just figments of his imagination. Ghosts and spirits did not exist, not even in New Orleans.

Or so he believed.

9

A CAST OF CHARACTERS

As the calendar turned to 1918, the persistent echoes of war still reverberated across Europe, casting a somber shadow over the world. Yet, despite these challenging times, the people of New Orleans stood on the threshold of anticipation, eagerly awaiting the arrival of Mardi Gras.

Mardi Gras, French for "Fat Tuesday," transcends mere revelry; it embodies a living tradition that weaves through the cultural fabric of New Orleans. This celebration, dating back centuries, unfolds like an intricate tapestry adorned with vibrant music, masked balls, and an array of social events.

The commencement of this grand season is marked by Twelfth Night on January 6th, also known as the Feast of the Epiphany. It serves as a symbolic overture, signaling the beginning of a cascade of festivities that crescendo as the calendar approaches Fat Tuesday - the day preceding Ash

Wednesday and the onset of Lent, with its own set of rituals, fasting, and sacrifices.

In the zenith of the carnival season, various Krewes emerge as the masterminds behind grand parades, orchestrating displays of opulent floats, captivating costumes, and whimsical throws that delight spectators, many of whom are themselves costumed. Adding to the rhythmic heartbeat of the celebration are the Mardi Gras Indians, African American dancers adorned in meticulously crafted costumes whose mesmerizing presence and magnetic energy captivate all those fortunate enough to witness their spirited procession.

Most importantly, beyond the dazzling displays, Mardi Gras in New Orleans is a profound community affair. Vibrant street parties pulse through neighborhoods, each reveler contributing to a collective mosaic of shared celebration. It becomes a familial affair, where generations enthusiastically join in, fostering a sense of unity that transcends the city's diverse populace.

However, the year 1918 brought a disheartening announcement from Mayor Behrman. Mardi Gras would be canceled due to the war. This decision reverberated across the social spectrum, disappointing not only the affluent members of Krewes like Comus, Proteus, Momus, and Rex, but also the Black members of the Krewe of Zulu. This collective disappointment underscored the shared sentiment and the profound impact of global events on the cherished local traditions of New Orleans.

But how does one stop Mardi Gras? The city can stop the parades, but how do you kill the spirit? Let's just say Mayor Martin Behrman did his best.

He stated in the press, "'Now that Mardi Gras season is approaching, I desire to repeat and to emphasize that masking of every kind and character will be strictly prohibited. This regulation is deemed essential because of the War and the opportunity that promiscuous and other masking would afford the enemy aliens and other evil disposed persons to commit crime while thus disguised.'"

The *Times-Picayune* noted that the purple, green and gold flags of Mardi Gras are not flying, *"but the Stars and Stripes have filled their place, and the flag of New Orleans has been raised."* Citizens complied to a degree. In lieu of carnival parades, they rallied around Liberty Bond parades, resulting in a remarkable sell-out of all liberty bonds.

Small victories indeed.

GIANCARLO CONTINUED WORKING ON HIS NOVEL WELL INTO THE spring. It had expanded from just a story of the crimes he had investigated into a narrative woven together with the history of the Sicilian immigrants to New Orleans, their fears, hardships, and successes. Throughout the book, he made mention of the many people who lived in the Quarter, both those still present, and those who had passed away, to give the reader a view of a slice of life in Little Palermo.

Little Palermo provided Giancarlo a trove of diverse personalities that he knew would fascinate his readers. Characters such as Enzo Ricci, a dreamy-eyed young man who was a cobbler by trade but who, with his easel and paint-stained hands, wandered the streets capturing the essence of Little Palermo on canvas. His artwork adorned local businesses' walls, portraying the neighborhood with vivid strokes. His studio, nestled above the cobblestone streets, served as a sanctuary for creativity, though his clandestine fame lay in his alluring nude paintings of prestigious citizens' wives.

And then there was Theresa Montalbano, who played the piano so beautifully and with such grace that she was often asked to play at debutante balls, the very balls that, as a Sicilian, she would never be able to attend as an invitee.

In the dimly lit corner of Pizzolato's Tavern, you could find Antonio Martino, fingers dancing over the keys of his accordion. Tony, as he was known, was the heartbeat of Little Palermo's music scene. His melodies, infused with the soul of Sicily, transported the patrons to another world. On weekend nights, the tavern echoed with the joyous sounds of accordion, mandolin, and laughter, creating a haven of celebration in the heart of Little Palermo.

He made sure to mention Mother Cabrini and the impact she and her sisters had on the Sicilian community of New Orleans. With heartfelt sincerity, Giancarlo painted vivid portraits of the moments he had witnessed firsthand: Mother Cabrini walking the streets of Little Palermo, her gentle smile offering solace to those in need; the orphanage on Esplanade Avenue, a beacon of hope for children left alone in the world by the scourge of yellow fever. Each sentence served as a touching tribute to her unwavering dedication and love, and her service to God. Through his words, Giancarlo immortalized the essence of Mother Cabrini's compassion and selflessness, ensuring that her memory would live on in the hearts of those who read his book.

And of course, Giancarlo mentioned Lucia di Napoli, with

her silver hair and wise eyes. She held court on a bench near the French Market. She was the neighborhood's storyteller, weaving tales of myths, legends, and the struggles of their ancestors in the old country. Children gathered around her, wide-eyed, as she transported them to a world where magic and reality danced together, and the echoes of Sicilian folklore resonated through the streets of Little Palermo.

Giancarlo enjoyed writing about many other people living in Little Palermo, but it was his crime stories that he knew would truly bring intrigue to the novel. He had completed his chapters on Walter Lamana's death and Marguerite's attack and suicide. He also completed stories on his other highly publicized cases, including the death of Philip Puma by the Black Hand and the interesting case of Fiona MacDugal, who killed three lovers with cyanide until her terrible deeds were pieced together by Giancarlo and she was arrested.

And then there was the intriguing case of David Billing, who, while in costume, pilfered precious gems from the wealthiest families attending lavish Mardi Gras balls. Giancarlo was able to unravel the mystery and return those gems to their rightful owners.

He also added the sad story of Evie Dupont, a strikingly beautiful young woman who worked in a brothel in the heart of Storyville. When her lifeless, mutilated body was discovered one night on the banks of Bayou St. John, it ignited a relentless pursuit by Giancarlo. Ultimately he unearthed a sinister connection leading straight to the doorstep of a formidable Louisiana politician, whose downfall Giancarlo orchestrated, ending with the powerful man's arrest.

Giancarlo began to debate with himself if he would

dedicate a chapter to the Cleaver and discuss the three cases from 1910 and 1911 that he believed to be interconnected. He was certain the story would make for a gripping narrative. However, a nagging doubt lingered in his mind.

He questioned whether including a chapter on the Cleaver attacks without a clear conclusion might disappoint his readers. With the Cleaver never being unmasked, it could lead to frustration among his audience. They would expect a resolution, closure, or some sense of finality to the story. He decided to postpone his decision on whether to include them or not.

While his book was coming along well, his health was declining even faster than his physician had first advised. His bad days, as he called them, instead of being just one or two times a month, were now at least once a week. When he was in the throes of it, he could not even get out of bed.

As for his apparitions, they did not go away either. When the ghosts of his past came, what he would see could not be predicted. Sometimes it was a victim, while other times it was the crime scene. He began to spend afternoons in the many bars of New Orleans, partaking of a few cocktails in an attempt to put the spirits out of his mind. It failed, and probably only added to the increased episodes with his heart.

Considering the increasing whirlwind of visions that danced through his mind, Giancarlo found himself pondering why the image of his wife never appeared among them. The longing to lay eyes on her once more became a deep ache in his soul. He yearned to behold her, to trace the soft curve of her cheek, to witness how her raven-tresses framed her exquisite face, and to experience once again the alluring sensuality that emanated from her very essence. But instead, his mind teemed with images of crime and criminals, of death and murder, and the haunting spectres from his past.

Giancarlo turned his storytelling to the fascinating tale of Pietro Giacona, the owner of a house at 1113 Chartres Street, located just across from the Ursuline Convent. The house had a rich history, dating back to 1826, and had once served as the residence of P.G.T. Beauregard, the renowned Confederate General from Louisiana.

Pietro Giacona had bought the property in 1904 and, along with his son Corrado, began selling wine out of the basement of the home. The Giaconas success did not go unnoticed by the Black Hand, and they demanded protection payments, as was their way. Initially, the Giaconas complied, but they eventually grew weary of the situation. They had immigrated to the United States to escape such criminal enterprises only to find them flourishing on the streets of New Orleans.

One evening, June 16, 1908, Pietro invited four members of the Black Hand to dine on the back balcony of his property. The night took a dramatic turn when Pietro Giacona fired upon all four Black Hand members, killing them. Giancarlo was tasked with investigating the shooting, and although both Giaconas were arrested, they were eventually found innocent, as it was determined they had acted in self-defense. Giancarlo concurred with the verdict, as did the rest of New Orleans' Sicilian inhabitants.

This case held immense significance, marking the beginning of the end for the reign of terror imposed by the Black Hand. It was a turning point in the fight against organized crime in New Orleans. Giancarlo became instrumental in putting the squeeze on its members and by

1917, the Black Hand had virtually disappeared, or so it was thought.

With the arrival of May, Giancarlo added the story of the death of a Jack Smith, a horseman. In the dimly lit stables of the renowned racing track, The New Orleans Fair Grounds, Jack Smith was found lifeless, strangled with a bridal, as his prized stallion Stormbringer neighed mournfully beside him. Giancarlo uncovered a web of jealousy and betrayal that led to the shocking truth behind the Smith's murder by a rival owner.

His thoughts then turned to a case he had handled in May 1912. It was the case of Anthony "Tony" Sciambra and his wife Johanna. The Sciambras were shot to death by a home intruder. The bullet intended for Tony Sciambra travelled through his body and struck his wife in her hip. He died at the scene, while Mrs. Toney, as she was called by her friends, died 10 days later in the hospital from an infection. Unlike all of the other stories in his novel, this one did not end with an arrest. The killer of the Sciambras was never found. Yet, Giancarlo believed his readers would find the story interesting, even with no triumphant conclusion. He decided he would write the chapter, and if it came out well, he would include it.

It took Giancarlo just two days to write the story of the Sciambras. Once finished, he read it from beginning to end, and was very much pleased with the result, even without the perpetrator being discovered. He was so thrilled with it that he began to believe that the chapter on the Cleaver attacks should be included as well. He decided he would sleep on it. He climbed into bed well after midnight.

It was May 23, 1918.

10

—————

THE MAGGIOS

While Giancarlo slept, Andrew Maggio, an immigrant to New Orleans from Sicily, sat contemplatively at a bar near his home nursing yet another gin and tonic. In his hand he held an unexpected telegram that bore the news that he had dreaded receiving. It was a telegram announcing that he had been drafted into the United States Army.

Earlier that day, Andrew, a skilled barber by trade, had reluctantly informed his family of his impending departure for boot camp. In an attempt to drown the unwelcome news, he declared his intention to embark on a memorable night out, or as he put it, "to put a bender on." In other words, he wanted one final hurrah before answering the call to duty. War was not his choice; he had abstained from volunteering when the initial plea for recruits echoed across the nation after the United States declared war on Germany. Destiny now dictated his path.

Andrew lived at 1901 Magnolia Street in uptown New Orleans in the residence of his brother, Joseph, and his brother's wife, Catherine. Joseph and Catherine Maggio owned a grocery store and saloon, and their residence adjoined the businesses. Andrew's bedroom sat next to the couple's room. The couple was awake when the drunken Andrew returned home around 2 a.m. He went straight to his bedroom and went to sleep. Joseph and Catherine both fell asleep soon thereafter.

It was a hot, sultry May evening. The moon was hidden behind clouds, making it dark outside the Maggio home. The night was still.

He came in the night.

THE DARK FIGURE MATERIALIZED IN THE SHADOWS AT THE corner of Upperline and Magnolia Streets. The silence was disrupted by the figure's humming of a jazz song, *At the Jazz Band Ball*. The haunting melody seemed to dance through the air, creating an eerie atmosphere in the dimly lit streets.

Fixated on the building before him, a large sign on the roofline announced the establishment's name: Maggio's Grocery. A sinister smile crossed his face before walking to the fence that surrounded the property. With a swift hop, he scaled it and made his way to an outdoor shed.

Stacks of firewood, vital for both cooking and winter warmth within the Maggio home and business, flanked the shed. Opening the shed door, he entered.

When he emerged, he held an axe firmly in his hand. It

was none other than the Maggio's own tool, casting a chilling prelude to a night of unspeakable horror.

The man proceeded to the kitchen door in the back of the residence. He removed his shoes, took out a screwdriver, and sat in the doorframe, where he began to chisel away at the bottom right door panel using the blunt end of the axe as a hammer. He hummed his jazz tune the entire time.

Something awoke Andrew at 4:30 a.m. He sat up in bed, listening. From his brother's room next door, he heard moaning. He banged on the wall but received no response.

He climbed out of bed as he fought the feelings of nausea that washed over him from his night of drinking. But through his drunken haze, he could sense that something was terribly wrong. Unsure what to do, he pulled on a pair of pants that were lying on the floor, and then hustled out the front door. He ran down the block to his other brother's home, Jake Maggio. He woke his brother and the duo went back to Joseph Maggio's home.

The brothers went around the home to the kitchen door. They both gulped hard when they saw one of the panels of the door lying up against the home, but the door was locked. They quickly made their way to the front door and then to Joseph and Catherine's bedroom.

What they saw would remain with them until the day they died.

WITHIN THE HOUR, CHIEF OF DETECTIVES GEORGE BOMBAY WAS standing in the bedroom of Joseph and Catherine Maggio. Also present was Chief Mooney, Arthur Marullo, and a young detective, Theodore Obitz. All of them were horrified by the scene in front of them. As they would state to the press later, "The crime was one of the most gruesome in the annals of the New Orleans Police force."

Obitz was placed in charge of the investigation. He initiated his inquiry with a comprehensive overview of the entire crime scene. Joseph lay lifeless on the bed, his feet dangling over the edge, while Catherine lay sprawled on the floor. Both figures were covered in blood.

As Obitz continued his investigation, he meticulously examined the bodies, as the brutal sequence of events unfolded in his mind's eye. Joseph, the initial victim, bore the signature of a ruthless assault, his throat slashed in a clean line, presumably by a barber's razor. Catherine, in a desperate bid to shield her husband, had become the assailant's next target, her face and body bearing numerous lacerations. The killer's final, merciless stroke claimed her life as the razor severed her throat so profoundly that her head hung precariously from her shoulders, almost entirely detached.

Yet, the horror did not end there. With the axe, the killer had unleashed his final savagery upon both of the lifeless victims. Catherine's head was split open, and Joseph's skull had been crushed by consecutive blows.

The room, once a space filled with the ordinary moments of a simple life had been transformed into a grotesque sea of blood, that had surged up the walls, leaving splatters reaching seven feet in height. A gruesome testament to the unspeakable violence that had occurred.

Chief Mooney, Bombay, and the other detectives on the scene stood in the bedroom, their faces etched with a mix of disbelief and grim determination. The lingering echoes of the savage act seemed to seep into the very essence of the space, leaving behind an indelible mark of evil.

Chief Mooney and the other detectives listened intently as Obitz provided his descriptions of the harrowing occurrence in a somber and measured tone. Each detail he recounted added another layer to the grim tableau, a chilling puzzle of violence and malevolence that demanded their collective attention and resolve.

Chief Mooney then ordered that the entire property, both inside and outside the home, be searched for clues to help unravel the mystery. George Bombay found the axe in the Maggio's bathroom. A bloody razor would be discovered outside in the yard. How the intruder had gained access to the property remained a mystery, as the kitchen door was locked, and the chiseled out door panel was too small for an adult to climb through.

To make the whole matter even more bizarre, Obitz stumbled upon a peculiar message scribbled in chalk on the sidewalk about a block from the murder scene. The message proved to be an enigma, its cryptic meaning eluding even Obitz's investigative instincts.

The detectives interviewed Andrew and Jake. They wondered how Andrew could have slept through it all. Because of the razor, all eyes looked to the barber as the prime suspect. Bombay disagreed as he believed the murders were the result of the Black Hand. Marullo sided with Bombay. However, most members of the police believed Andrew Maggio was responsible. Mooney came to believe this as well.

Before long, Andrew Maggio was arrested for the deaths of Joseph and Catherine Maggio.

MICHAEL DEVLIN, AN ENGLISH IMMIGRANT TO NEW ORLEANS, was a twenty-three-year-old reporter for the *Times-Picayune*. Although he loved journalism and was diligent in his job as a reporter, his true dream was to write novels one day. Deep down, he had a love of storytelling, and through his work as a reporter, his writing skills were being honed.

He had a reputation of fairness, and his reporting was deemed accurate. He was motivated by a sense of justice, and he hoped his reporting in some way could assist in bringing it about in all of his crimes he reported on. At 23, he was already a seasoned crime reporter.

His brief article on the Maggio murders appeared in the afternoon edition of the *Times-Picayune*. It spoke of the horrific scene inside the bedroom, as well as the use of a razor and axe in the killings. Mention was made of the cryptic message in chalk, but the article did not say what that message said.

Giancarlo was in Giorlando's grocery that afternoon, speaking with Augustino and Lila Davis, a Black woman who was a friend and neighbor to both men. The news of Giancarlo's retirement and its underlying cause had just been shared with Lila. Given her reputation as a well-known spiritual healer in the neighborhood, she kindly offered her services to try and help him. However, despite his fondness for Lila and his friendly demeanor towards her, he held reservations about such spiritual practices and preferred not to partake in them.

With a persuasive tone in her voice, Lila said, "Mr. Giancarlo, I've seen my remedies work wonders for many. Let me help you through this challenging time."

But he demurred, "Thank you, Lila. I appreciate your kind offer, but I believe I'll find my own way through this."

Just then, a young man arrived in the store carrying copies of the afternoon edition of the *Times-Picayune*. Augustino was holding a box of oranges, so Giancarlo took the papers from the young boy. As he did so, the atmosphere grew heavy as Giancarlo's gaze fixed on the headline: *Sicilian Grocery Owners Brutally Murdered in their Home.*

Quickly placing the papers down on the counter, Giancarlo pulled the top one off the stack and stuck it under his arm. He then reached in his pocket and pulled out his money, placing it on the counter. He told Augustino and Lila goodbye and headed upstairs to his room.

He read the article by Devlin three times in a row. As he read, a feeling of dread washed over his entire body – a feeling he remembered well during the Cleaver attacks. What did the chalk message say? Was it from the killer? He had to find out.

He knew the young reporter and liked him a lot. He was a reporter one could trust, a man who kept his word. Surely, the reporter had to know what the message said. There was one way to find out.

Two hours later, Giancarlo was seated in a chair in the waiting area of the *Times-Picayune*. On his lap was the paper he had purchased. Michael Devlin walked into the waiting area and extended his hand towards him.

Giancarlo stood. "It's nice to see you again, Michael."

"Same detective. How is retirement?"

"I'd rather be working," Giancarlo confessed.

Devlin nodded. "They said you wanted to see me."

"I did. Can we speak somewhere quietly?" Giancarlo asked.

"Sure. We can step right over here into this office," Devlin suggested, gesturing towards the nearby room.

Right off the waiting room was a small office with a round table inside. The walls were bare. Giancarlo took his seat while Devlin shut the door. He then sat down across from Giancarlo.

"What can I do for you?" Devlin asked.

Giancarlo laid the paper on the table. He pointed to the article.

Devlin sighed. "Gruesome scene from what Obitz told me. As a matter of fact, I've never seen so many officers traumatized by what they saw."

"I'm interested in the message that was found at the scene."

"Ah, the chalk message," Devlin replied.

"It was Obitz who found it?" Giancarlo inquired.

"Yes, he and his partner."

"Your article did not say what that message said."

"Obitz asked me not to report it," Devlin explained.

"But you know what it said?" Giancarlo pressed.

Michael Devlin stroked his chin, deep in thought, before saying, "Of course. And you are here because you want me to tell you."

"Yes."

"Why?" Devlin Questioned. "You're retired,"

"Let's just say I have a keen interest in the matter."

"You always treated me fairly. You always provided information to me and respected my role in your investigations," Devlin remarked. He paused, stroking his chin again, but then went on, "Of course, I will deny that I ever told you this, okay?"

"Of course," Giancarlo agreed.

"Scribbled on the sidewalk, the unsettling message declared, 'Mrs. Joseph Maggio is going to sit up tonight just like Mrs. Toney.' What that means I have no idea."

Giancarlo, overtaken by a sense of foreboding, sank back into his chair, feeling an oppressive tightness in his chest. The name "Mrs. Toney" echoed in his mind, like a haunting refrain.

Suddenly, Giancarlo rose abruptly from his chair, and began to pace. The gravity of the message weighed heavily on him, and with every anxious step, the reality of what it might mean settled upon him.

Devlin stared in silence at his agitated friend, a mixture of confusion and concern flickering in his eyes. The tension in the room was palpable as Giancarlo's restless movements betrayed his inner turmoil.

After a moment, Devlin finally broke the silence by

asking, "What is it?" The question lingered, waiting for a response from the retired detective, who appeared burdened by unspoken dread.

Lost in his troubled thoughts, Giancarlo murmured, "Oh my God," aloud, paying little attention to the question.

Devlin asked again, more urgently, "Giancarlo, what is it?"

Giancarlo stopped pacing and turned and faced the reporter. "Before I answer, can I ask you two questions."

"Sure. I will try to answer."

"How did the killer enter the Maggio's home?"

"The police are not sure," Devlin replied.

"But there was a chiseled out a panel on the kitchen door?" Giancarlo queried further.

Confused as to how Giancarlo would know that, Devlin responded, "Yes. But the door was locked, so they don't know how he entered."

Giancarlo placed his hands on the table and leaned over it. He then looked directly at Michael Devlin and asked, "Did the killer wear shoes?"

"I feel like you already know the answer that I'm going to give you. They found sock prints in the blood on the bedroom floor. So, he did not wear shoes. It seems after the deed, the killer actually took off his shirt and socks, both covered with blood, and left them rolled up in the bedroom where the murders took place. Detective Rabito, I ask you again, what is your interest in this case?"

"I know what the message is referring to."

Surprised, Devlin asked, "What?"

Giancarlo proceeded to tell the young newspaper man the

story of the Sciambra murders, and, in particular, Johanna Sciambra, whose nickname was "Mrs. Toney."

When Giancarlo finished, the young reporter sat in shocked silence in the little room. He finally asked, "So you think this killer was involved in the murder of the Sciambras back in 1912."

"I do. Although the way the Maggios were murdered doesn't match how the Sciambras were killed. He used a revolver to murder them."

Devlin quickly responded, "A revolver was found lying by the killer's clothes in the Maggio's bedroom, but it was not used in the crime. It was a razor blade and an axe."

The vision of the Cleaver at the top of his stairs near his apartment came into Giancarlo's mind. "My God, he has returned."

"Who has returned?"

Not paying attention to the question, Giancarlo said, "And now we know he was involved in the killing of the Sciambras. How did I miss that?"

"Giancarlo, I'm very confused. The police truly believe they have their man. They think Andrew Maggio killed his brother."

Giancarlo said with emphasis. "They have the wrong man."

"Then who did it?"

Michael Devlin was mesmerized as the master detective laid before him the connections between the Maggio murders and the Sciambra murders, and how they could all be connected to the earlier attacks by the Cleaver, including the death of Joe Davi. With the chalk writing found, Giancarlo finally could bring closure to the Sciambra case in his mind. They met their deaths at the hands of the Cleaver. And now, all these years later, the Cleaver had come out of the shadows and attacked again. Why the delay in the attacks? Giancarlo had no answer. But there was no doubt that this was the same man.

"Giancarlo, you're saying this killer, this man who killed the Maggios, is the same Cleaver from so long ago?"

"Indeed I am."

"I never heard about those attacks; I was still over in England when they all occurred, so I'm not surprised about that. You really believe this is him?"

"Yes, the Maggios are his first attack after all these years."

Devlin shook his head. "That may not be the case. What I am about to tell you, I tell you in the utmost of secrecy. This was never even reported in the papers."

"What is it?"

"Back in December, there was an attack. An attack on Sicilian immigrants who ran a grocery, the Andollinas. I was just told about that attack from Obitz this morning. The Andollinas were attacked by an axe wielding crazed man. They survived. Obitz wondered if that attack was connected to the murder of the Maggios. But his thoughts were shut down by those above him. No one wanted to investigate the connection between that attack and this latest one - not Mooney, not Marullo, not Bombay, none of them. Mooney and his other detectives pegged the crime on Andrew Maggio, while Bombay and Marullo believe it is the work of the Black Hand.

Giancarlo chuckled. "Maybe Mooney should have held onto his job at the railroads."

"In over his head, you think?"

"I guess we will find out."

"I know Bombay and Marullo are convinced the Andollina attack and the murder of the Maggios are the work of the Black Hand."

"Of course, they do," Giancarlo replied. "I can tell you with certainty that this is not the work of the Black Hand."

"How can you be so sure? I know you're Sicilian, so I don't mean any disrespect, but the police have had a very hard time controlling crime in the Italian enclaves of the city. Perhaps the Black Hand lives once again."

"I know how the Black Hand works. I know their every move. They do not kill women. Period. They are not involved. Without a doubt, the Cleaver has returned."

"Who is he? Why does he kill?" Devlin inquired.

"Those are answers that the police, the press, and all of New Orleans need to answer, and soon."

Devlin then asked, "I have one question for you?"

"What?"

"Why did you retire? You have a gift."

Giancarlo pointed to his chest and said, "Bad ticker."

Devlin stood up from the table. "I'm going to let Obitz know what you think the message is referring to and the connections to the earlier murders."

"Obitz is a good man. He may believe you, but he will have a tough time convincing Chief Mooney that they arrested the wrong man for killing the Maggios. Eventually Mooney may come to his senses, if he'd only look at the facts, and realize the truth. Let's just hope it's not too late."

"If this killer is related to the earlier attacks, will he strike again?" Devlin asked.

"He will, but will it be in a week, a month, a year, or seven years? Who knows? I'm afraid that answer only remains with him, and we will only learn of it when the next attack happens. I do thank you for trusting me with your information."

"Your retirement is a loss for all of us."

Giancarlo extended his hand. Devlin shook it as their meeting came to close.

WAR ON JAZZ

After his conversation with Michael Devlin and the surprising discovery of the contents of the chalk message, Giancarlo was grappling with a mix of emotions. The shock of the return of the man he knew as the Cleaver weighed heavily on him. The fact that this elusive killer had resurfaced after so many years and claimed more victims burdened Giancarlo's conscience, as the strange vision of the Cleaver outside his apartment door replayed over and over in his mind. As he tried to make sense of it all, a knot formed in his stomach, and the gravity of the situation began to sink in.

The urge to run to Chief Mooney and beg for his badge back, to make another attempt at uncovering the madman's identity, surged within him. However, a sense of resignation settled in; he knew it was too late for that now. The opportunity for redemption had passed, slipping through his fingers like grains of sand.

Despite the turmoil, Giancarlo held onto faith in Detective

Obitz. Perhaps with his fresh perspective and new set of eyes, Obitz could bring closure to the matter that Giancarlo never could. Putting aside thoughts of returning to the police department, Giancarlo turned his attention to his book. Now that he had some closure to the Sciambra murders, he could write a satisfying ending to their story.

Equipped with the newfound connection to the Cleaver, Giancarlo intended to revise the chapter on the Sciambra murders. The inclusion of the Cleaver in that story added an even more chilling narrative. This tale would offer readers insight into the earlier Cleaver attacks. His vivid descriptions of the gruesome murder scene within Joe Davi's bedroom would undoubtedly send shockwaves through even the most unflinching readers. He would show how all of these attacks spread out over the years were the result of the elusive Cleaver.

Meanwhile, Michael Devlin followed through with his promise. He informed Detective Obitz of the connection between the chalk message and the Sciambra murders. Obitz quietly pulled the investigation files from that murder and reviewed them very carefully.

Obitz also shared his concerns regarding the possible connection to the murders to Bombay and Marullo. Frustrated, Obitz could see that even with this new information, those two detectives still held the wrong belief that the Black Hand was responsible for the attacks. And yet, Obitz had been an investigator on the Andollina attacks. He was starting to believe the same as Giancarlo Rabito, that the Sciambra murders, Andollini attacks, and the Maggio murders were all related, and were not the result of the Black Hand. And although he knew nothing about the Davi attacks from his own experience, he trusted Giancarlo's assertion that they were all linked to the mysterious Cleaver. The man clearly knew what he was talking about.

The Maggio murders deeply unsettled the citizens of New Orleans, particularly the Sicilian community, renewing a sense of unease and tension. Discussions about the attacks and expressions of fear reverberated among Sicilian-owned restaurants, produce stands, and grocery stores.

Obitz was busy chasing leads, while Devlin was unyielding in questioning Chief Mooney. The young reporter theorized the arrest of Andrew Maggio had been a mistake, and he was relentless in asking the chief if he had the wrong man behind bars. As Giancarlo predicted, Chief Mooney, based on the chalk message and the connection with the Sciambra murders, finally came to believe they had arrested the wrong man after the Maggios' killing. Andrew Maggio was released from custody, under the Chief's orders.

But with no suspects to take his place, Mooney began to feel the heat from the press to provide closure to the Maggio case. His one hope was that Detective Obitz could make a breakthrough and bring the matter to a conclusion, just as he had done in the Rydell matter a few months earlier. Mooney's hopes were soon dashed just a week later.

Detective Obitz was shot and killed while chasing a robber late one evening. Grief quickly took hold inside the entire police department, while the citizens became resolved that the murderer of the Maggios would never be found.

Giancarlo was devastated when he heard the news of the death of Detective Obitz. With the killing of Chief Reynolds and now Obitz, he knew the men on the police force had to be reeling. Added to that was the mounting pressure on the entire department to find the murderer of the Maggios. Giancarlo's grief at the loss of Obitz, aided by the revelation of the return of the Cleaver, turned quickly to depression. There lay a heavy and ominous pall over his already burdened heart.

He spent the next day in bed, his heart ailment taking its toll once again. It was almost as if his body wanted to make sure that any thoughts of coming out of retirement were extinguished forever.

TWO DAYS LATER, FINALLY FEELING BETTER, GIANCARLO STOOD across the street from the Ursuline Convent, its weathered walls resonating with the weight of history. It was a beautiful afternoon, but inside the adjacent St. Mary's Italian Church, the funeral of Joseph and Catherine Maggio was taking place. He watched solemnly as men carried their flower-strewn caskets out of the church, down the stairs, and onto carriages which would take the couple to their final resting place. He made the sign of the cross, kissing his thumb at its conclusion, and prayed that their killer would be brought to justice soon.

As he walked home, the evocative sound of a piano and a saxophone drew his attention to the small saloon on the corner. The melodic strains of the jazz music provided him with a gentle reminder that in New Orleans, even amid death, music prevailed.

The music whispered to his soul, enveloping him like a warm blanket and inviting him into its embrace. He made his way into the saloon and took a seat at the far end of the bar.

After the bartender poured his drink, Giancarlo quickly got lost in the music. In its pulsating rhythms, he became more and more aware of the connection this music had to the heart and soul of New Orleans. Giancarlo spent the next couple of hours taking in the sounds of his city, drinking more than a few cocktails, trying to distance himself from the Maggio murders and the return of the Cleaver.

As his feet tapped to the beat of the music, his troubled soul became soothed by the enticing melodies. Lost in the seductive allure of jazz, he found solace in its rhythm and harmony. While listening to the talented musicians pour forth their emotions into this music, Giancarlo thought about the current push by some to put an end to the art form. How, he wondered, could anyone be opposed to this music?

Little did he realize that soon, in the coming weeks, what had initially begun as mere whispers of opposition would rapidly evolve into an all-out assault against jazz. Against the backdrop of his personal struggles, a larger cultural war unfolded across the city, as the harmonious notes of jazz clashed with the dissonant tones of those seeking to silence it. The leaders of this movement were the elitist reformers, who saw jazz as a threat to the established order.

NEW ORLEANS HAD A LOVE AFFAIR WITH MUSIC. MUSIC WAS PART of the social fabric of life in the Crescent City. Though the city had been a leading slave port before the Civil War, and segregation persisted long after slavery was abolished, people of different races mixed much more freely in New Orleans than other American cities in the early 20th century.

Cultures blended together as music evolved to accommodate them all.

All different types of music came together: spiritual, opera, blues, classical, military, and ragtime, America's most popular music for a time in the early 20th century. From all of these musical genres, New Orleans musicians began adding their own improvisation, and jazz was born.

Frank Douroux's Little Gem Saloon was located in the 400 block of South Rampart Street. This small, intimate establishment was often regarded as the birthplace of jazz. All of the early jazz greats played here, like Buddy Bolden, Sidney Bechet, Bunk Johnson, and Jelly Roll Morton.

As jazz became more and more popular, a reform movement rose up to meet it. For years, these reformers had declared war on vice in the city and were trying to bring a more ordered society to New Orleans. By 1918, the reformers' campaign, primarily driven by the privileged white elite, had seen success, aided immensely by the rules and restrictions on civilian life promulgated by the Defense Department during World War I.

The US Navy ruled that no houses of prostitution could be near a military site. With the Port of New Orleans being a vital asset to the US government to get troops and supplies to Europe, Storyville, the famous red-light district near the French Quarter, succumbed to the rules of war. It was closed and torn down.

And yet, amidst this backdrop of societal change, there was one element that survived and thrived, and its echoes could still be heard around the city, and that was jazz music. In the face of attempts to suppress various forms of entertainment and expression, jazz continued to resonate, symbolizing resilience and cultural resistance, placing it front and center in the reformers' war.

For the elite, jazz was a symbol of the decay that they felt had crept into and festered in their society. They considered it vulgar, and the musicians who played it faced disdain from the elite, who viewed their talent as illegitimate, since they were lacking in a formal musical education. And worst of all, in the view of the elite, the exponents of that jazz sound were the Blacks and the Sicilians, the lowest of the low in their imagined social hierarchy, and the root of all the problems in the city they believed belonged to them.

It's true, jazz, the rebellious lovechild of ragtime and blues, of spiritual and traditional American ballads, first emerged in the city's African American and Creole communities, where it inherited its rhythm and tempo. However, New Orleans Jazz music also has Italian blood running in its veins, where its musical voice is heard loud and clear through Italian brass tunes. Sicilian musicians learned syncopated rhythms and blues tonalities from their African Americans neighbors, while Black players absorbed popular Italian melodies and the lyrical Italian trumpet sound.

The campaign against jazz went beyond a mere disdain for what the elite perceived as vulgar music. It was an effort by the elite to assert their authority and relegate Blacks and Sicilians to subordinate positions, resolidifying their control over New Orleans.

On June 20, 1918, the war against jazz was placed directly in front of the citizens when an editorial appeared in the *Times-Picayune*. Giancarlo awoke that morning, picked up a paper, and was amazed at what he read. With a killer on the loose in the city, the paper decided it would use its editorial power to enter the musical debate. They sided with the traditionalists and declared war against jazz, or jass as they referred to it.

The article was not only an attack on jazz, but it was also an attack on the class and race of the vast majority of musicians who were the leading exponents of jazz in the city.

The article began by stating that jazz, at its inception was listened to behind closed doors and drawn curtains, but it soon spread out into public spaces - *"… like all vice, it grew bolder until it dared decent surroundings, and there, was tolerated because of its oddity."*

Then the article turned to comparing jazz to the more traditional, highbrow music of the city. Stating that there are *"many mansions in the house of music,"* the more traditional style of music found its home at the French Opera House, or as the article called it, *"the first great assembly hall of melody."*

So where did jazz fit in in this so-called house of music? *"In the house there is, however, another apartment, properly speaking, down in the basement, a kind of servants' hall of rhythms. It is there we hear the hum of the Indian dance, the throb of the Oriental tambourines and kettle drums, the clatter of the clogs, the click of Slavic heels, the thumpty-tumpty of the negro banjo, and, in fact, the native dances of the world."* Acknowledging that the city was the birthplace of jazz, the article than moved to its conclusion with its declaration of war.

"In the matter of jass, New Orleans is particularly interested, since it has been widely suggested that this particular form of musical vice had its birth in this city - that it came, in fact, from doubtful surroundings in our slums. We do not recognize the honor of parenthood, but with such a story in circulation, it behooves us to

be last to accept the atrocity in polite society, and where it has crept in, we should make it a point of civic honor to suppress it. Its musical value is nil, and its possibilities of harm are great."

There was much debate throughout the city after the release of that editorial. Was jazz music something that should survive, or should it be stomped out, as a means of civic honor as called for by the *Times-Picayune*? There were strong feelings on both sides.

Giancarlo cherished opera, classical music, and jazz equally. He saw room for all these art forms in the city. He recognized that opera was a deeply passionate art form, and he believed that the Black and Sicilian communities brought forth that same intensity of passion in jazz. Their passion permeated every facet of life, encompassing love, cuisine, festivals, art, business, and especially music. Giancarlo vehemently disagreed with the *Times-Picayune's* editorial stance and embraced the diversity and vitality that these musical expressions brought to New Orleans.

The jazz loving attacker of the Maggios read the editorial, too. He took note of every word and swore vengeance against the *Times-Picayune.* Someway, somehow, he would get the editorial board as well as all of the citizens of New Orleans to understand the importance of jazz.

For the inhabitants of the city, the debate about the article and the future role of jazz was cut short. Just days later, there was another attack.

THE STRANGE CASE OF THE BESUMERS

In the early morning hours of June 26, 1918, Louis Besumer and his wife were attacked by an axe-wielding man who had entered their residence, which was attached to their grocery store located on the corner of North Dorgenois and Laharpe Streets.

Both survived the attack.

Louis had been struck once across his face, but Mrs. Besumer's injuries were even more serious, including a cracked skull. The bloody axe was lying on the bedroom floor, and a chisel used to remove a bottom panel from the door lay on the back steps. Yet how the perpetrator gained access perplexed the investigators.

Within an hour of the attack, Chief Mooney, Detective Marullo, Detective Bombay, Assistant District Attorney Ben Daly, and Coroner Joseph O'Hara were all crammed inside the humble residence, fully engaged now that there had been yet another axe attack. Mrs. Besumer claimed that it was a young, dark person who attacked her.

Meanwhile, Michael Devlin was anxious to get information. While waiting on some word from the police, he spoke to neighbors and quickly got the idea that there was a lot more to the story of Louis Besumer and his wife, who he learned were Eastern European immigrants to New Orleans.

Thanks to Mrs. Besumer's statement, the police arrested Lewis Obichon, a Black handyman who had worked for the Besumers. However, over the course of the next few days, the narrative of the attack as laid out by the Besumers changed many times. Mrs. Besumer suddenly remembered that it wasn't a Black person who attacked her, but a white man. She then later changed her story again and said that her husband had attacked her. The police threw their hands up, and despite the discrepancies and changes in her story, not to mention the fact that Mr. Besumer was himself a victim, this would ultimately lead to the arrest of Mr. Besumer.

Chief Mooney was convinced the Besumers were hiding something. Mooney even allowed Michael Devlin to interview Mrs. Besumer in the hospital to see if the young reporter could make any sense of the whole matter.

Some members of the police force believed the attack was nothing more than a domestic fight. Others believed it was the Maggio killer who had struck again. Thanks to the investigatory work of Michael Devlin, eventually more information was released. It was learned that the couple were not married. Mrs. Besumer's real name was in fact Harriet Anne Lowe, and she was Irish. Also, Louis Besumer had always said he was Polish, when in reality, it was discovered that he was German.

The investigation turned bizarre, and the entire matter became a media circus. Letters were discovered inside the residence that led investigators to believe Louis Besumer was a German spy. At the height of the Great War raging in Europe, this caught everyone's attention. It was obvious Mooney was in over his head, so the Department of Justice stepped in to interview the perceived spy. It became quickly apparent that they could not make a spy case against him. However, Louis Besumer remained in jail for the alleged attack on his wife.

The whole Besumer incident was strange. Everyone tried to follow the story daily in the papers, but it was hard to keep track of the new, legitimate information.

Giancarlo's bad days now were running consecutively. During most of the Besumer investigation, he stayed in his apartment, following the story in the *Times-Picayune*, and in particular, the reporting of Michael Devlin. Based on that reporting, Giancarlo believed the attack was a result of the same attacker as the Maggios, even though some of it did not match up. While they were grocery owners, they were not Italian. And the woman in this case had taken the more brutal beating than the man.

Devlin tried his best to trumpet to the citizens that the attacks were connected. On June 28, he wrote an article in the *Times-Picayune* that included this passage: "*In the same manner in which Joseph Maggio and his wife, Italians, were chopped to death with a hatchet as they slept behind their grocery store at Upperline and Magnolia Streets a month ago, Louis Besumer and his wife were chopped with a hatchet early Thursday morning as they slept in their quarters in back of their grocery store at Dorgenois and Laharpe Streets. Police believe the hatchet user in both crimes was the same man. The latest hatchet victims are in Charity Hospital in critical condition."*

Bombay and Marullo were furious that Devlin linked the two attacks together. They still believed that the Andollina and Maggio attacks were the result of the Black Hand, and they had been so vocal with this opinion, they could not afford to change their minds now. As for the Besumers, the detectives were unsure if it was a robbery gone bad, a domestic brawl, or if it was connected to Mr. Besumer's alleged German spy activities. There was one thing that was certain in their minds, it was *not* connected to the murderer of the Maggios.

As for Chief Mooney, he was uncertain of the connection, but did not rule it out. He needed more information and was determined to keep an open mind. Where the facts led him, he would go.

Giancarlo read the article about the Besumers with interest, but with the turn of events in the investigation, he knew the story of the attacker would fall by the wayside. The story would be overtaken by the sensationalized story of the Besumers. Instead of being a warning to all of the citizens about a killer on the loose, he knew the citizens would get lost in the sensational stories of espionage. He did meet with Augustino Giorlando and his wife and informed them of the latest attack on a grocer in the city. He advised them to take precautions.

Giancarlo wondered if the attacker followed the news reporting after his attacks. For if he did, the weird turn of events and the reporting now focusing on Louis Besumer being a potential German spy, meant one thing. He would feel compelled to strike again, and soon.

Giancarlo was correct.

On Monday night, August 4, 1918, Mary Schneider, nine months pregnant, had just put her three children to bed inside the home that she shared with her husband, Edward, at 1320 Elmira Street in the St. Claude neighborhood. Her husband worked the late-night shift at the Southern Pacific wharf, so he was not at home.

The moon hung low in the sky on that fateful night, casting a pale, eerie glow over the quiet St. Claude neighborhood. Unbeknownst to Mary Schneider, a sinister presence lurked in the shadows, watching, and waiting for the perfect moment to strike.

The air inside the house on Elmira Street was heavy with an oppressive stillness, broken only by the soft snores of Mary's sleeping children. As Mary settled into her bed, her weariness began to envelop her, lulling her into a vulnerable state of slumber.

Time passed, and the darkness deepened. Then, a noise, barely audible, pierced the silence. Mary stirred, a mother's senses awakening her, as she instinctively reached out to welcome her husband, happy for his early release from work. But to her horror, she found herself face to face with an unknown figure, whose features were obscured by the cloak of night.

A surge of terror coursed through Mary's veins, as she let out a piercing scream, a desperate plea for help. A forceful blow crashed against her skull, sending searing pain radiating through her body, as darkness descended upon her. She fell unconscious on the bed.

When Mary eventually regained consciousness, she had a nasty gash across her forehead and broken teeth spilling from her mouth. The intruder was gone. And there, in the darkness, clutching her pregnant belly, she unleashed a round of shrill screams, desperately crying out for help.

As usual, Chief Mooney, Detective Bombay, and Detective Marullo stood in the residence soon thereafter. Mary was at Charity Hospital where doctors were trying to save her and her baby.

After checking the property, the investigators were perplexed. There was no visible sign of entry. The weapon used against Mary seemed to have been a bedside lamp, which lay broken on the floor, and with Mary's blood on it. And the Schneider's axe was missing from their storage shed. Some of the drawers of the dresser had been rummaged through.

Bombay said to Mooney at one point, "The Schneiders are not Italian and they don't own a grocery. The weapon was a lamp, not an axe. There is no connection."

Mooney replied, "People said they heard her scream. Perhaps our man was startled and grabbed the lamp to shut her up."

"And the axe?"

Mooney pointed to his mouth. "The injury to her mouth and teeth didn't seem to be the result of the lamp. That's just my opinion. I think he used the axe as well. I think we are dealing with the same man."

"Well, I disagree with you. I think the axe was taken after the fact to make people *think* it was the same killer of the Maggios. This is a case of a simple burglary."

Mooney smiled. "No matter what we say, the citizens will hear of another attack, and they will put their blame on the boogeyman they have conjured up."

"I still wonder how the perpetrator got in here."

"Strange. Very strange. Let's go talk to the press. They will want some information."

THE AFTERNOON EDITION OF THE *DAILY STATES* PRINTED A VERY interesting interview. Unnamed detectives within the police had sat down with Mark Gilson, a reporter. They proceeded to ridicule and call into question the belief that these latest attacks were all the actions of one individual. Each attack was separate and distinct, they opined.

Chief Mooney was incensed that these unnamed men would go behind his back and assure the public that the attacks were unrelated, when his belief was tending toward the fact that they were in fact connected. He stood in the kitchen inside his home early that evening, drinking an Old Fashioned to relieve the sting of betrayal.

The attack on Mary Schneider was not just a burglary. That's what his gut was telling him. While he did not have the instinct of a policeman who had earned his stripes working the beat as a young man, something was just gnawing at him. Of course, the pressure to find the culprit or culprits and put an end to the attacks was weighing harder and harder on him. It was then and there he decided he needed to know once and for all what the connections were between all these crimes. He knew there was one person who could assist him. One person who others had told him had an uncanny knack for explaining crimes. That person was Giancarlo Rabito.

He called the retired detective and asked if they could meet at an uptown saloon on Magazine Street, Henry's Bar. Mooney thought it was a perfect location to speak in private about the most pressing of matters with someone who had been intimately involved in the earlier investigations.

Giancarlo said he would be there, and the conversation ended.

Mooney hung up the phone and checked his watch. He would be meeting with Rabito in two hours. He fixed himself another drink, savoring it before leaving for his meeting.

HENRY'S BAR HAD BEEN OPENED AT THE TURN OF THE 20TH century by Irish immigrants James Lee and Margaret Tully Lee. It was an unassuming, neighborhood spot, which was beloved by its dedicated patrons.

Giancarlo walked in. It was not crowded that night. Giancarlo saw Mooney seated at a table. The Chief was dressed in a white shirt and khaki pants, not in his police attire. He stood up from the table when Giancarlo approached.

"Nice to see you again, Chief," Giancarlo said, as they shook hands.

"Same, Giancarlo. And please, call me Frank. Can I get you a drink?"

"Sure, what are you having?"

"An Old Fashioned."

"I'll have the same," Giancarlo replied.

Mooney turned toward the bartender and yelled out, "George, bring another one for my friend."

The bartender nodded his head and then turned to begin making his creation. Giancarlo and Mooney took their seats.

"Thanks for coming to see me, Giancarlo. Before we begin, how are you feeling?"

"Good days and bad days, you know how it goes."

"Well, I hope you have more good days in your retirement." Giancarlo nodded. "Me too."

"Well, like I said, I wanted to meet with you and get your assistance on a matter."

"Sure. And what matter is that?" Giancarlo inquired.

Mooney leaned forward over the table, and in a whisper, said, "There is a killer on the loose in our city. But I think you already knew that."

"When I heard about the Maggios' murder, I wondered if the Cleaver had risen again and was on the hunt. And then, when I learned of the attacks on the Andollinas, Besumers, and Mary Schneider, I had no doubt. He is back."

"Just recently I learned of the original Cleaver murders. Terrible business. You are sure it's the same man?" Mooney pressed.

"I do think they are all related. The Crutti, Rissettos, and Davi attacks were all committed by him. Now I believe this new string of victims are his, too."

Just then George came over carrying two drinks. He placed one in front of Giancarlo and put the other next to Mooney's other half full glass.

Mooney said to Giancarlo, "Such a good bartender. Brings a drink when he knows I will need another soon."

George smiled, and said, "Chief, with the crime in this city, I would have to drink a few of these a night if I was in your position."

Mooney raised his glass, and George left them alone to continue their conversation.

Mooney looked back toward Giancarlo. "So, you were discussing his connection to the other attacks."

Giancarlo nodded his head. "Yes, and I would add in the Sciambra murders, even though a revolver was used. Of course, the chalk message linked it to the others."

"I wanted to meet with you to get more information on those earlier attacks. Has his *modus operandi* changed? What the hell are we dealing with?"

"A killer," replied Giancarlo. "That is what we are dealing with. A sick, cold blooded, killer."

Giancarlo went into great depth, explaining each of the attacks of the Cleaver. His attention to detail was astonishing. He spoke about the smallest clues and nuances that the Cleaver had left behind at the crime scenes, demonstrating an uncanny ability to recreate the scenes. His explanations were not only informative but also delivered with a sense of reverence for the victims, as if he were determined to bring justice to their memories. Mooney was in awe. This was a *real* detective.

When Giancarlo finished, Mooney said, "So this Cleaver,

you believe, is the same man killing and maiming people now with an axe."

"Yes. And we now have a good idea of how he works. His method from back then to now has not changed much. In most instances, he looks for a grocery with a barroom attached. He removes a panel from the backdoor. How he slips in I'm not certain as he has been described as a large man and only ever carves out a small entrance. The attacks occur at around 3 a.m. The weapon he uses on his sleeping victims is usually the owner's own property, an axe."

Mooney listened attentively to Giancarlo's explanation, and as the pieces of the puzzle fell into place, a sense of clarity washed over him. The pattern Giancarlo described was chillingly consistent, and Mooney had to admit that it made a compelling case for the Cleaver being the same individual responsible for the recent attacks.

Taking another sip of his drink, Mooney couldn't deny the weight of the evidence. Giancarlo had expertly connected the dots between the attacks of the past and these current ones. The method, the timing, and the choice of weapon, all pointed to a disturbingly consistent *modus operandi*. Any doubts that lingered in Mooney's mind disappeared. He was convinced that New Orleans had a madman on its hands. A madman who thirsted for blood.

Placing his glass back on the table, Mooney leaned forward, his gaze fixed on the retired detective. His voice was steady, but the gravity of the situation pulled at his words as he asked, "Who is he?"

Giancarlo sighed. "That has been on my mind since 1910. These are some of my conclusions to date. He's a middle age white male. Working class. I think at one time he was a simple burglar. He knows how to get into places quietly. I often wonder if his disappearance for six years was a result of being in jail for a robbery. Perhaps our killer has been sitting in a New Orleans jail these past six years, biding his time to get out and kill again."

"Why does he attack Italians mostly? I mean except for the Besumers and Mary Schneider, they were all Italians."

Giancarlo replied, "Why Italians, and grocery owners at that? Not sure. Perhaps his war is against the success of immigrants. But that's just a guess."

Chief Mooney added, "There are some on the force who believe it's the Black Hand."

"It's not," Giancarlo replied with conviction.

"I don't think so either. Some of my other detectives say they are robberies gone bad. Separate and distinct, not the work of a single man. I'm sure you saw the recent article where they spit forth their crap."

"I wondered if they were speaking on your behalf. I didn't think so."

"Absolutely not," Mooney replied. "They didn't even give their names, those cowards."

"You asked me who he is? I'll say it again. He's a madman who needs and wants blood. He can't control his urge to kill. Of this I am sure: he will kill again."

Giancarlo's words cast a grim shadow over their conversation. Mooney was silent, before picking up his glass and gulping down the rest of his second drink. Mooney broke the silence with a matter-of-fact question. "Are you saying that we have a Jack the Ripper type lunatic on the loose in our city?"

Giancarlo nodded solemnly, his expression mirroring the

gravity of the situation, as he replied, "Yes, Chief, that's precisely what I'm saying."

"I've begun speaking to some men who study the behavior of criminals. Trying to get any help I can in uncovering this madman's identity. I have even contacted a detective with the Pinkerton Agency. I am leaving no stone unturned in trying to stop him. Until we can discover who he is, I need to increase the patrols late at night; particularly around Italian grocery stores."

"I agree, even though his last two attacks were on non-Italians. By the way, how is Mary Schneider?"

"She is recovering. She gave birth to a beautiful and healthy baby girl."

"That's wonderful news," Giancarlo replied, his face breaking out into a smile.

"I can't thank you enough for meeting with me. For my detectives to go behind my back and put forth a theory that I know is inaccurate, is hurtful to me, my department, and our investigation."

"The citizens have already made the link. They will not listen to that erroneous account."

"Exactly, and that's why they never should have said what they said. I was stopped this morning by a young reporter for the *Times-Picayune*. A man named Devlin. He sees the link, at least between the current attacks. I was careful what I said to that reporter. I didn't reveal or deny anything. One good thing is he has not connected these recent attacks to the Cleaver, or so I believe."

Giancarlo said nothing as he picked up his glass, taking a swig. He did not want to tell Chief Mooney that he had had already made that connection for Devlin some time ago.

The Chief continued. "I think it best, for now, that we don't let the public know about that connection. I fear if we did, then they would come to believe that we may never be able to stop him. I need to assure them that we will catch this lunatic, to prevent our fellow citizens from going into hysterics. I am certain that by the morning, this Devlin will make the connection that the Schneider attack was done by the same man who attacked the Andollinas, Maggios, and Besumers. Eventually, I fear, he will connect them all to the Cleaver attacks."

"Perhaps the people should know," replied Giancarlo.

Now it was Giancarlo's turn to gulp down the rest of his drink. Mooney turned both of his hands palms face up, a pose of supplication, signaling for Giancarlo's input.

But when Giancarlo looked up, he was suddenly taken aback, as the man seated at the table was not Frank Mooney but James Reynolds, the deceased police chief. Giancarlo's mouth dropped open as he stared into the face of his old friend. Then he heard a voice, Frank Mooney's voice, and the image of James Reynolds disappeared as Mooney asked, "Are you ok?"

Rubbing both of his temples, Giancarlo said, "I'm sorry. It passed. Not feeling great, but I'm ok."

"Well, I was asking if you want to come back and work as a special investigator?"

"You're joking, right?"

"No. I know you're unwell, but the offer is there," Mooney said with a grim expression. "Your city needs you."

Giancarlo smiled. "I spend more time than you can imagine in bed. Which means I would be of little service to you."

"You were a good cop, Giancarlo. You are a good cop. So, what does one do in retirement?

"I'm writing a novel. A novel about the crimes I was involved with during my career."

"I hope when you finish, your novel is brought to the end with the capture and arrest of our madman."

"Me too, Frank. Me too."

THE NEXT MORNING, CHIEF MOONEY'S PREDICTION PROVED correct. The headline of the *Times-Picayune* screamed:

POLICE BELIEVE AXMAN MAY BE ACTIVE IN THE CITY

Michael Devlin's article that morning connected the Schneider attack with the earlier attacks on the Andollinas, Maggios, and Besumers. Chief Mooney was relieved to see that Devlin's reporting did not discuss any connection to the Cleaver attacks. But the Chief knew the headline was enough to stir immense anxiety among the citizens.

And for the first time, the killer was a given a name in public, a name that would soon bring fear to the entire city and, in particular, the Sicilians: The Axman of New Orleans.

13

ALMOST AS IF HE HAD WINGS

The *Times-Picayune* headline made the residents fearful. Was there really an axman on the loose in the city? Why was he attacking grocery store owners? These questions were pondered by all, particularly the inhabitants of Little Palermo and the Sicilians living in other parts of the city.

Some even began to speak once again of the attacks of the Cleaver, who terrorized the residents so long ago, adding to the already chilling atmosphere. However, even they could not imagine that the same individual responsible for the past horrors was responsible for these latest attacks. The realization that they were facing a relentless and cunning killer from their darkest nightmares only deepened the sense of dread. The entire city was on edge.

The routine activities that once brought comfort and a sense of normalcy now carried an air of trepidation. Grocery store owners felt a deep sense of vulnerability. Their establishments had become potential targets of the mysterious axman. The mundane act of buying essentials became an exercise in caution, as customers scanned their surroundings and hurriedly completed their purchases.

The recent brutal attack on the pregnant Mary Schneider had shaken many residents to their core, raising even more questions and adding to the confusion surrounding the investigations. Notably, Mary Schneider, like the Besumers, did not belong to the Sicilian-Italian community, which perplexed both the inhabitants of Little Palermo and those attempting to uncover the truth. Some speculated about whether the Axman had expanded his targets beyond the confines of the closely-knit community. A few Sicilians hoped it might mean they were now safe from the Axman's gaze and his blade.

Those thoughts were dashed mere days later. The Axman struck again, and this time his victim, Joseph Romano, was a man of Italian descent, dispelling any illusions of safety for the Sicilian-Italian community. Little Palermo was once again thrust into a state of collective dread, desperate for answers and longing for an end to the reign of terror that now plagued their lives.

***

IN THE WEE HOURS OF AUGUST 10TH, THE MOON SAT OVER Gravier Street, a densely populated street a few blocks off Canal Street. On the corner of Gravier and Tonti Streets sat a modest grocery store that held the hopes and dreams of Lilly Bruno and her family. Lilly and her two young daughters, Pauline, fifteen, Mary, thirteen, lived in the building. Lilly's widowed sister, Rosie, lived with them and ran their little grocery store with unwavering dedication. Lilly's uncle, Joseph Romano, a barber and the main provider for the family, also lived on the property. Lilly, Rosie, and Joseph had all emigrated to New Orleans from Sicily.

The family was poor, but worked hard in their different jobs, all contributing together to try to make their way in the world. Their immigrant journey was like many others, a testament to the strength of family ties and the pursuit of a better life amidst the challenges they encountered as new Americans.

As the moon continued to cast its gentle glow over Gravier Street, inside the home, young Pauline Bruno turned over and over in her bed. She couldn't sleep, as all of her thoughts were concentrated on the dreaded Axman of New Orleans. She had been thinking about the Axman over the past few days. She had heard the stories of his attacks on grocery store owners, which only ratcheted her fears. She tried not to awaken her sister sleeping next to her, but she could not lie still in the heat of that August night as her mind raced with her fears of the Axman. Finally, just before 3 a.m., she drifted off to sleep, unaware of the evil that lurked outside. Despite her fears, she had never truly believed in the imminent arrival of a dark force to her own home. His presence would shatter the tranquility of the family and plunge them all into a harrowing ordeal.

For on that night, the Axman came to the Brunos.

He slithered out of the shadows and hopped a fence in the backyard of the property at 2336 Gravier Street. He immediately made his way to the tool shed in the backyard. He wore a dark jacket and pants, with a black hat pulled down low over his face. Under his breath, he hummed a jazz tune, *Tiger Rag*, the jazz melody twisted into a nightmarish symphony.

He opened the shed and pulled out an axe. He then proceeded towards the back door. As he reached into his pocket to pull out a chisel, he noticed an open window, beckoning to him as an invitation to his macabre dance.

Silently, the Axman climbed in through the window, defying gravity with a haunting elegance. The air in the home grew heavy, the very walls recoiled from the evil presence.

He walked down a small hallway and came to the first bedroom, the bedroom of Joseph Romano. He opened the bedroom door and entered. Silence took hold and time stood still, as if bracing for the unspeakable act that was about to occur.

***

Chief Mooney and Detective Marullo were inside the little residence within the hour. The family was quite shaken. Mooney interviewed them all personally while a young detective, Mike Miller, took notes. Chief Mooney's attention soon focused on fifteen-year-old Pauline Bruno, who said she had heard a noise that morning around 3 a.m. coming from her uncle's bedroom.

Sitting at the table beside her, Chief Mooney asked her to provide him with every detail she could remember. She told Chief Mooney that when she heard the sound, she sat up in bed and saw a man standing in her doorway. Chief Mooney made her repeat her description twice, then instructed

Detective Miller to write it down with specificity. "Every detail counts," he told his young detective.

Pauline described the intruder as white, she thought, but really couldn't be positive. He was tall and wearing all black clothes. She screamed when she saw him, which awoke her sister and the rest of the house. "Then he just… disappeared." That's how she put it.

Pauline then continued relating the events of that night. "After he left, my Uncle Joseph stumbled out of his bedroom and passed by our bedroom door. My sister and I ran from the room and entered the kitchen. Uncle Joseph was holding his head."

"Can you describe his injury?" inquired Mooney.

Pauline explained what she saw. Joseph Romano had a severe gash that ran across the top of his head with blood pouring down his face. He yelled out to them both to call an ambulance before collapsing into a chair. He was taken to Charity Hospital. The intruder was already long gone.

While Mooney continued interviewing Pauline, Marullo was inside Joseph Romano's bedroom. The man's pillow and sheets were soaked in blood. A bloody axe lay on the floor.

Newspaper reporters began arriving as word spread of the attack. Neighbors stood outside as fear, anxiety, apprehension, and grief took hold.

Chief Mooney continued his discussion with Pauline, the sole witness who had encountered the intruder inside the home. Meanwhile, Joseph Romano, the other potential witness, was receiving medical treatment at the hospital, and Chief Mooney planned to interview him later in the hopes of shedding light on the intruder's identity. Mike Miller stood nearby, diligently taking notes as the interview concluded.

"So, Ms. Pauline, if I understand correctly, the intruder left the residence after you yelled," Chief Mooney summarized.

"Yes, I guess so."

"And he said nothing to you?" Chief Mooney inquired, hoping for additional details.

"No."

"But you never saw him leave."

"No, sir."

"Can you describe for me one more time how he left?" Chief Mooney pressed.

"He… he just kinda vanished," Pauline replied.

Chief Mooney stroked his chin. He leaned in and asked, "Is there anything else that stood out about him? Anything that might help me identify him?"

Pauline took a deep breath. "He moved… almost as if he had…wings," she replied, her voice trembling slightly.

The implication of Pauline's words hung in the air, leaving Chief Mooney momentarily speechless. Mike Miller stared at the words he had just transcribed on his notepad, realizing that the investigation had taken an unsettling turn. Were they dealing with an entity that defied rational explanation?

Chief Mooney, trying to convey a sense of reassurance, said, "Thank you, Ms. Pauline, for your cooperation and your courage in sharing this with us."

Mike Miller nodded in agreement, still trying to comprehend the meaning of what had been said.

Detective Marullo walked into the room and came over to the Chief.

"I'll head to the hospital now to speak with Joseph

Romano," Chief Mooney stated. "Perhaps he can provide us with some leads or shed light on this mysterious intruder."

However, just then Detective Bombay walked in and pulled Chief Mooney off to the side.

"I just left the hospital," he told the Chief. He leaned in closer and said, "Joseph Romano died from his injuries. The single blow he received fractured his skull."

"Oh, my Jesus," Chief Mooney exclaimed.

Collecting himself, Chief Mooney approached the grieving family, mustering the strength to deliver the heartbreaking news. With a heavy heart, he informed them of Joseph Romano's passing, their faces becoming masks of sorrow and disbelief.

After consoling the family as best he could, Chief Mooney stepped outside. The recent events weighed down his mind. He knew he had to address the press, as they were hungry for updates on the investigation. Taking a deep breath, he prepared himself to deliver a statement. A statement that he hoped would ease the frayed nerves of his city.

ABOUT SIX REPORTERS WERE STANDING OUTSIDE THE CRIME SCENE, including Michael Devlin. Mooney's conversation with Giancarlo at Henry's Bar the other night was fresh on his mind. He would use this opportunity to set the record straight. He spoke to the press in an authoritative tone.

"Joseph Romano was attacked this morning and he later died as a result of those injuries. He was attacked in his bed with an axe. As these axe murders have grown in number, I have been forced to believe that they are all the work of a single madman. I'm convinced that the Romano murder is the work of that same madman, an axe wielding degenerate. I further believe he is a sadist. I have consulted many prominent persons who have made a study of crimes and criminals, and most of them are under the opinion that these crimes are the work of one man whose obsession is to hack people with an axe. Take this as gospel. But do not fear; we're going to get him yet! I'm doing everything in human power to run down this murderous maniac."

As the cameras flashed and the questions ensued, Chief Mooney remained resolute, his commitment to protecting his city and seeking the truth was unwavering. He hoped that by standing firm in his conviction that the perpetrator would be caught, the residents of the city would keep calm.

As the press event ended, Chief Mooney was unaware that his young, note-taking detective, Mike Miller, was off to the side speaking to a reporter, too. What Miller said to that reporter would offset any hope that Chief Mooney had in dousing the fears of the residents of New Orleans.

BY THAT AFTERNOON, THE NEWSPAPERS ACROSS THE CITY WERE trumpeting the latest attack. The citizens of New Orleans began to ponder just who this madman was. For some, they agreed with Mooney; the Axman was simply a crazed individual. But for others, they believed the reporting of the newsman who had printed Pauline Bruno's chilling words that the intruder had moved "as if he had wings." They took this as proof that the Axman was a phantom. That's how he entered the houses. That's how he committed his crimes without being heard by others in the home. That's why he has never been caught and never would be.

The headline of the *Times-Picayune* newspaper the next day convinced Chief Mooney that his words had had no effect on the frayed nerves of the city. At the same time, the headline sent chills throughout Little Palermo.

WHO'LL BE NEXT, IS THE QUESTION ITALIANS ARE ASKING

The reporting of the Romano murder and Mooney's statements about an axe murderer sent the city into a full-fledged panic attack over the next few days. Gun sales increased. The *Item* was soon reporting that *"A literal reign of terror has swept through many quarters in New Orleans, where inside Italian households, members of the family divide the night into regular watches and stand guard over their sleeping kin, armed with buckshot-loaded shotguns."*

Makeshift alarms with the residents using water bottles or crates up against the doors were set up inside their homes. The coming of night was dreaded by all.

The most predominant belief among the non-Italians was that all of it, every attack, was the result of the Black Hand. It was more palatable for them to believe the attacks were the result of the Sicilians and their own form of justice and vendettas. Some even believed they had it coming to them, as they were low-class, crime-ridden degenerates.

One man in the city kept hearing the whispers and growing sentiment against his community, and he felt an obligation to set the record straight. That man was Giancarlo Rabito. He placed a phone call to Michael Devlin and arranged a meeting with him at the Old Absinthe House.

His objective was to lay out the entire case for a single madman and show the connection between all of the attacks, including those dating back to the time of the Cleaver. He reflected back to his conversation at Henry's Bar with Chief Mooney and was convinced the Chief's approach was wrong. Even though Giancarlo knew what he would say would most likely cause the citizens to move from panic into hysteria, he truly believed they had to know the truth. They had to be ready to protect themselves. They had to be prepared to kill the Axman when he slithered into their homes.

14

THE INTERVIEW

The Old Absinthe House sat on the corner of Bourbon and Bienville Streets. Its name was derived from a drink made famous by its one-time bartender, Cayetano Ferrer, who learned his trade working the bar at the French Opera House. The drink he developed in 1874 was known as The Absinthe House Frappe, or as it was called by the locals, "the green monster." The drink was a mixture of sugar, water, and absinthe, an anise-flavored spirit. People flocked to partake until 1912, when the U.S. Government declared war on absinthe. Officials likened it to cocaine and the spirit was outlawed.

Even so, the bar retained its name. Originally constructed in 1806, the building was an integral part of New Orleans history and lore. Supposedly, in a secret room on the second floor, General Andrew Jackson enlisted the help of the pirate Jean Lafitte in the imminent invasion by British forces during the War of 1812. With a promise of pardon for his illegal activities, Lafitte agreed, and on the battlefield in Chalmette, Louisiana, the woefully undermanned American forces turned back the British by inflicting heavy losses.

Of course, some residents claimed The Old Absinthe House was haunted, with sightings of Lafitte and Jackson climbing the stairs, and even the Voodoo Queen of New Orleans, Marie Laveau, seated at the second story window, peering down upon Bourbon Street.

Giancarlo arrived at The Old Absinthe House before Michael Devlin. He found a table off in the corner and sat down. A single, orange-colored glass held a burning candle inside, casting a flickering glow in the dimly lit bar.

The bartender came over and extended his hand. "Detective Rabito. It's been a while. How goes it?"

"Fine, Jeffrey. Fine."

"Your friends better be careful. The Axman is on the loose," Jeffrey warned, his tone carrying a note of concern.

"I know. It's a bad time for everyone," Giancarlo acknowledged somberly, his mind preoccupied with the recent string of gruesome murders.

Just then, Devlin walked into the bar and came over to the table.

"Jeffrey, this is Michael Devlin," Giancarlo said as Devlin took a seat.

The bartender extended his hand and asked, "The reporter?"

Shaking hands, Devlin replied, "Yes. That's me."

"Can I get you both a drink?" Jeffrey offered.

"Sure, I'll take a rum," Devlin replied.

"And I'll have a Sazerac."

The bartender slapped Giancarlo on his back. "Good

seeing you Detective." With a nod, Giancarlo acknowledged the gesture as the barman walked away.

Turning towards each other across the table, Giancarlo said, "Thanks for coming to meet me. I need to set the record straight."

"Tensions are high across the city after the Romano murder. Most believe it's the Black Hand. They disagree with the Chief."

"The Chief is right, although even what he said is tempered. Tempered by the fact that he feels an obligation to reassure the public," Giancarlo remarked thoughtfully. "I am under no such obligation. They need to know. They need to know the *whole* truth. When one is retired, one can spend a lot of time studying. I've read every report that has come out about every case. I need you to report to the citizens what I tell you today."

"Do you want to make a statement, or do you want me to ask questions?" Devlin inquired.

"You can ask me questions, and I leave it to you as to how you want to write the article."

"Fair enough. Wait, here are our drinks," interjected Devlin.

Jeffrey placed the drinks on the table and then left to wait on another customer at the bar. They both took a drink before Devlin fired his first question.

"I remember when we first spoke at my office after the Maggio murders, you mentioned the attacks many years ago. Is it your belief that the Axman is the same person who committed the crimes back in '10 and '11?"

"There is no doubt in my mind," affirmed Giancarlo.

"Back then, he was known as The Cleaver."

"Correct," Giancarlo confirmed. "The Axman is the same person bringing a new reign of terror to New Orleans."

"Why is he doing this?" Devlin pressed.

"He is a Jekyll and Hyde type. He's a criminal of the dual personality type. He may be a respectable, law-abiding citizen, but then the impulses come upon him, and he must obey them. He is akin to Jack the Ripper because his actions seem compulsive and random," Giancarlo explained.

Giancarlo then discussed at length each of the attacks, dating back from Crutti all the way up to Joseph Romano, connecting them all to the Axman.

When he finished, Devlin asked, "Chief Mooney says this man will be caught. What do you think?"

"Jack the Ripper was never caught. These types of criminals are cunning and very hard to catch. They have their plans laid out before attacking." Giancarlo paused, and then said, "It would not come as a surprise to me if the police were unsuccessful in bringing this killer to justice."

Michael Devlin took a deep breath before asking, "You want me to put that response in the paper? People may lose all hope."

Giancarlo nodded. "They have to know what we are facing. Jack the Ripper was not stopped by the police. He, most likely, was only stopped by his death."

"What about the fact that most of the Axman's victims are Italian?"

Giancarlo had been waiting for this question, a chance to set the record straight. He chose his words carefully. "There has been no known motive for any of the Axman attacks. However, it is a plain fact that practically all of the victims were Italians. I know many in our city blame the Black Hand for this reason." Giancarlo paused.

Devlin could see this part of the conversation was very close to the retired detective's heart.

Giancarlo looked directly at him, his gaze unwavering as he spoke with conviction. "This is the reason I wanted to speak with you. You need to get the word out. My community deserves the truth to be known. The *Mafia* does not kill women, period. In fact, you could not get a *Mafia* agent to murder a woman under any circumstances. On top of that, the *Mafia* would not leave a person they attacked alive. They kill so that the person can not offer testimony against them. These attacks are not connected to the Black Hand or the *Mafia*."

"I will put that in my story. I will make sure they know your belief that neither the Black Hand nor the *Mafia* is involved. I will mention that the Chief is of the same opinion," assured Devlin.

"Thank you," responded Giancarlo gratefully.

"Giancarlo, I can hear the dread in your voice. You are fearful for the citizens of New Orleans."

"I love these people. All of them. But of course, I have a special place in my heart for the Sicilians. They came to this country with nothing. They forged a life for themselves and their families here. They deserve to live in peace and to have a chance for prosperity. Not to face death at the hands of a lunatic," Giancarlo expressed with emotion.

Devlin took a sip of his drink, contemplating Giancarlo's words before asking, "What should people do to protect themselves?"

"The killer comes during the dead of night when his

victims are sleeping. He quietly enters their yards and then somehow enters their homes where he commits his terrible deeds. If I were them, I would get a dog and put it in my yard. That might scare the Axman away," Giancarlo advised.

"You mentioned that he somehow enters their homes. Is it true the police don't know how?" queried Devlin.

"We know he chisels out a door panel. But the opening is too small for a normal man to crawl through. The door is locked from the inside. So how he gains entry is a mystery," Giancarlo explained, his tone tinged with frustration at the perplexing nature of the case.

Devlin sat up straight in his chair, hesitating for a moment before speaking. He knew what he was about to say went against the conventional norms of society. "You do know there are many citizens who believe he's no man at all. They believe he is a phantom. They take to heart the words of Pauline Bruno that he moved as if he had wings and use that as proof of their belief."

"Throughout my career, I lived by a saying, a saying that has always proven to be true," Giancarlo began, his voice carrying a sense of solemnity. "The murderer is just a real as the murdered. This killer, this maniac, is a man, not a phantom." Giancarlo's tone reflected a determination and a belief in his words born from his years of experience and conviction.

"Giancarlo, thank you for reaching out to me. I will put a story together forthwith."

"Thank you," replied Giancarlo. "Thank you for meeting me."

"Detective Marullo mentioned to me that you are writing

a novel," Devlin said, shifting the conversation away from talk of the Axman.

"I am. It's about my time as a detective. But the book has taken on a life of its own. It's also a testament to the Sicilian men and women who came to New Orleans. They sacrificed everything to try for a better life."

"I hope to be a writer one day," Devlin shared, his voice tinged with aspiration.

"I've read and studied every one of your articles. You already are a gifted writer," Giancarlo complimented sincerely.

"Is your book almost done?"

Giancarlo sat quietly for a moment, contemplating. Then he said, "I would like to close the book with the capture and arrest of the Axman. So, for now, I'm still working on it, waiting for the event to happen that will bring it to a close. So you see, perhaps I have hope after all."

"I'd love to read it one day. I hope you can finish it soon. It would mean closure for so many. Thanks again for meeting me."

They both took a large swig of their drinks. Devlin knew the article he was about to put out to the public would send the city into a frenzy, and also put him at odds with Chief Mooney in reporting Giancarlo's belief that the killer may never be found. But he also knew he had a job to do, and Giancarlo was right. The citizens had to know the truth.

15

AXMAN HYSTERIA TAKES HOLD

*D*evlin's article appeared in the paper the next day. Indeed, it set the entire city into a frenzy. Chief Mooney at first was incensed when he read the words of Giancarlo. But he quickly came to understand that the retired detective, like him, was trying to achieve the same result: find the Axman and bring him to justice. They were both trying to protect the citizens of New Orleans.

Over the next few days, the police received numerous reported sightings of the Axman. One grocery owner discovered chisel marks on his back door but claimed the thick wood thwarted the attempt. An axe was found in his backyard. Another grocery owner heard noises by his back door one night, which woke him up. He grabbed a gun and shot through the door. When he checked the yard, there was no sign of anyone but an axe was lying on his steps.

The very next night, a grocery store owner reported that his makeshift alarm of a crate of tomatoes leaning up against the back door had worked. The sleeping grocer was alerted and scared off the perpetrator. A chisel was found on the back steps. They'd come close to death, but thanks to their vigilance, they lived to tell the tale.

In the area of Tulane and Broad, it was reported that the Axman was spotted, and the witness claimed it was a woman, or at least a man wearing woman's clothing. A search party was quickly put together, but nothing was found. Just two days later, the Axman was thought to have been seen hopping a fence in the dead of night. But again, a search turned up nothing.

Fear gripped the citizens, and there were many a sleepless nights as the residents listened for a sound, any sound, to indicate an intruder. Families would divide the night into shifts, each adult family member taking a turn sitting in a chair with a loaded shotgun.

In an attempt to loosen the mood and bring more people to their store, the Piggly Wiggly market took out a full one-page ad in the *Times-Picayune*. It read:

Attention Mr. Mooney and All Citizens of New Orleans: The Axman will appear in this City on Saturday, August 24th. He will ruthlessly use the 'Piggy Wiggly' axe in cutting off the head of all High-Priced Groceries. His weapon is wonderful and his system is unique. Don't miss seeing him.

The advertisement failed miserably, as the Sicilians and many of the other citizens of New Orleans did not take kindly to the joke.

AUGUST IN NEW ORLEANS IS STIFLING DUE TO THE HEAT AND humidity. Giancarlo continued working on his novel, rereading and perfecting the stories he had already written, and adding new stories. He had recently added the tale of a forbidden romance between a Creole woman and a wealthy businessman that led to a scandalous murder in the heart of the Garden District. Another new chapter recounted the case where Giancarlo found himself entangled in a web of corruption when he stumbled upon a secret gambling den hidden beneath the vibrant brothels of Storyville, exposing a network of high-stakes gambling and bribery among the city's elite.

His work on his novel stopped when he suffered two consecutive "bad days." But by the weekend, he was feeling better. The August heat that Saturday was almost unbearable. He decided to take a trip out to the western part of the city, to the area of Spanish Fort, located on the banks of Lake Pontchartrain. The locals loved going here during the summer heat to catch the lake breezes.

The area was so named for a now abandoned small fort that sat where Bayou St. John meets Lake Pontchartrain. The fort was built by the French in 1701 and expanded by the Spanish in 1788, but it never saw battle. The location was still an integral part of New Orleans history. It was at this site that Bienville, the founder of New Orleans, first made encampment in 1699. The fort was the location where, in 1814, General Andrew Jackson arrived to defend the city from the coming British invasion, before being paraded through the streets to Antoine's Restaurant for a celebration dinner. And it was the location where many New Orleanians would use the electric rail from the city to this area. They could take in the sights and sounds, and eat, drink, and dance the night away under the ancient oaks. Over the years, the area of Spanish Fort had evolved into something of an adult playground, so much so that Spanish Fort became known as the "Coney Island of the South."

There were an amusement park, casino, theatre, dance pavilion, cabarets, and several fine restaurants, including Over the Rhine, a German restaurant and beer garden. The other restaurant was Tranchina's Italian Restaurant, which had a nightly band conducted by Terry Tranchina himself in the pavilion overlooking the lake.

Spanish Fort played an important part in the development of jazz. Early jazz musicians performed here, sharing ideas and techniques, nurturing the new musical genre.

Giancarlo sat at a table by himself at Tranchina's. He had just finished a meal consisting of minestrone soup, lasagna, and a cannoli. Terry Tranchina was leading the band through some jazz favorites, but every third or fourth song, he would play a Neapolitan love song, which the crowd loved to hear. Many sang along.

As Giancarlo paid his bill, Terry played the Neapolitan love song *Non ti scordar di me*. It was Giancarlo's favorite, and after the death of Piccolini, it had a special place in his heart. It reminded him of his love, and it also made him think of his life in Sicily so long ago and of his now deceased parents. Sitting at the table, he began to sing along, as his eyes welled up with tears.

When the song was over, he wiped the tears from his eyes and left the restaurant. Although it was a very hot night, he decided to take a walk before making his way back to the city on the electric rail that ran along the banks of Bayou St. John.

Spanish Fort was crowded that night, with people mingling about, listening to a band near the main pavilion. Some were seated at tables, while others were dancing on the makeshift dance floor directly in front of the band. The band was pounding out jazz tunes that brought smiles to everyone listening.

As he passed the outskirts of the dance floor, he noticed Charlie Cortimiglia and his wife, Rosie, dancing. They waved to him and he walked over.

"Great to see you, Giancarlo," Charlie said, wiping the sweat from his brow, the result of dancing in the August heat.

"Great to see the both of you. What brings you over to Spanish Fort from Gretna this evening?"

"It's our anniversary," Rosie replied, as she leaned in and hugged her husband.

"Happy Anniversary," replied Giancarlo.

"Yes, we left Mary with a relative for the night," she added.

"Is she two yet?"

"Almost," replied Rosie.

"Giancarlo, how have you been feeling?"

"I've been ok. Some bad days, but all in all, not too terrible."

"And how is your book writing."

"It's hard, but it's coming along." He paused, and then said, "You know, I've been following the Axman case very closely. Please be careful, particularly late at night."

"Fearful times," replied Charlie. "Rosie is scared when midnight comes. I keep telling her we are safe in Gretna. All of his attacks have been in New Orleans."

Rosie interrupted, "No. We are Italian grocery store

owners. We fit the description, I keep telling him, but he is a … *testa dura*. A hard head," she said as she knocked her knuckles on the side of her head.

"But not New Orleans grocery owners," Charlie added.

"Well, be careful just the same," replied Giancarlo. "Happy anniversary and please enjoy your evening."

Charlie extended his hand and said, "We will. *Ciao*, Giancarlo."

The couple turned, took a few steps, and began dancing to the music once again. As Giancarlo began to walk away, he thought of his wife, and how he would have loved to be dancing with her. He missed her so.

Giancarlo walked toward the remnants of the old fort. It was a moonless night. While he was walking toward the fort, he ran into Salvatore D'Antoni.

"Detective Rabito, what brings you out to Spanish Fort this evening?"

"Just dinner at Tranchina's."

"Wonderful. I'm playing later tonight in a band at Frolics. I add a little Italian touch to the music, I like to say."

"Great."

"Stay and come hear us."

"No, I need to get back."

"Detective, I read your interview in the paper about the Axman. You still think he's a man, not a ghost?"

Giancarlo smiled. "I do. A crazed lunatic, who at times can act as normal as you and I. But when the darkness comes upon him, he can't control his urge to kill."

"I agree with what you said that he will never be found. But the reason is because he is not of this world. He is a phantom. A spirit. I saw where Mooney said in the paper that he has been communicating with a detective from the Pinkerton Agency. What a waste of time. He needs to consult with people connected to the spirit world to find a way to drive this phantom away."

They walked up to the abandoned fort together. Once a symbol of resilience, the fort now stood as a weathered relic, its crumbling walls evidence of the weight of time. In front of the fort sat its sole occupant, a solitary grave inside of a rusting wrought iron fence, a silent witness to the centuries.

Salvatore asked, "You don't believe in spirits, Detective. Yet, you live in New Orleans, the most haunted of all American cities. Take this grave. Do you know who is buried here?"

Giancarlo looked down at the weathered headstone. Time had eroded the inscription, rendering the identity of the occupant obscure. "No, but I'm sure you are going to tell me."

"It is the resting place of a Spanish officer, the commander of the army stationed here. His name was Sancho Pablo. In 1741, he fell in love with the daughter of a local Native American chief. The chief opposed the union and killed him. To this day, on moonless nights, people say they can hear the mysterious sound of a woman weeping at the old fort. It is the princess crying for her lover. In New Orleans, Giancarlo, spirits live."

Giancarlo shook his head. "You know what is fact? Sancho Pablo, if that is indeed who is buried here, is dead. Of that, I am certain. Neither he nor his lover have anything more to say."

"If you or the police want to capture the Axman, you must enter into the spirit world. That's where you will find him, this demon from hell. That's where you can confront him, and hopefully, destroy him. He kills during the devil's hour."

"The devil's hour?" Giancarlo asked.

"Jesus died at 3 p.m. on Good Friday. To mock Jesus, the devil flipped it. He does most of his deeds at 3 a.m. That's the devil's hour."

"And how does one tap into the spirit world?"

"I would start at a tomb."

"A tomb?"

"Yes. The tomb of Marie Laveau in St. Louis Cemetery No. 1."

"The Voodoo Queen?"

"Go there, place three X marks on her tomb, spin around three times, knock on the tomb, and ask her permission to enter the spirit world. If you truly believe, she will grant your wish. And then you can look for the Axman and find him."

Giancarlo laughed. "If you know the way, why not do it yourself, and rid us of the Axman?"

"I know my limitations, Detective. Even if I could find him and confront him, I could not stand up to the Axman. It would be the end of me. But you, you have a strength, and a fight inside of you that makes me believe you could take him on and defeat him."

"It's getting late. I'm going to walk over to catch the train. Good luck with your performance tonight. Nice seeing you again."

"Nice seeing you as well. Heed my words, Detective. Mooney and his cohorts will never do what needs to be done to stop this killer. You can. You must. You are the only hope our community has in ending this terror."

They went their separate ways.

As Giancarlo walked under the oak tress close to the fort, a slight breeze blew in from the lake. He laughed under his breath as he pictured himself standing in front of Marie Laveau's tomb, chalk in hand.

The wind wrestled the leaves on the oak trees above. Suddenly, within the sound of the wind in the trees, just for a moment, Giancarlo thought he heard the sound of a woman crying. But before he could listen more closely, it disappeared. All he could hear was the gentle sound of the breeze.

16

DEATH AT EVERY DOOR

Giancarlo continued working on his novel, weaving in the story of the *doped bottled beer* incident into his narrative. The event, etched into the annals of history, unfolded on November 27, 1906 inside Willie Piazza's brothel in Storyville. Amongst the high-end gamblers and notable figures of the police department, a sinister act transpired. One of the policemen, John Paderas, surreptitiously laced the drinks of some of the women with drugs, purportedly passing it off as a jest. The festive atmosphere took a sinister turn when the unsuspecting ladies fell victim to the concoction, necessitating urgent hospitalization to ensure their survival. Giancarlo was the man who fingered Paderas as the culprit, and had him dismissed from the police department and charged with conduct unbecoming an officer.

As the weeks passed following the Romano murder, there were no further Axman attacks. The frenzy began to settle down. Then, an unforeseen turn of events altered the entire landscape. A new terror emerged, overshadowing the Axman attacks and erasing them from the news and collective consciousness of the citizens of New Orleans completely.

On September 5, 1918, the oil tanker, *Harold Walker*, left Boston's Commonwealth Pier headed for New Orleans. On board were 15 sick crew members. All of them were suffering from flu-like symptoms. Three of them would die during the trip.

The boat docked in the port of New Orleans and brought the Spanish flu to the city.

THE DISEASE SPREAD LIKE WILDFIRE THROUGH NEW ORLEANS. BY October, there were 8,000 cases reported. Just weeks later, that number would jump to 25,000.

The New Orleans Superintendent of Health, with Mayor Martin Behrman's consent, ordered the closing of all schools, along with churches, theaters, movie houses, and other places of amusement. The French Opera House's remaining season was canceled. Public gatherings such as sporting events, public funerals, and weddings were prohibited. Streetcars were ordered to run at half-occupancy to prevent overcrowding, which was difficult because many streetcar operators were sick themselves. Street lamps were extinguished to prevent nighttime gatherings of people. Citizens began wearing masks in public to protect them from the disease.

With the closure of so many businesses, many of the jazz greats began to move away from the city to find other places to ply their trade, in particular Chicago. The jazz men who stayed behind, even the great Louis Armstrong, were forced to find odd jobs to make ends meet.

The police, at least those who were not ill, were pulled from their regular duties to enforce the city's mandates. This all resulted in the investigations into the Axman falling by the wayside. The flu, the bringer of so much death, changed the focus of the newspapers.

By All Saints' Day, the disease had taken its toll on every facet of New Orleans life. Although there were mandates in place and the city government was trying to prevent large gatherings of people, even Mayor Behrman knew there would be no stopping the All Saints' Day celebrations.

All Saints' Day in New Orleans is a celebration unlike any other. It is a true celebration of life and death, exactly what the grieving population needed.

Brought from France as *La Toussaint*, All Saints' Day is a Holy Day of Obligation for Catholics. The day is dedicated to the saints of the Church, all those who have entered heaven, including saints who are recognized by the Church and those who are not. But in New Orleans, the Day is when the living remember and care for their deceased relatives. And what better way to do that than to visit their tombs?

The day begins with residents attending Mass to seek spiritual solace and guidance. Following the religious observance, many individuals make their way to the renowned French Market, a bustling hub where they acquire flowers and religious items. Laden with these tokens, thousands then converge upon the cemeteries scattered throughout the city to pay homage to their departed loved ones.

The act of cleaning the graves takes center stage as families and friends meticulously tend to the resting places of their beloved. With heartfelt reverence, they scrub away dirt and debris, restoring a sense of dignity and care to the tomb. In this serene and sacred environment, prayers are offered, words of remembrance are spoken, and quiet moments of reflection are cherished.

To further express their enduring love, visitors leave behind meaningful offerings. These may include flowers, symbolic beads, prayer cards, or other personal mementos, each carrying the message that the departed are remembered and honored. Through these heartfelt gestures, the residents of New Orleans create a profound bond between the living and the dead, affirming the everlasting ties of love and remembrance on this sacred day.

Giancarlo woke up early that November 1st and went to Mass at St. Mary's Italian. The church was packed as the Sicilian residents began their long day praying to the Lord for the souls of their departed loved ones.

He was not feeling great that morning, and he knew cleaning his wife's grave would be too strenuous. Instead, he carried in his hand a simple prayer card dedicated to St. Joseph, the patron saint of Sicily, that he would leave on her grave.

His wife was buried in St. Louis Cemetery No. 1, located on the outskirts of the French Quarter. It's the oldest cemetery in the city.

When Giancarlo entered, the entire cemetery was awash in excitement. The residents were busy washing their loved ones' tombs. Some decorated the gravestones with colorful flowers. Others, with their work complete, were playing tunes on trumpets or clarinets, honoring their loved ones with a favorite song.

Giancarlo walked down the cramped aisles lined with above ground tombs, until he came to that of his wife. This was her family tomb. It sat next to one of the more colorful and famous people to ever call New Orleans home, Paul Morphy, perhaps the greatest American Chess Master. Rumors said that he had been born in the very same house on Chartres Street that General Beauregard had lived in and where the Giacona incident with the Black Hand occurred, a story Giancarlo had related in his novel.

Giancarlo walked up to the door of his wife's tomb, the tomb of the Mastracchio family. Engraved on the door were the names of all the deceased members of his wife's family, including her mother, Rosalie, and father, Frank. The last two names on the door were Piccolina and "an unnamed baby girl." Giancarlo's wife and daughter.

He knelt down on the steps leading to the door. He placed the prayer card on the entrance. As he was about to pray, he glanced at the tomb. Parts of it were dirty, which had turned the white stone to an almost greyish color, while other parts of the tomb had weeds growing from cracks in the stone.

"I promise I will clean it, Piccolina," he said, before adding, "when I'm feeling better."

He then began to say his prayers to his wife and his daughter. His last prayer was reserved for the Virgin Mary. He pleaded to the mother of Jesus, "Please let me see my wife one more time. Please let me gaze at her again." When he finished, he reached out and ran his finger over his wife's engraved name on the tomb.

"*T'amo*, Piccolina. I miss you so much."

He stood and, after one final glance at the tomb, he slowly walked down the aisle and turned the corner heading toward the exit. As he passed one of the aisles, he happened to glance over at the most visited tomb in the cemetery, that of Marie Laveau. He thought of his conversation with Salvatore D'Antoni at the Spanish Fort.

"The spirit world," he mumbled incredulously under his breath, as he continued walking toward the exit.

DURING THE FALL OF 1918, 54,000 PEOPLE IN NEW ORLEANS contracted the Spanish flu, making up fourteen percent of the entire city's population. Of that number, some 3,500 died.

Giancarlo had avoided getting sick. That was until mid-November. It started with a cough, and then high fever. He became very ill, which exacerbated his underlying heart problems.

During his terrible illness, he was visited by Salvatore D'Antoni, Augustino Giorlando, Charlie Cortimiglia, Sebastian Mandina, and Michael Devlin, who all checked in on him now and again. However, it was the compassionate care extended by Augustino's wife, Maria, and Lila Davis, his middle-aged Black neighbor, that became Giancarlo's lifeline.

Lila, a woman of African descent with a deep connection to her ancestral roots, was a renowned healer in Little Palermo. With her radiant presence and an air of ancient wisdom, Lila embodied the essence of spiritual healing. A graceful poise and an aura of tranquility characterized her appearance. Her almond-shaped eyes, filled with warmth and wisdom, sparkled with an inner light that mirrored her deep connection to the healing arts. She wore a simple white dress, symbolizing purity and spiritual cleansing, and a white turban. Around her neck she wore a large, African-style gold necklace. Along with Maria's, her nurturing presence and dedicated attention became an essential source of support and aid, offering Giancarlo comfort and hope during his most trying moments.

When he was at the height of his sickness, the visions of the cases he had worked on and the images of those who had been murdered came over him with a vengeance. The darkness and violence that Giancarlo had witnessed throughout his life seemed to intertwine with his own physical suffering. The lines between reality and his fevered imagination blurred as the murder scenes and the faces of the victims appeared before him with relentless persistence. Each detail, each haunting image, branded itself into his consciousness, deepening his sense of unease and worsened his physical symptoms.

And yet by Saturday, November 11, Giancarlo had turned a corner. His fever had finally departed, and his overall condition began to improve. He was in bed that morning when outside his window, the city resounded with the joyous peals of bells. His room was filled with the distant sounds of jubilation as Lila Davis entered, taking a seat by Giancarlo's bedside.

In a soothing, gentle tone, she said, "Mr. Giancarlo, I can hear the city singing with joy today. The streets are alive with celebration. It's a historic day, a day of great victory."

Curious, Giancarlo inquired, "What is happening out there, Lila?"

With excitement evident in her voice, Lila said, "Oh, my

friend, today is a day of triumph! The war in Europe is over. Germany has surrendered and our brave soldiers are coming home. The city is rejoicing, filling the streets with jubilation."

Giancarlo's eyes widened as he processed the news. "Is it true? Is the war over?"

Lila's eyes shone with pride. "Yes, indeed. Can you hear the cheers? The shouts of victory and relief?"

"It's over," Giancarlo murmured. "It's finally over."

Reaching out to touch his hand, her voice filled with reassurance as she said, "The world has triumphed over evil, and so shall you. Brighter days lie ahead for you."

"Thank you, Lila. I will forever be in debt to both you and Maria for your kindness."

"Ah, Mr. Giancarlo. Piccolina was always such a kind, welcoming soul to me. The same as you. It's my pleasure to help you."

"You are a true healer, Lila. I never have asked you, as I guess I took it for granted. Do you practice Voodoo?"

Chuckling softly, Lila responded, "No. I do not. I use healing techniques that my ancestors used in Africa, passed down from generation to generation. But I have great respect for the those who practice the healing aspects of Voodoo, learned from the greats such as Marie Leaveau and Mama Vévée."

"I know all about Marie Leaveau. But who is Mama Vévée?"

"You've never heard of the one of the greatest healers this city has seen? You might not know her, but I know you know her son."

Curiosity piqued, Giancarlo questioned, "Who?"

"Mama Vévée was a Creole woman from a long-established New Orleans family. She was very close to an Italian man. Very close," she reiterated with a wink. "They had a son together. He has been here to check in on you. He's your friend, Salvatore D'Antoni."

A sudden realization dawned on Giancarlo; the eerie ghost stories Salvatore had shared over the years now making sense. In disbelief, he exclaimed, "You're kidding?"

Lila shook her head. "No, I'm not kidding. Mama Vévée was Salvatore's mother. As a child, he lived with his father, so not many know his true lineage. But he loved his mother fiercely and would see her often. He dabbles in Voodoo that he learned from her. And that means he learned from one of the very best. She has passed away, now only a memory of the past."

"I had no idea."

"Rest now, Mr. Giancarlo. While the city celebrates, I will be here tending to your recovery. Soon, you will able to join the joyous melody filling our streets, marking your own triumph."

As Giancarlo drifted into a much-needed rest, the sound of jubilation outside continued to weave its way into his dreams, fueling his determination to overcome his illness and emerge into a world now ablaze with hope and liberation.

BY THE END OF NOVEMBER, GIANCARLO HAD FINALLY recovered. At the same time, the flu finally released its death grip, and by December the city began to loosen many of the mandates that had been in place. Although weakened,

Giancarlo had survived. The same could be said of New Orleans.

The calendar turned to 1919. All had been quiet on the Axman front. No attacks since Joseph Romano. The panic and fear of the Sicilian community had diminished, as had the rising numbers of ill from the Spanish Flu. The city was slowly pulling out of the pandemic.

But yet again, Mardi Gras was cancelled, at least the balls and parades, as a precaution. Mayor Behrman knew he could not stop the citizens from celebrating their beloved festival two years in a row. He announced that on March 4th, Mardi Gras Day, the city would remain open and work would continue, but individuals could "celebrate Mardi Gras if they pleased."

Many New Orleanians donned masks and costumes and took to the streets. Smaller Carnival organizations, such as the Jefferson City Buzzards, the Easy Riders, the Magazine Market Swells, and the Mysterious Babies held impromptu street parades. The Loyal Order of Moose even held a masquerade ball Mardi Gras night.

The city felt alive again. The war was over. The pandemic had finally loosened its hold. The streets came to life with the vibrant sounds of music. Jazz, the soulful rhythm that defined the city, began to fill the air, drawing people together in celebration. In saloons, bars, and music halls, talented musicians unleashed their creativity, improvising melodies that resonated with the renewed spirit of the people.

And on top of all of that, the dreaded Axman of New Orleans had not been heard from for over seven months.

Chief Mooney in particular felt great relief. He would no longer have to use his officers to enforce the draconian mandates that had been put in place. He also took credit when he could for having increased police patrols around Sicilian grocery stores since the Romano killing. Perhaps, he suggested, that's why the Axman had not been heard from.

Or so he had hoped.

Just four days after Mardi Gras, the Chief's feeling of relief would be turned upside down and reach into the darkest part of his soul.

For on March 9, 1919, the Axman returned.

17

THE AXMAN CROSSES THE RIVER

The little Italian grocery store on the corner of Jefferson and Second Streets in Gretna always opened at 5 a.m. On that Sunday morning, the first patron arrived at 5:10 a.m., but finding the door locked and the store not yet opened, left. A few more people showed up that morning to pick up groceries, but they also found it locked and left.

Around 7 a.m., Hazel Johnson, a Black teenager who lived in the same Gretna neighborhood, was sent by her mother to pick up a few items from the grocery. She approached but the door was locked. She knocked but received no answer. She knew the owners very well and would often go over and play with their two-year-old daughter. She did not want to return home empty handed, so she walked down the side alley toward the back.

When she reached the backyard, she approached the back door. It was then that she noticed the missing panel on the lower half of the door. The panel that had been removed was lying on the ground nearby.

She was puzzled, and quickly went to the front of the store again, where she saw a neighbor she knew well, Edward Jackson. She led Edward to the door with the missing panel.

"It is strange," Edward said looking at the panel. "Why don't you slip inside and take a look around?"

"In there?" Hazel asked hesitantly.

"Well, I certainly can't fit through there. Only a small child could."

"Okay, but promise me you will stay right here."

"I promise, Hazel."

She walked up to the door, got to her knees, and then crawled through the area of the door with the missing panel. She stood up in the kitchen. The room was dark and quiet.

"What do you see?" Edward yelled through the open panel.

"Nothing."

"Open the door and let me in."

She turned the handle, but the door was locked from the inside. "It's locked, and there is no key."

Just then she heard a faint sound, the sound of someone whimpering. "Wait," she said. "I hear something."

Having been inside the home numerous times, she could tell the sound was coming from the owners' bedroom. She made her way down the hallway.

Edward was on his hands and knees, peering into the kitchen through the open panel. Suddenly he heard the most blood curdling scream he ever heard in his life. Then he saw

Hazel running back into the kitchen. She climbed through the panel, screaming at the top of her lungs.

Edward gently grasped her trembling shoulders, attempting to calm her down as best he could. "Hazel, breathe, my child. Take a deep breath," Edward urged, his voice filled with genuine concern. "What happened? What did you see?"

"They are dead!" she exclaimed, her voice trembling with horror. "They are dead!"

Hazel struggled to regain her composure, tears streaming down her face. Between sobs, she managed to convey what she had witnessed inside. The details were gruesome and horrifying.

Her screams had caught the attention of the neighbors, Iorlando and Frank Jordano who owned the grocery across the street. They were one-time rivals with their neighbors, but now they considered the Cortimiglias to be friends.

Father and son came running over, and Hazel told them what she had seen. On the ground in the yard, Iorlando noticed two axes, one covered in blood, the other in mud. Frank ran to the back door and with a few swift kicks, gained access to the home. He and his aging father went into the home to the bedroom of Charlie and Rosie Cortimiglia.

When they entered, they found Charlie lying on the floor, half-conscious, his head bleeding profusely from a brutal attack. But it was Rosie who brought the younger man to his knees. She was seated in a chair, whimpering loudly, holding the lifeless body of her daughter, Mary. The child had a deep cut across the top of her head, with blood still oozing out of the wound, spilling onto both Rosie and the floor. Rosie herself had a wicked cut across her own face. Blood was all over the bed, floor, walls, and ceiling. The attack must have been truly vicious.

Frank's heart pounded with a mix of fear and urgency as he rushed over to where Charlie lay on the floor. Gently shaking him, he called out to his neighbor, desperately hoping for a response.

Charlie opened his eyes and recognized his neighbor. "I'm dying, Frank. Get my brother-in-law." He then passed out.

Charlie and Rosie Cortimiglia would be rushed to Charity Hospital, while their beloved daughter would be sent to the morgue.

———

THE CORTIMIGLIA'S STORE WAS SITUATED IN GRETNA, ACROSS THE Mississippi River from New Orleans in the Parish of Jefferson. That meant the investigation would be conducted by Jefferson Parish police and not Orleans Parish. The men in charge of the investigation were Gretna Police Chief Peter Leson and Jefferson Parish Sheriff Louis Marrero. It was obvious that this attack and murder were a result of the same killer from New Orleans, the Axman of New Orleans. It had the same *modus operandi*. And yet Leson and Marrero didn't need or want the assistance of the New Orleans Police.

They hinged their entire investigation on two things. There were two axes found, and, in their erroneous view, the feud between the Jordanos and Cortimiglias had never truly ended. From the beginning of their investigation, the Jordanos were the number one suspects in the attack. They failed to consider other possibilities, even the one staring them in the face.

WORD SPREAD QUICKLY ACROSS NEW ORLEANS THAT MORNING of the Gretna attack. With the death of two-year-old Mary Cortimiglia, this was the cruelest of the Axman's attacks. Most of the citizens of New Orleans came to believe the Axman was the culprit, even though the police in Jefferson Parish failed (or did not want to) make the connection.

Giancarlo had spent that Sunday morning going to Mass, and then making his usual stop at Brocato's. While he was seated at a table, Michael Devlin came into the store. Augustino had told the reporter where he thought Giancarlo could be found when Devlin had stopped at the apartment.

Devlin did not mince any words. He said straight out, "The Axman has attacked again."

"When? Last night? Where?" Giancarlo asked urgently.

"Gretna. Last night, yes."

"Gretna." Giancarlo repeated, as he thought of his friend, Charlie Cortimiglia, and how upset Charlie would be with that news.

"I wanted to come find you. He attacked Charlie Cortimiglia and his family," Devlin continued.

Giancarlo's face went white. "My God. Please tell me they were not too badly injured?"

"Both of them were seriously wounded. They are in Charity Hospital. But Giancarlo, Mary, their daughter, was asleep in her mother's arm in bed. He killed that child with a single blow that crushed her skull."

"Fucking animal," Giancarlo hissed, his anger palpable. Giancarlo had said it loud enough for others in Brocato's to hear him, but he paid no heed, as he repeated again, "He's a fucking animal."

"I heard the scene inside the bedroom was horrific," Devlin added grimly.

"Missing panel? Used an axe?" Giancarlo inquired, already piecing together the details.

"Yes exactly. Two axes were found in the yard. One bloody, the other with mud. The Sheriff of Jefferson Parish is investigating the neighbors as possible suspects."

"The neighbors. Not the Jordanos?" Giancarlo questioned.

"Yes," confirmed Devlin.

"He's stupid. They did not do this," Giancarlo stated firmly.

"I know. I'm going to meet with Chief Mooney in a bit. He wants me to relay to him what I learn of the crime scene."

"Can I come with you?" inquired Giancarlo, his determination evident.

"I don't see why not," Devlin replied.

"I want to catch him. I want to catch him and bring him to justice. Can you do me a favor?" pleaded Giancarlo.

"Sure, what?" Devlin asked.

"Can you get me copies of the crime scene photos, and your news articles from all of the attacks. I want to piece together everything I know to assist Mooney in tracking this killer down."

"Yes, I will have it all delivered to your home. Let's go. I'm meeting Mooney near Canal Street," Devlin said, as they both headed out with a shared sense of purpose.

MANDINA'S

Mandina's sat at 3800 Canal Street. Its owner Sebastian Mandina had emigrated to New Orleans from Sicily in 1898. After arriving in the city, he soon purchased a house at the corner of Canal and Cortez streets and opened a bar and grocery store on the ground floor.

Sebastian, a compact and muscular man, had a commanding presence despite his short stature. His stockiness was deceiving, for he was athletically built, possessing a strength and agility that his appearance belied. The rich timbre of his Sicilian accent added a touch of old-world charm to his character, a reminder of his heritage. He lived above the business with his beloved wife, Frances, and their two sons, Anthony and Frank.

What had begun as a modest grocery store had evolved into a bustling pool hall, famous not only for its lively games but also for the mouthwatering sandwiches crafted with love by Sebastian himself. For years, after the closing of the grocery, the patrons of the pool hall had passionately urged Sebastian to convert his establishment into a full-fledged restaurant, a testament to the sheer deliciousness of his creations. He had toyed with the idea but so far hadn't made a firm decision.

Sebastian looked up from behind the bar, his eyes widening as Giancarlo and Devlin walked into his establishment. Chief Mooney had not yet arrived.

Giancarlo spoke in hushed tones, his voice laced with concern. "Sebastian, you won't believe the news. There's been an attack over in Gretna."

Sebastian's face turned pale, and he leaned in closer, anxiety plain on his face. "Oh, shit! Not Charlie?"

Giancarlo nodded gravely. "Yes, Charlie."

Sebastian's gaze swept across the pool hall, taking in the long bar, the in-use pool tables, and the few scattered groups of people savoring his famous sandwiches. "How is he?" Sebastian asked.

Giancarlo breathed deeply and then said, "He and his wife are in critical condition, but their daughter was murdered."

Determination blazed in Sebastian's eyes as he clenched his fists. "I'll put a bullet through his skull, through his fucking skull, I tell you. My God, poor Charlie and Rosie. How could anyone kill a child?"

Giancarlo replied, "That's the same question we are asking. He must be stopped. In the meantime, I know you no longer have the grocery store, but be careful, Sebastian. A madman is preying on Sicilians."

Sebastian said again, "Poor Charlie and Rosie."

Devlin added, "We are all praying for their lives."

Just then, Chief Mooney walked into Mandina's. "Gentlemen," he said as he approached.

"Chief, we were just telling Sebastian the news," Devlin responded, as the others acknowledged Mooney's appearance.

Sebastian, his face still drained of color, spoke with apparent shock, "I stand before you, Chief, in utter disbelief. The magnitude of this tragedy is beyond comprehension."

Mooney, his expression serious, said, "It's a grave situation indeed."

Sebastian, ever the host, offered a measure of solace, "I'll prepare some sandwiches for all of you. Please, take a seat."

"Thank you, Sebastian," replied Mooney.

Sebastian excused himself and left the trio of men as they took their seats at a table. Devlin proceeded to unload the harrowing details of the case. His voice carried the weight of the tragedy as he narrated the gruesome events, just as they had been reported to him.

When he described the horrific wounds inflicted upon the unfortunate family, especially the tragic fate that befell their young daughter, a chilling hush fell over the table. The atmosphere grew colder and darker, with an air of profound dread that thickened around the three men, shrouding them in an inescapable unease. The grim imagery Devlin presented intensified the terror that had gripped them all, making it seem as though a fog of fear and grief enveloped them.

Devlin sighed heavily, an audible manifestation of the burden they shared. "I'm afraid we all know who the culprit is," he admitted. "The method of entry is always the same, and the brutality is relentless. This individual is cunning, always managing to evade capture."

Mooney, who had been hanging onto Devlin's every word, leaned in, his face reflecting both curiosity and dread. He confessed, "I had suspected it was the Axman even before I heard any evidence. Now, listening to you, I'm convinced."

Giancarlo, who had been silently absorbing the grim details, joined the conversation with a firm declaration. "There is no doubt."

Mooney said, "I have offered my services to Jefferson Parish in any way I can."

Giancarlo inquired, "What about the Jordanos, Chief?"

"The sheriff over there is convinced the Jordanos are the culprits. I'm afraid they have the Jordanos in their sights."

Devlin interjected, "But that's preposterous. They were *friends*."

Giancarlo implored, "Chief, you can't allow that to happen."

Mooney gave his solemn assurance, "I'll do all that's within my power. But as you know, the case is beyond my jurisdiction."

Giancarlo pressed on, "You must convince Leson and Marrero to not arrest them."

Mooney's promise was unwavering. "I will try. You have my word."

Sebastian returned with a tray of sandwiches and joined them at the table. His gaze settled on Chief Mooney; his worry was palpable. "Will this madman, this child killer, ever be brought to justice?"

Mooney's response was filled with a haunting uncertainty. "I'll be honest with you; I don't know. I hope so, but I genuinely don't know."

Giancarlo's voice was resolute. "He must be stopped. This killer must be brought to justice. No stone should be left unturned. Every resource should be deployed to end his killing spree. He took the life of a child. He will kill again."

Mooney sighed, his responsibility weighing heavily on him. "We have thrown everything into the investigation. But we've hit dead end upon dead end. The longer he walks the streets, the more victims there will be. That's what keeps me awake at night."

Giancarlo, with a somber nod, empathized, "I know the feeling well, Chief. Too well."

When the meeting came to an end a little while later, Giancarlo's heart sank as he reflected on the devastating news. Charlie and his wife had been attacked, and their daughter murdered. Murdered by a fiend.

Chief Mooney asked Devlin to come meet with some of his detectives so they could hear the descriptions of the crime scene. Giancarlo, meanwhile, left Mandina's in a cab by himself.

As the cab journeyed through the city streets, Giancarlo's mind replayed the harrowing descriptions of the Cortimiglia's bedroom Devlin had painted. The bloodstained scene, burned into the fabric of his consciousness, left an indelible mark on his soul. The tragedy pressed upon him, and the solitude of the cab offered a moment for the profound darkness to sink in.

When the cab reached the intersection of Canal and Royal Streets, he asked to be let out. Giancarlo hoped that a quiet walk along Royal Street might provide some clarity.

Yet, with each step, the grip of depression only seemed to tighten. Grief clung to him, refusing to dissipate. The city's usual charm and vibrancy had given way to a haunting stillness that mirrored the turmoil within Giancarlo's soul.

Unable to escape, he found himself instinctively drawn to a small saloon on Conti Street, right off Royal Street. Giancarlo took a seat at the end of the bar, a sense of emptiness pervading his thoughts. He ordered a martini, not for the taste, but for the comfort it might bring in that somber moment.

Giancarlo sought solace in the depths of that martini, its cool bite offering a temporary respite from the anguish that enveloped him. But the alcohol could not drown out the questions that plagued his mind. He beckoned to the bartender for another drink and requested a pencil and a napkin.

The bartender obliged, and Giancarlo's hands traced the outline of a crude map of New Orleans. With each stroke of the pencil, he marked the locations of the Axman's attacks as best he could. As he looked down at the map, the locations confirmed what he always believed to be true. The attacks seemed scattered and random. There was no discernible pattern to the madness that gripped the city. And now, with the horrifying incident in Gretna, the Axman had crossed the river, spinning his web ever larger.

Giancarlo ordered another martini and then another. Why would he kill a child? What kind of monster is this man?

Devlin had told him how Hazel Johnson was the first inside. And how she was sent in because no one else could fit through the missing door panel. And further, how she confirmed the door was locked from the inside.

He ordered another drink. Almost always a missing panel? How did the Axman gain access? How did he fit through such a small hole in the door? He moved "as if he had wings." Those words from Pauline Bruno rolled around in his brain with a haunting resonance.

Amidst the haze of alcohol, a glimmer of memory stirred within him, recalling his conversation with Salvatore D'Antoni, a man whose beliefs veered into the supernatural. A man who, as he had learned from Lila Davis, was the son of a woman steeped in the world of Voodoo.

"What if Salvatore was right?" Giancarlo whispered to himself, his inner voice filled with uncertainty. Could it be that the Axman was not a mortal but rather a phantom lurking in the shadows? A slinking agent of the devil operating at 3 a.m.? The thought of a blending of the tangible and the ethereal realms sent shivers down his spine.

He remembered his conversation with Salvatore the very same night he had seen the Cortimiglias on the night of their anniversary at Spanish Fort. *"If you or the police want to capture the Axman, you must enter the spirit world."* Words he had once dismissed as the ramblings of a fervent mind now resurfaced with newfound relevance.

Drunk yet resolute, Giancarlo was determined to try anything, even venture into a world he had never believed existed. The series of gruesome killings and brutal attacks had to stop. Mooney had related his frustration that he had faced nothing but dead ends in his investigations. Perhaps the time was ripe for a change. Giancarlo was willing to push the boundaries of his belief to bring an end to the terror that had plagued New Orleans.

Giancarlo stumbled off the bar stool and walked out of the saloon. He took a deep breath and it helped steel his resolve. He knew the time had come to embark on a journey, a journey that would test his limits in the physical world and, perhaps, beyond it.

His transformation from a skeptic to someone willing to explore the supernatural world was a dramatic shift, proof of his unrelenting desire for justice and to avenge the heinous acts committed by the Axman. He welcomed the uncertainty that lay ahead. If the spirit world truly existed, he was willing to venture into the uncharted territory of that world. He would go on a quest to confront the slinking agent of the devil who had inflicted unspeakable horrors upon the innocent people of New Orleans. And it would be inside that world where Giancarlo would find the Axman and unmask him. He would bring the murderer to justice.

Giancarlo walked away from the saloon, his footsteps echoing along the street. The air crackled with a sense of anticipation; purpose hung around him like a shroud. Giancarlo's heart thudded in his chest, the rhythm of a war drum, as he ventured into the abyss.

As he walked, the memories of the Axman's deeds flashed his mind like grotesque paintings of despair. The victims cried out for justice, and it was Giancarlo who now shouldered the burden of their retribution. He knew that the journey ahead could be perilous. But he had reached his breaking point, a juncture where the pain of inaction outweighed the fear or absurdity of what lay ahead. He was prepared to face whatever challenges the spirit world had in store for him. His journey would be a collision of justice and vengeance, of light and darkness.

Justice guided him. With each step, he moved closer to the heart of the unknown, where his fate would be decided, and the agent of the devil would finally be confronted.

19

THE TOMB OF MARIE LEVEAU

It was dusk when Giancarlo arrived at his destination. St. Louis Cemetery No. 1 was empty of visitors. Giancarlo walked through the gates, placing his hand on the pillar to his left to steady himself. His afternoon of heavy drinking had taken effect.

He walked directly to the tomb of Marie Laveau. X marks could be seen all over the tomb. Some were circled, which meant Marie Laveau had granted the person's wish, and they had returned to thank the Voodoo Queen by placing the circle around the marks they had left. That was what Marie Laveau demanded. And if you believed in her powers, then you knew you must obey her command.

Marie Laveau, a Creole, had been born in New Orleans in 1801. By trade, she was a hairdresser. She was a devout Catholic. But in her day, she also became known as a dedicated practitioner of Voodoo, healer, and herbalist. She was often consulted by her fellow citizens to help them with personal matters ranging from finances to health to family disputes. She aided anyone from condemned prisoners to politicians. Her reputation was well known around the entire country.

Yet, there were differing opinions about the source of her knowledge and power. Some believed her abilities were derived from her deep connection to the world of Voodoo. According to the skeptics, however, women often shared their secrets and gossip during their hair appointments, and Marie Laveau was an astute listener who paid attention and took note. They attributed her supernatural knowing skills learned while doing her work as a hairdresser.

Marie Laveau's legacy lived on even after her passing in 1881. In death, as in life, people continued to call upon her, believing that she held the power to grant their wishes and offer guidance.

Giancarlo stood in silence before her tomb. Whether or not this ritual would yield any results remained uncertain, but his determination to find and confront the Axman burned unwaveringly in his heart. He was willing to try anything.

He leaned down and picked up a piece of stone from the ground, a token of the tradition steeped in history, a practice that held deep significance in the realm of Voodoo and spiritual rites. He walked up to the tomb, and after taking a deep breath, he held up the stone and with deliberate care, scratched out three X marks in a row on the tomb. It was a gesture that transcended the ordinary. It was a step into the unknown.

He then did three quick turns, which made him feel quite dizzy thanks to the martinis. He knocked on the tomb and yelled, "Grant me passage into the spirit world. Let me find the Axman."

And then, nothing. All was silent.

Giancarlo wasn't sure what he had been expecting. Maybe a big gust of wind, or a clap of thunder, letting him know that his wish was granted. He dropped the stone to the ground. His shoulders slumped, and a wave of self-doubt washed over him. What was he even doing here? What had compelled him to engage in such a desperate and futile act? These thoughts echoed in his mind, leaving him perplexed and unsure of his next steps.

As Giancarlo turned away from the tomb, ready to leave this fruitless endeavor behind, he was taken aback to find a man standing directly behind him. His features held a certain timeless quality, an otherworldliness. Clad in garments reminiscent of a bygone era, his presence exuded an air of mystery and intrigue. The stranger's deep blue eyes were captivating. Giancarlo acknowledged the man with a nod, still startled by his sudden appearance.

The man asked, "Do you know where the Vignes tomb is?"

"No. I do not."

With a weary sigh, the stranger turned away and silently retreated into the shadows, his brief, enigmatic presence leaving Giancarlo both puzzled and intrigued. As the mysterious figure disappeared into the night, Giancarlo couldn't shake the feeling that he had just brushed against the edges of another world, one far more complex and mystifying than he had ever imagined.

"I need to stop drinking," he said out loud, as he shook his head and took a deep breath, attempting to clear his mind of the fog that both the alcohol and the bewildering encounter had created. He turned once more to the tomb of Marie Laveau.

The air became still and silent.

His gaze fell upon the X marks he had drawn on the tomb, each one a symbol of his determination and his plea for passage into the spirit world. Frustration welled up within him, and he muttered, "Spirit world. Thanks for nothing." Disheartened, he turned away from the tomb, ready to face the reality of his struggle alone.

But as he took a step forward, his body froze in place. Directly in front of him stood a striking woman adorned in a brown turban that concealed her hair, and a shawl draped gracefully around her shoulders. Recognition surged through him as he realized who stood before him, a figure he knew from countless portraits he had seen throughout the city.

It was Marie Laveau. The Voodoo Queen herself.

In her arms, she cradled a girl child. Giancarlo's breath caught in his throat as he beheld the child's delicate face, marred by a horrifying split across the top of her head. Blood stained her innocent features. A chill ran down his spine as he recognized the child as Mary Cortimiglia, the young victim of the Axman's brutality. Shock and disbelief mingled as he struggled to comprehend the ghastly manifestation.

Before he could fully process this macabre sight, the child vanished into thin air. The woman, once cradling the child, now held an axe in her hands.

Giancarlo's head began spinning. He felt as if everything was upside down except for him and the woman. His chest began to tighten. His hands began to shake, as did his knees. He felt like he was falling, but he could not take his eyes off the woman in front of him. He went to his knees to steady himself.

The woman's gaze bore deep into his eyes. She nodded her head in a welcoming sort of way. Then, there was a huge flash of light, and the image before him disappeared. He grabbed his chest and fell back onto the ground, unconscious.

WHEN GIANCARLO AWOKE, HE FOUND HIMSELF LYING IN BED IN A large room with other beds occupied by other men. As his eyes fully opened, they were able to focus on the man standing over him. It was Augustino Giorlando.

"Welcome back, Giancarlo. We thought you were gone."

"I'm here, wherever here is."

"You're at Charity Hospital. A cemetery worker found you and called for help. An ambulance took you here."

"A cemetery worker?" Giancarlo's mind raced as fragments of memories from his drinking at the saloon to his visit at the cemetery resurfaced. Images of the man asking about the tomb and of Marie Laveau danced in his head. Although the events were hazy, he couldn't shake the feeling that there was more to it than just a drunken stupor.

"Yes, they found you lying on the steps of your wife's tomb," explained Augustino, his voice tinged with concern.

"My wife's tomb?" Giancarlo exclaimed, startled. He remembered placing the X marks on Marie Laveau's grave, and his plea to be allowed entrance to the spirit world. But how did he end up at his wife's tomb?

"Yes, by her tomb," Augustino confirmed.

"How long have I been out?"

"It's almost 9 a.m., so you've been out most of the night."

Giancarlo sighed. "Have you heard the Axman attacked the Cortimiglias and killed their daughter."

"We know. It's awful, just awful. They are here at the hospital, although the police won't let me see them. How are you feeling? The doctor said you had, as he put it, a panic attack, which is not a good thing for someone like you to have."

Giancarlo rubbed his temples.

Augustino asked, "Head hurts? Well, that can be expected. The doctor also thinks you drank too much."

He remembered drinking heavily at the saloon in an attempt to forget about the death of Mary at the hands of the Axman. "I remember now. I was stupid."

"What were you doing in the cemetery?" inquired Augustino, his tone laced with curiosity.

"I don't know. But I was found by my wife's tomb, you're sure about that?"

"Yes," Augustino affirmed with a nod.

Giancarlo wanted to tell Augustino what had happened and what he had seen, but he knew he would sound like a lunatic. Was what happened real or a result of his drinking? And how the hell had he ended up at his wife's tomb? He had no memory of anything after seeing the woman. That woman. He knew her. Marie Laveau. It had to be.

His thoughts were interrupted when Augustino asked him, "Will we ever catch him? The Cortimiglia's attacker."

As the memory from the day before became clearer, Giancarlo knew that his visit to the cemetery had been impulsive and irrational, fueled by alcohol and despair. He decided to believe that events at the cemetery were a manifestation of his intoxicated state rather than a genuine connection to the supernatural. He dismissed all other thoughts of ghosts and spirits. He had never believed in the spirit world, so why start now.

With a deep breath he responded to Augustino's question, his voice laced with determination. "The Axman is a man. A simple man. He is not a ghost. He is not a phantom. He is not a spirit. We need to outsmart him. Study his attacks in the past, hopefully find him, and kill him."

"Well, you need to get better first. Why don't you try to rest. I'll wait outside your room until the doctor comes."

"Thank you, Augustino."

Augustino patted Giancarlo on the shoulder and then left the room.

LATER THAT MORNING, ROSIE CORTIMIGLIA'S CONDITION improved enough to be seen by Leson and Marrero. After intense questioning, she told them she was unsure who had attacked her and her family. When she was later released from the hospital, Marrero had her arrested as a material witness. Under even more intense questioning, being asked over and over again if Frank Jordano was the attacker and the killer of her baby, Rosie Cortimiglia finally broke and said, "He did it. He's the man who hit me, attacked my husband, and killed my daughter."

That was all Leson and Marrero needed. They immediately arrested Iorlando and Frank Jordano.

Chief Mooney was incensed when he got word of the

arrest. He knew a child lay dead, and the murderer was the Axman, not the Jordanos.

The citizens of New Orleans believed the same, and so did the press. *The New Orleans Daily States* asked in their newspaper story the questions that almost every New Orleanian was asking. *"Who is this Axman and what is his motive? Is the fiend who committed the Gretna butchery the same man who executed the Maggio and Romano murders and who made attempts on other families? If so, is he a madman, robber, vendetta agent, or sadist?"*

Mooney knew the pressure on him to find the culprit would be even more intense now. But he had no leads, no one in custody, and no evidence. Since becoming police chief, it was as if the Axman was laughing at him and his inability to catch him. It was an embarrassment to both him personally and to his department.

Soon the Axman would bring that embarrassment to the doorstep of all of the citizens of New Orleans.

THE LETTER

Giancarlo was released from the hospital on Tuesday morning with orders from the doctor to take it easy and stop drinking. When he arrived back home, he found stacks of newspaper articles, photos, and reports on the Axman attacks that had been placed outside of his apartment door by Michael Devlin. He brought them inside and began the painstaking process of working through them. He thought if anything, they would at least make his novel better.

He began by placing a map of the entire city on the wall of his apartment. He then put a picture from each crime scene on the map over the area where the event had happened. Next, he began putting the newspaper articles in order and slowly reading them, while taking notes. He believed that somewhere within all of this information was the one clue that could lead to finding the Axman. Over the course of the next two days, he never left his apartment; he did nothing but study each and every crime.

Little did he know that he, along with all of the citizens of New Orleans, would soon be hearing from the Axman.

It was late in the afternoon on that Friday. Giancarlo was working through his articles and crime scene pictures. He had told himself that reading everything was not strenuous, so he was obeying his doctor's orders to take it easy.

There was a knock on the door. When he opened the door, Michael Devlin was there.

"Good afternoon, Michael."

"Good afternoon, Giancarlo. Hope you don't mind my stopping by."

"No, not at all. Come on in," Giancarlo said, as he opened the door wider.

Devlin came into the living room. He looked at the wall and saw the map of the city with the crime scene photos placed on top. "You've been hard at work, I see," he remarked.

"I have."

"I'm so sorry about the Cortimiglias. Those poor people."

"Terrible," Giancarlo murmured, his voice heavy with sorrow.

"They arrested the Jordanos," Devlin continued. "I'm outraged."

Throwing his hands up, Giancarlo remarked, "I was

expecting it. It's completely ridiculous," expressing his frustration at the news of the Jordanos' arrest.

"Mooney told me he will speak to Leson and Marrero. He will try to get the Jordanos released, and the charges dropped," Devlin informed Giancarlo.

"I'll speak with Charlie once he recovers."

"I'm sorry for disturbing you today. I heard about your hospital stay. I sure hope you're feeling better," Devlin said with genuine concern.

"I am. What can I do for you?" Giancarlo inquired politely.

"I'm seeking your advice. I didn't know what to do, so I thought it best to come see you and get your opinion. I've never been confronted with anything like this before," Devlin admitted.

Intrigued, Giancarlo leaned forward. "What is it?"

"I received a letter. A letter addressed to me. A letter the author is asking to have it published in the newspaper. A letter the likes of which I have never read before. I know I should have spoken to my editor first, but I'm not sure what he will want to do with it. I believe it needs to be published, but first I wanted to see what you think."

"Who sent the letter?" Giancarlo questioned, curious about the mysterious correspondence.

Devlin pulled out an envelope from his jacket pocket. On the front of the envelope were the words, "To Michael Devlin." He reached into the envelope and pulled out the letter, saying, "Here it is."

"But who sent it?" Giancarlo pressed

"It's from him," Devlin replied cryptically.

"Who?"

"It's from the Axman," Devlin revealed.

Giancarlo's mouth fell open in shock. "From the Axman himself?" he asked.

"Yes, and like I said, I've never read anything like this in my life. Here, read it," Devlin insisted, handing Giancarlo the letter.

Taking the letter, Giancarlo studied it intently. The handwriting was distinctive, filling the entire page. With a mix of trepidation and intrigue, he began to read the words out loud written before him, unsure of what to expect from the notorious Axman's communication.

Hell, March 13, 1919

> *Esteemed Mortal of New Orleans:*
>
> *They have never caught me and they never will. They have never seen me, for I am invisible, even as the ether that surrounds your earth. I am not a human being, but a spirit and a demon from the hottest hell. I am what you Orleanians and your foolish police call the Axman.*
>
> *When I see fit, I shall come and claim other victims. I alone know whom they shall be. I shall leave no clue except my bloody axe, besmeared with blood and brains of him whom I have sent below to keep me company.*
>
> *If you wish you may tell the police to be careful not to rile me. Of course, I am a reasonable spirit. I take no offense at the way they have conducted their investigations in the past. In fact, they have been so utterly stupid as to not only amuse me, but His Satanic Majesty, Francis Josef, etc. But tell them to beware. Let them not try to discover what I am, for it were better that they were never born than to incur the wrath of the Axman. I don't think there is any need of such a*

warning, for I feel sure the police will always dodge me, as they have in the past. They are wise and know how to keep away from all harm.

Undoubtedly, you Orleanians think of me as a most horrible murderer, which I am, but I could be much worse if I wanted to. If I wished, I could pay a visit to your city every night. At will I could slay thousands of your best citizens (and the worst), for I am in close relationship with the Angel of Death.

Now, to be exact, at 12:15 (earthly time) on next Tuesday night, I am going to pass over New Orleans. In my infinite mercy, I am going to make a little proposition to you people.

Here it is:

I am very fond of jazz music, and I swear by all the devils in the nether regions that every person shall be spared in whose home a jazz band is in full swing at the time I have just mentioned. If everyone has a jazz band going, well, then, so much the better for you people. One thing is certain and that is that some of your people who do not jazz it out on that specific Tuesday night (if there be any) will get the axe.

Well, as I am cold and crave the warmth of my native Tartarus, and it is about time I leave your earthly home, I will cease my discourse. Hoping that thou wilt publish this, that it may go well with thee, I have been, am and will be the worst spirit that ever existed either in fact or realm of fancy.

-The Axman

"My God," Giancarlo said when he finished reading. "I too have never read anything like this. And you want to publish this?"

"I do," Devlin replied resolutely. "The citizens need to know what we are facing. He is threatening an attack next Tuesday night."

Giancarlo's brows furrowed with concern. "Do you believe this is really from him?"

Devlin shrugged his shoulders before posing the question back, "Do you?"

"I know we are dealing with a lunatic. It's very difficult to know how lunatics are expected to act. Jack the Ripper taunted the police so I can't say for sure. I would act under the belief that it is from him," Giancarlo reasoned.

Devlin sighed. "I agree, and that's why I think it needs to be published. Just imagine if there were an attack that night, and it comes out later that we had received this letter."

"I can't believe I'm going to say this, but I agree with you. It should be published. Do you think your editor will allow it?" Giancarlo pondered.

"This letter will be a sensation," Devlin advised. "He will publish it when he realizes how many newspapers he will sell by printing it. I just wanted to get your opinion and see if you agreed with me. I value your advice."

"Did you notice he says 12:15 Tuesday night is when he will pass over the city? You know what day that is? St. Joseph's Day, the most important of days for Sicilians, the celebration of the patron Saint of Sicily," Giancarlo pointed out, the significance not lost on him.

"The poor Sicilians have been through so much," Devlin lamented, his empathy evident. "It's chilling to think that such a sacred day could be tarnished by such a heinous act."

But amidst the urgency of their conversation, Giancarlo couldn't shake the disturbing revelation about the Axman's affinity for jazz. It was a piece of the puzzle that added a new layer of complexity to an already twisted case.

"And what about his remark about jazz," Giancarlo interjected, his voice heavy with concern. "We have a jazz loving killer on the loose?"

"If a household is playing jazz that night, he will not kill the members of the household. What will people think?" Devlin's question hung in the air, thick with apprehension.

Giancarlo's expression darkened as he contemplated the implications. "They will think they have to obey to survive," he replied somberly, his voice mirroring Devlin's unease. "I think in every house, saloon, and dancehall, all of New Orleans will be listening to jazz next Tuesday."

"I guess you have convinced me that my feelings are correct. I'm going back to work to meet with my bosses, to show them this letter, and lay out why I think we should publish it. Thanks so much for seeing me. I'm sorry for disturbing your recovery."

Giancarlo gestured toward the map and pictures on his wall. "You didn't disturb my recovery."

"I heard you were found in the cemetery. What were you doing there? What happened?"

Giancarlo was silent for a moment. He wanted to tell someone of what he had seen that night. But who would believe him? Hell, he didn't even believe it. He had come to believe that it was just another vision that was playing tricks on his brain. He simply replied, "I went to see my wife's tomb. That's all I remember."

"Well, I'm glad you're feeling better. Take care, Giancarlo. Be careful." He paused, before adding, "And whatever you do, listen to jazz Tuesday night."

Giancarlo chuckled. "This letter will catch the attention of all of New Orleans. And I believe jazz will shake the walls of many a home and establishment."

They walked toward the door to the apartment. As Giancarlo opened the door, Devlin said, "Take care of yourself, my friend."

With a smile, Giancarlo said, "I will obey my doctor's orders."

"Good evening, Giancarlo," Devlin said as he left the apartment.

Alone once again, Giancarlo fell into his chair, the weight of recent events settling upon him. His gaze drifted towards the wall adorned with the haunting memories of the Axman attacks. Each photograph, each newspaper clipping, served as a reminder of his unsuccessful chase to uncover and stop this madman over all these years.

As he stared at the wall, Giancarlo's mind replayed the chilling words of the Axman's letter. The words echoed in his thoughts, stirring up a mix of emotions - anger, frustration, and a lingering sense of dread. But amidst the turmoil, a spark of determination ignited within him.

This letter, this ominous warning of an impending attack, presented a chance - a chance to finally confront the Axman, to bring him to justice once and for all. It was an opportunity Giancarlo couldn't afford to pass up. After years of tirelessly pursuing this elusive killer, this was his moment to find closure, to end the reign of terror that had plagued New Orleans for far too long.

But as he contemplated his next move, another memory surfaced in Giancarlo's mind, the memory of his supposed encounter with Marie Laveau, the legendary Voodoo Queen.

He suddenly remembered the desperate plea he had made to her, the request to enter the spirit world in search of answers, of justice.

With a firm resolve, Giancarlo made up his mind. He would not sit idly by and wait for the Axman's next move. No, he would take action. He would be there on the night referenced in the letter, ready to confront the Axman, to stop him in his tracks, and to bring an end to the nightmare that had consumed the city.

As he stood up from his chair, a sense of purpose coursing through his veins, Giancarlo knew that the road ahead would be perilous. But he was prepared to face whatever challenges came his way. Remembering his beloved Sherlock Holmes stories, he felt like the game was afoot once more, and this time, he was determined to emerge victorious. For him, this was more than just a chance, it was a mission, a mission to finally bring closure to the chapter of the Axman once and for all.

21

THE AXMAN'S JAZZ

On Sunday, March 16th, the Axman's letter appeared in the *Times-Picayune*. The reaction of the citizens of New Orleans was varied. Some thought the letter to be a joke. Others, Sicilians in particular, took the letter to heart, and people could be heard all over Little Palermo whispering the news that "The Axman is coming."

Giancarlo sat in his apartment later that afternoon. He had tacked the Axman's letter on his wall. He was certain there had surely been a contentious debate among the newspaper staff regarding whether or not to release it. But Devlin must have finally pushed it through. Giancarlo wasn't positive what to think of the letter. But there was one thing he knew for certain. The closer they got to St. Joseph's Day, the more people would pay heed to the letter, even those who did not believe it was from the Axman.

On Monday, two advertisements appeared in the newspaper, promoting a new jazz composition. The ads said,

"WAIT - WATCH THE AXMAN'S JAZZ" and *"COMING MYSTERIOUSLY, THE AXMAN'S JAZZ."*

The ads had been placed by Joseph Davilla, a thirty-five-year-old local Italian songwriter and businessman. He owned his own music publishing company and had numerous hits with his jazz compositions. The Axman's letter had inspired him to write his latest.

That same day, the Jordanos were officially arraigned in court for the murder of Mary Cortimiglia and the attack on her parents. Their trial was set for May.

TUESDAY ARRIVED. THE RESIDENTS OF NEW ORLEANS PREPARED for St. Joseph's Day. For the Sicilian community, St. Joseph's Day was the biggest celebration of the entire year.

The devotion to St. Joseph dated back to their time living in Sicily. The story goes that there was a terrible drought in Sicily. The residents were starving. The only consistent food they had to survive on were dried fava beans. They prayed to St. Joseph, the rains came, and the drought ended. They set up altars with food in celebration of what St. Joseph had done for them. They would recreate this scene every year on St. Joseph's Day.

This tradition remained with them when they came over to America. And in New Orleans, with its love of food, the altars that were set up were magnificent. These "altars" would be decorated with candles, flowers, and statues of the saint. Placed around the table were all sorts of food, which included fish, breads, cakes, pastries, wine, and of course, dried fava beans for good luck, since that was the food that had helped sustain them in Sicily.

St. Joseph's Eve was usually the busiest of nights for the Sicilian community as they prepared for the celebrations the next day. It was also the night of the Axman's promised attack.

GIANCARLO LEFT HIS APARTMENT AT 11 P.M., HIS REVOLVER discreetly tucked into his waistband. The city, known for its vibrant spirit and love of revelry, was pulsating with energy like never before.

If there is one truism in life, it is this: New Orleans knows how to throw a party. The love of food, music, and the deep desire to "let your hair down" on a night of fun, ran through the fiber of every New Orleanian. This night of all nights, New Orleans came to life.

The soulful melodies of jazz filled the air, weaving a tapestry of sound through homes, cafes, dancehalls, and saloons alike. It seemed as if every establishment had become a stage for the enchanting tunes of jazz, its rhythm and brass echoing through the streets, inviting people to embrace the moment and let their inhibitions slip away.

Families gathered around pianos in homes, fingers dancing across the keys, creating their own melodious renditions of jazz classics. The joyous notes echoed through the walls, intertwining with the laughter and conversations of loved ones. Others relied on the phonograph, its mechanical voice breathing life into the iconic jazz compositions, filling the rooms with an infectious rhythm that transcended the boundaries of their dwellings.

For the Sicilian community, which had lived in fear in recent months due to the looming presence of the Axman, this night offered a delicate balance between liberation and vigilance. As they immersed themselves in the festivities, their senses alive with the sights, sounds, and flavors of New Orleans, they remained watchful, keenly aware of their surroundings, ready to safeguard their loved ones from the agent of the devil.

The jazz players in town were thrilled to be hired all across the city. With the closing of Storyville and the war against jazz by the reformers, gigs had been tough to come by, but not this night. Everyone was looking to hire anyone who could pound out a jazz tune on a piano, trumpet, clarinet, or saxophone.

As Giancarlo had predicted, some of the residents who were skeptical of the letter but were scared enough to play along came out in droves to listen and dance to jazz that night. They would rather be safe than sorry.

For others who believed from the start that the letter was a hoax, they still used the night to have a good time. One group of young men uptown even invited the Axman to their stag party. Their invitation advised him to just walk in, as "it will not be necessary to remove any panels, for all of the doors will be open."

Giancarlo walked down the streets of New Orleans that night as the syncopated sounds of jazz pulsated on every block. Listening to the jazz and taking in the sights through the windows of the buildings where he could see party after party gave him no doubt that people believed the Axman was coming. Walking with a purpose, the weight of his revolver pressed against his skin, as his resolve to confront the Axman intensified. If the Axman was on the prowl tonight, Giancarlo would find him.

Chief Mooney was skeptical of the letter. But he was also smart. He and his department had been taking a beating for not catching the killer. With the appearance of the letter, he knew he had to prevent any further attacks at all costs. He increased patrols all night across the entire city. He was even walking the Quarter himself.

As jazz pulsed through the veins of the city and the shadows of fear danced alongside the revelry, Giancarlo and Chief Mooney embraced their respective roles, united by a shared mission: to safeguard the innocent, confront the darkness, and bring an end to the reign of terror that had gripped their beloved New Orleans.

By midnight, the revelry throughout the city surged with an even greater fervor. And then, the clock struck 12:15 a.m. This was the Axman's fateful hour. The atmosphere crackled with a mixture of exhilaration and fear. Anticipation fell over the city. Hearts beat faster. Breaths were held. The revelers, caught between exhilaration and apprehension, wondered if the Axman's threat would manifest before their eyes. The city seemed poised on the edge of a precipice, teetering between celebration and chaos.

As the minutes passed without any sign of the Axman, a collective sense of triumph and relief washed over the citizens. The anxiety that had hung heavy on their shoulders dissipated, replaced by an overwhelming feeling of victory. They realized that their unity, courage, and determination had thwarted the looming threat. They danced with renewed fervor, their bodies moving to the infectious rhythm of jazz, each step a celebration of their collective resilience.

In homes, husbands and wives kissed, as they pulled their children close, providing a sense of security. In bars and saloons, glasses were raised in toast, and voices rang out in harmonious chorus. The sense of community grew stronger as neighbors clinked their glasses, sharing laughter and hugs. Barriers dissolved and strangers became friends, bound by the exhilaration of overcoming a common threat. The vibrant spirit of New Orleans reverberated through every corner, uniting the city in a moment of triumph.

Aware of the Axman's notorious tendencies to strike during the Devil's hour, the celebration continued well into the night. The jazz played on, a resilient anthem against the darkness, as the revelers danced with passion. The hours passed, and as the clock approached 4 a.m., a collective sigh of relief swept through the crowd. They had made it through the night, unscathed by the Axman's attack.

Giancarlo watched as the citizens were now in the streets, making their way home. Many, while passing, would say, "Good night, Detective." He was well known and respected. While they walked, many hummed jazz tunes. They would do so all the way home.

At 4:30 in the morning, when the night had faded into the early hours, Giancarlo began his own journey home. The streets, once alive with laughter and music, had emptied. The houses, saloons, and dancehalls were shrouded in darkness, their doors and windows closed, marking the end of a memorable night. With a sense of weariness, Giancarlo walked the quiet streets, the echo of jazz tunes still resonating in his mind.

Unbeknownst to Giancarlo, a mysterious presence loomed in the shadows near the French Opera House. The figure stood cloaked in darkness, concealed within the doorway of a nearby building, dressed inconspicuously in dark attire. With a hat pulled low over his face, observing the street with an intensity veiled by the shroud of secrecy, he hummed the haunting jazz melody of *After You've Gone* under his breath, the tune blending with the night.

The mysterious presence had spent the entire evening immersed in the captivating melodies emanating from the various buildings within the Quarter. The night had reaffirmed what he had long believed. He held dominion over the entire city.

From the concealed vantage point of the doorway, the figure's gaze followed Giancarlo as he passed by. The cover of darkness provided a shield, rendering the lurking presence invisible, even to Giancarlo's watchful eyes.

As Giancarlo continued his path, the figure seized the opportunity and stealthily slithered down the street in the opposite direction, a phantom dissipating into the night. His movements were swift and deliberate, leaving no trace of his presence behind.

Giancarlo was now walking directly in front of the French Opera House. Suddenly, an icy chill coursed through his veins, sending a shiver down his spine, and settling deep within his bones. The unexpected chill seized Giancarlo's senses, evoking an eerie and foreboding sensation. It was as if an invisible presence whispered through the night, a whisper that sent a ripple of unease through his being. It was at that moment that he saw her.

Amidst this ominous backdrop, Giancarlo's gaze was drawn to a figure walking through the closed doors of the French Opera House. Her presence seemed to materialize out of thin air, a specter emerging from the depths of the night. The doors to the opera house had never opened. Illuminated by a faint, ethereal glow, she was a vision both mesmerizing and unsettling.

Her attire, a white dress tattered and torn, draped her form. Strands of long, flowing white hair cascaded down her back. Yet, it was her eyes that seized Giancarlo's attention, piercing and fiery red, radiating an otherworldly intensity.

In her right hand, she clutched a single red rose, a stark contrast against the pallor of her complexion. The vividness of the flower stood out, its crimson hue a stark reminder of passion and danger.

Giancarlo's instincts urged him to step back, to maintain a safe distance from this figure who now stood before him. Recognition flickered in his mind as the pieces fell into place. Marguerite, the witch of the opera house, was here.

As Marguerite approached Giancarlo, the air crackled with tension. Slowly, she lifted her hand, her finger pointing ominously over his shoulder. Her voice, raspy and haunting, whispered, "The Axman cometh. It is he."

Giancarlo's heart skipped a beat, his senses sharpening as he turned to face the direction she indicated. There, amidst the shadows cast by the balconies on Bourbon Street, he caught a glimpse of a figure moving with an eerie grace. A chill surged through his veins, memories of Charlie

Cortimiglia and the heartache that befell his family flooding his mind.

"Take the shot," she commanded, her voice carrying the weight of destiny.

Instinctively, Giancarlo's hand went to his waistband. He pulled out the revolver, his grip tightening around the handle. Just as he was about to begin to run down the street to try and confront the individual, an icy touch descended upon his shoulder. Startled, he turned his gaze back to the enigmatic woman, her cold hand resting upon him. The touch sent a jolt of electricity through his body. There were supernatural forces at play.

"Take the shot," she commanded again, her voice carrying the weight of destiny.

Her instructions went against all of his training as a police officer. Yet, as Marguerite's chilling words pierced the air, Giancarlo raised his revolver, his grip steady and his aim true. Time seemed to slow as he focused on the figure walking down Bourbon Street, a silhouette dancing in the moonlight.

In that fleeting moment, Giancarlo's resolve solidified. The memories of the Axman's atrocities, the anguish of the victims' families, and the love he had for his city coalesced into a singular purpose. With unwavering determination, he squeezed the trigger, unleashing a thunderous gunshot that shattered the stillness of the night.

JUST A HALF BLOCK AWAY ON TOULOUSE STREET, THE SHARP crack of the gunshot caught the attention of two police officers. Reacting swiftly, they sprinted onto Bourbon Street, their firearms at the ready, prepared to confront any threat that awaited them.

As they approached the scene, they noticed Giancarlo standing alone in the middle of Bourbon Street, holding his weapon, its barrel still pointing down the empty street from which they had arrived.

"Drop the gun," one officer yelled, running toward him.

As if shaken from a trance, Giancarlo raised both of his hands, pointing the gun up in the air.

"Drop the gun," the other officer screamed.

As some of the residents of Bourbon Street gathered on their balconies, drawn by the sound of the gunshot, a collective murmur spread through the night air. Their eyes scanned the scene below.

Giancarlo, his heart pounding, placed the gun down on the ground as instructed by the officers. He turned, looking behind him to see Marguerite, but she had vanished, His mind raced with adrenaline-fueled questions, his voice trembling as he repeated his inquiry, "Did I hit him? Did I hit him?"

The first officer, maintaining a composed demeanor, approached the discarded weapon and picked it up. With a sense of authority, he turned his attention back to Giancarlo, his voice calm but inquisitive. "Who? Who were you shooting at? There is no one on the street." As he got closer, he was able to see Giancarlo's face. "Detective Rabito? Are you ok?"

Giancarlo's eyes strained to see past the officer, his gaze fixed on the empty expanse of Bourbon Street. His heart sank, and a wave of disappointment washed over him.

The arrival of more police officers added to the growing

crowd on Bourbon Street. The first officer, still holding Giancarlo's firearm, reiterated his question, his voice tinged with curiosity and concern. "Why did you shoot your gun?"

Before Giancarlo could formulate a response, a familiar face emerged from the group of arriving officers. It was Benjamin Gill, a fellow officer who knew Giancarlo well. His presence offered reassurance to Giancarlo in this disorienting moment. With a voice filled with urgency and genuine care, Benjamin said, "Giancarlo, it's Benjamin. What happened?"

Giancarlo's hands trembled as he turned to face Benjamin. "I saw him. I saw the Axman. I fired at him."

Benjamin's brows furrowed in disbelief. He pressed further, seeking clarification. "The Axman? Where did you see him?"

Giancarlo's gaze shifted, his eyes fixating on the spot just up the block where he believed he had witnessed the ominous figure. With a resolute tone, he responded, "Just up the block. I was certain he was there, lurking in the shadows."

Benjamin followed Giancarlo's gaze, his finger pointing in the direction Giancarlo had indicated. He asked for clarification, "That way?"

"Yes."

Benjamin looked at the first two officers on the scene. One of the men replied, "My partner and I were at the other corner. There was no one on the street." The other officer agreed and added, "If there was somebody there to shoot at, we would have seen him. No doubt."

Giancarlo rubbed his eyes, repeating, "I saw him. I swear I saw him."

Benjamin reached out, placing a comforting hand on

Giancarlo's shoulder, saying, "C'mon Giancarlo, come sit down."

As Giancarlo went to sit down on the curb, one of the officers asked Benjamin. "What do we do with him? Arrest him?"

Benjamin shook his head, his conviction clear. "No. Chief Mooney would not want that. We will make sure he gets home. We will take his gun though. Ya'll can leave. We have this under control."

As the people retreated from their balconies back into their homes and the officers gradually dispersed from the scene, quiet returned to Bourbon Street. Giancarlo sat on the sidewalk, his head bowed.

Benjamin took a seat beside Giancarlo. He spoke softly, his voice filled with understanding. "We are going to take you home. Are you okay?"

Giancarlo raised his head slightly, his eyes reflecting a mixture of gratitude and apology. "I'm sorry for disturbing everyone. I'm fine. Yes, please, take me home."

Benjamin helped him up and then he, along with his partner, began their walk back to Giancarlo's apartment, their pace slow and steady.

Meanwhile, a figure emerged from the confines of a business doorway on the next block of Bourbon Street, right where Giancarlo had fired his shot. The figure, shrouded in shadows, stepped onto the deserted street. With a haunting jazz tune lingering on his lips, he resumed his journey down the dimly lit thoroughfare, his presence blending seamlessly with the darkness that enveloped him.

22

DON'T SCARE ME, PAPA

As the sun rose over the city of New Orleans, its inhabitants held their collective breath, eager for news and reassurance. To their relief, the morning brought a sense of calm and respite. The city had remained untouched; there were no reported attacks from the notorious Axman.

The *Times-Picayune* had a cartoon called *The Witching Hour – 12:15 a.m.* in the paper that morning. It depicted a family all playing music inside the home while the mother stood guard by the window waiting for the appearance of the Axman.

In the vibrant neighborhood of Little Palermo, the residents awoke with a sense of joy and relief. The news that there had been no Axman attacks had spread like wildfire, igniting a spirit of celebration and gratitude among the tight-knit community. Today, they would come together at St. Mary's Italian Church to commence the festivities of St. Joseph's Day, an occasion of great significance and reverence.

As the church bells rang out signaling the start of the

day's celebrations, families dressed in their finest attire made their way to the church. The aroma of freshly baked bread and pastries filled the air of Little Palermo, intertwining with the spirit of faith and camaraderie. Inside the ornate walls of St. Mary's, the voices of the congregation rose in unison, offering prayers of thanks for the safety bestowed upon their beloved city.

Giancarlo did not go to Mass. He slept in until about ten that morning. As he lay there, he attempted to piece together the fragments of the night before. His memory was a jumbled mess, like a puzzle with crucial pieces missing. The echo of the gunshot still reverberated in his mind. He had fired his gun. He knew that for certain because the police had heard it. That much was true. But the question of why he had taken the shot against all of his training made him consider elements that eluded his understanding.

First, Marie Laveau at her tomb and now Marguerite outside the opera house. He thought back to Marguerite's command to shoot his gun. Did that really happen? Did he really see her? He wondered if he was losing his mind.

He got out of bed and made his way to his living room. He looked at the wall in his apartment, lined with the map, crime scene photos, and the letter from the Axman. The items bore witness to Giancarlo's desperation and stood as a testament to his desire to stop the Axman.

Standing before the wall, his frustration and confusion boiled over. In a fit of despair, he tore down each piece of evidence. As his frenzy reached its crescendo, his gaze fell upon the photograph of Mary Cortimiglia. Her eyes seemed to pierce through him, a haunting reminder of the lives disrupted by the Axman's reign of terror.

Overwhelmed, he crumbled to the floor. Tears flowed freely as he thought not only about the victims, but the realization that the answers might never come. The room echoed with his sobs, the floor around him littered with the pictures and maps torn down from the wall.

By Thursday, the citizens of New Orleans were ready to settle back into a routine. The past few days had been a whirlwind.

Meanwhile, news of the night of jazz and the reason behind it made its way around the country. Not everyone thought publishing the letter had been the best idea.

The *Herald* could not believe that the *Times-Picayune* did not *"think of the great amount of harm it has done to the ignorant classes who are superstitiously inclined and believed to a certain extent that this axman would visit certain families who did not have a jazz band."* It went on to criticize the cartoon that ran as *"a tasteless joke."*

A new musical composition, Joseph Davilla's jazz tune, was released that day and kept the entire episode front and center in the citizens' minds. Davilla called his work *The Mysterious Axman's Jazz* or *Don't Scare Me, Papa*. He hired a piano player to ride in the back of a wagon and played his song up and down Canal Street. He even convinced the *Times-Picayune* to allow him to use the *Witching Hour* cartoon on the front of his sheet music. Over the course of the next few months, Davilla sold thousands of copies, and his music could be heard everywhere throughout the city. His music had made him so much money that there were some people who were skeptical of the letter from the Axman and truly wondered if it had been written by Davilla himself in order to sell his music.

Giancarlo stayed in his apartment all weekend. He had begun to experience more and more "bad days." But by Monday he was feeling better, enough at least to get out of his apartment.

Giancarlo's first destination was a nearby café, a cozy spot tucked away in a charming corner of Little Palermo. Familiar faces and friendly greetings from the staff welcomed him. He ordered his usual cup of strong black coffee and settled into a booth, observing the ebb and flow of the bustling café.

Giancarlo took out a binder that held the pages of his novel. He began to read his manuscript from the beginning. When he reached the chapter on Walter Lamana, he remembered the vision of the man sitting in the doorway with Walter's head on his lap. And then, when Giancarlo read the chapter on Marguerite, her appearance on the night of jazz flashed in his mind.

Were these images real or just figments of his imagination?

While sipping his coffee and delving into his writing, he couldn't shake the nagging feeling that he needed to confide in someone about his experiences. The encounters with Marie Laveau and the vision of Marguerite had left him questioning his own sanity with no clue where to seek answers.

He decided there was only one person he could speak to, and that person was Salvatore D'Antoni.

Finishing his coffee, Giancarlo closed his binder. With determination in his eyes, he made his way through the familiar streets of Little Palermo, heading towards Salvatore's home.

SALVATORE'S APARTMENT WAS LOCATED IN THE MIDDLE OF THE French Quarter at 624 Pirates Alley. The Alley, paved in cobblestones, was only 16 feet wide and 600 feet long. The Cathedral sat on one side and the Cabildo on the other, with Jackson Square on the east end and Royal Street on the west. At the Royal Street end of the alley were the exquisite gardens of St. Louis Cathedral, surrounded by an iron fence. Across from the garden was located the elegant Fleur de Paris hat shop.

Pirates Alley's name was derived from the legend that pirates would use the Alley as their quick escape route back to their ships docked in the Mississippi River to avoid the authorities.

At an intersection midway down the alley, directly across from a single gas lantern, stood the Creole House. However, from 1769 until it was demolished in 1837, this was the location of the infamous *Calabozo,* the Spanish jail from whence the pirate Jean Lafitte had once escaped and which had been known as a place of terrible deeds and horrific living conditions for its prisoners. Many people believed Pirates Alley was and remained one of the most haunted places in New Orleans.

During Spanish control, that intersection was the only place in the entire world where the center of religion, government, and law were all within 20 feet of each other.

Giancarlo turned off Royal Street and walked down

Pirates Alley. He arrived at Salvatore's apartment. He knocked and his friend let him in.

SALVATORE'S APARTMENT WAS ON THE FIRST FLOOR. UPON entering, Giancarlo was met by a large table cluttered with mysterious objects: tarot cards, dice, jars of herbs and spices, caged animals, bones, mummified bats, candles, and pictures of a few saints of the Catholic Church. Giancarlo thought back to his conversation with Lila Davis and knew that Salvatore was a purveyor of Voodoo, the religion brought to New Orleans with enslaved Africans, mixed with the traditions of Haitians who had come to the city, and the superstitions of Catholicism.

After a few pleasantries, Giancarlo, all the while looking at the table, said, "Salvatore, Lila Davis told me about your mother. Who she was and what she did. Would you please tell me about your parents?"

"My father did not emigrate to New Orleans with the masses of Italians in the last few decades. He was here long before that, running a citrus trade between America and Sicily back in the 1850s. It was here where he met my mother, a free woman of color, a Creole. She was a wonderful woman, deep into the spiritual world, and the world of Voodoo. She had uncanny powers to foretell the future, to look deep into men's souls, and to enter the spirit world. She was best known as a healer and people would seek her out to cure them."

Still looking at the table, Giancarlo asked, "Are these objects hers?"

"Some. I've also acquired some objects of my own," Salvatore replied.

Giancarlo, intrigued, probed further, "Are you, I don't know how to say it, into Voodoo?"

Salvatore laughed. "I'll put it this way. I'm a believer. And I find it interesting. I study it. I love to learn about Voodoo priestesses from the past and what they did. I consider myself more of a historian who dabbles in the world of Voodoo. What brings you to my house tonight? Is it the Axman?"

"More like the spirit world. I want to learn more about it."

Salvatore smiled large. "You have dabbled my friend. I can see it in your eyes. You visited her tomb, like I told you to."

"I was desperate after the attack on the Cortimiglias and the death of their daughter. Desperate and drunk, to be fair. But yes, I did what you told me to do," confessed Giancarlo.

"So, you come to me because you saw something?" inquired Salvatore.

"I want to understand," explained Giancarlo earnestly.

Salvatore gently urged, "Tell me what you saw."

Giancarlo told him about the events of that night, beginning with the strange appearance of the man in the cemetery looking for a tomb.

Salvatore chuckled at the mention of the odd appearance, saying, "You met Henry Vignes. He is a sailor from centuries ago."

"Centuries?" Giancarlo exclaimed, astonished.

"Indeed. The legend says he had given his important papers to his landlord while he was off on his travels around the globe. While gone, she sold his family tomb. He wanders the cemetery now for eternity, trying to find rest," Salvatore explained, adding a layer of eerie history to Giancarlo's supposed encounter.

Giancarlo rubbed his temples, not sure what to think. He then told Salvatore about the appearances of Marie Laveau, and of Marguerite. And finally, the firing of his gun at the supposed figure of the Axman. He held nothing back. He ended his summary by saying, "I don't think what I saw is real. I think they were hallucinations, figments of my imagination. At least that is what I keep telling myself."

"When one confronts the spirit world for the first time, it's difficult to comprehend. The easy way out is to disbelieve. But it's real. It's all real. You have made the connection to the spirit world. You have opened the door, and in doing so, the spirits can visit you at will."

"I have so many questions," replied Giancarlo thoughtfully. "Both about what I have seen, and what it means going forward."

"What do you mean?" questioned Salvatore.

"Can I control who I see? Can I dictate who comes to me?" Giancarlo asked, his voice tinged with uncertainty.

Salvatore shook his head. "No. Such power is reserved for the most formidable spiritualists. Marie Laveau and my mother could do this, to a degree. They, in some respect, not only made the connection, but they had an element of control over it. In contrast, you are more like a vessel, a slave to that world and therefore subject to its whims and rhythms. You have no dominion over it."

Giancarlo sighed, the weight of disappointment settling on his shoulders. "I was afraid that would be your answer."

Salvatore smiled knowingly, his gaze piercing. "Your question betrays a deeper longing. It suggests that your desires extend beyond merely locating the Axman. You also harbor the hope of reuniting with someone dear to you. You came to me to understand the realm you sought permission to enter, but beneath it all, your heart aches for one last glimpse of someone. Your wife, no?"

Giancarlo hung his head down, as he whispered his admission, "I would do anything to see her again."

Salvatore's tone softened, offering reassurance, "The spirit world knows your deepest desires. They know what brought you into their world. The journey ahead, the experiences you will have, and where they lead you remain shrouded in uncertainty. But have faith, my friend. The path will unfold in due course. Your sole obligation is to maintain your belief."

"That's the hard part. I don't know what to believe," Giancarlo acknowledged.

"My friend, you have opened the door. You have seen now the spiritual world firsthand. There is no going back now. The spirits will continue to come to you, but when and where you will have no idea. Marguerite came to you to point out the Axman to you. They know why you came into their world. You have called upon them for help. They have answered that call."

"For the past few months, I have seen things. Even before the encounter at the tomb. Things I did not want to believe were real. I'm not willing to say that what I am seeing now is any different. I fear I am a sick man, Salvatore. Sicker than you know. My mind and body are tired. I've seen much in my life that no human should ever have seen."

"There is nothing I can say today that will convince you. But rest assured, this is a fact, a truth. Spirits are real. We will leave it at that, for now."

Giancarlo reached down on the table and picked up one of the tarot cards. He looked at it. It depicted a skeleton dressed in black armor, riding a white horse and wielding a sickle.

Salvatore said, "You have chosen the death card, the Messenger of Death."

"What does that mean? I'm going to die soon? I don't need a card to tell me that," Giancarlo replied with a hint of bitterness.

"It does not mean physical death, my friend," Salvatore explained calmly. "This card is interpreted differently. It means the death of a way of thinking, a change of a belief, a change from an old way into a new way. The death of the old way of thinking gives life to the new."

Giancarlo placed the card back on the table. "I'm sorry for disturbing you. I guess I just wanted to tell someone what I had seen. Thank you for your time."

Salvatore nodded understandingly. "You're always welcome here, Giancarlo. Remember, understanding will come with time."

It was dusk when Giancarlo stepped out of the front door and onto Pirates Alley. A fog had rolled in off the river, enveloping the entire alley in mist.

He turned toward Salvatore who stood in the doorway. Giancarlo extended his hand to him. "Thank you for helping me try to understand."

Salvatore clasped Giancarlo's hand firmly. "It will become clearer."

Giancarlo nodded in gratitude, then turned and walked down Pirates Alley, draped in the dense fog.

23

THE TRIALS

By April, the Spanish flu had all but disappeared from the city. And since the attack of the Cortimiglias and the letter to the *Times-Picayune*, there was silence on the Axman front, no attacks and no more letters.

Giancarlo had no other visitors, sightings, visions either. He still did not know what to make of it all. He still wondered if he was losing his mind.

As the Spanish flu and fear of the Axman receded into the background, the residents of New Orleans began to turn their attention to two events that would soon take control of the city's interest. The trial of Louis Besumer for the attack on his wife and the trial of the Jordanos for the death of Mary Cortimiglia were on everyone's minds. The Besumer trial was set to begin in Orleans Parish by the end of April.

Giancarlo took a keen interest in the newspaper articles leading up to the Besumer trial, particularly, Devlin's jailhouse interview of Louis Besumer who maintained his innocence. Devlin made sure to point out to his readers that the evidence against Besumer was largely circumstantial. He provided his opinion that one man was responsible for the axe attacks and made clear that he believed Besumer's claim of innocence.

About a week before trial, Giancarlo met Michael Devlin for dinner at Arnaud's, a recently opened restaurant in the city.

From the moment Devlin saw Giancarlo, he was overwhelmed with concern about the detective's health. He looked much thinner, his color was pale, and he seemed very agitated. After they enjoyed an appetizer of Shrimp Remoulade, their talk turned to the upcoming trials.

Giancarlo said, "Your interview of Besumer was very sympathetic and was very well done. I agreed with all of your points. I would add that not only is Besumer innocent, but so are the Jordanos. None of these people in jail committed the crimes they are accused of. The person responsible is the Axman, and none of these people are that fiend."

"I've learned that Chief Mooney is expected to be called in the Besumer case as a witness for the defense. The prosecutors are seeking the death penalty. I credit Chief Mooney for getting involved to correct this wrong. I'm going to testify as well; They are going to question me about my interview of Harriet Lowe in the hospital."

"Don't say anything, but I am meeting with Chief Mooney in a few days to discuss the possibility of both of us being called as witnesses for the Jordanos for their upcoming trial in May. They believe there was a feud between the families which resulted in the attack. I know firsthand that the feud was long over. They were friends, not rivals. The jury needs to know the truth. The jury also needs to know the truth about the Axman. That's why Mooney wants to testify. He wants to share evidence that the killer was the Axman, not the Jordanos."

Devlin said, "The Axman. His appetite for blood must have been satisfied. There has been nothing from him for a few weeks."

Giancarlo smiled. "He's biding his time. The urge to kill is not upon him yet."

"I know you studied the crime scenes. I'm guessing they revealed nothing. Have you given up?"

Giancarlo fell into a somber silence before whispering, "I saw him."

"Saw who?"

"The Axman."

Devlin's eyes widened. "When?"

"The night of jazz. He was by the French Opera House. I pulled my revolver and took my shot."

"What are you talking about?"

"I fired at him. I know what I saw, but the police who were on the street say there was nobody there. They say I fired my gun down the empty street. They let me go home, but they took my gun."

"How do you know it was him? Where did he go?" pressed Devlin.

"You will think I'm crazy if I told you. Hell, I think I'm crazy."

"What is going on with you, Giancarlo? You have me concerned."

Giancarlo hesitated briefly, wondering if he should reveal

his recent experiences to Devlin. After his candid conversation with Salvatore, he felt emboldened to venture into this surreal territory. Pointing a finger at Devlin, he asked, "Do you believe in spirits?"

"Ghosts?"

"No, spirits. They are a different entity."

"I don't know. Do you?"

"I've seen… things," Giancarlo said cryptically.

Devlin stroked his chin. "What kind of things?"

"Let's just say I've been having visions."

"Of people?"

"Yes. People from my past. Victims from my cases, as well as others. I know you must think I'm off my rocker."

"Just a bit," Devlin admitted with a laugh, lightening the mood. "Do you think these visions were real or just memories that come to the forefront of your mind in times of stress, making you think they are real?"

"I don't have an answer to that question. I believe and hope they are just conjured up images from my past. But I'm just not sure anymore. Trust me, I know how strange this all sounds."

"Look, I can't even begin to imagine the things you saw in your years of work as detective. It would not surprise me that those events would remain with you, seared into your memory for the rest of your life."

Giancarlo sighed, before asking, "Do you know the story of the Witch of the Opera House?"

"That old wives' tale, how a ghost haunts Bourbon Street?"

"That's the one. Years ago, I investigated her death and the murder of her lover and his mistress."

"Really? You must have been a newly minted cop back then."

"I was," Giancarlo confirmed. "So, I know all about her."

"What does this have to do with our conversation?"

"She appeared to me."

"The witch?" Devlin asked, surprised.

"Yes, she not only appeared to me, but she pointed out the Axman walking down the street. She told me to take the shot."

Devlin swallowed hard, then he sat back in his chair. When he leaned forward again, he said, "But the police saw nothing… no witch and no Axman."

"No, nothing," Giancarlo agreed.

"Do you concede it could just be your mind playing tricks on you?"

"Of course, in fact, I *believe* this is just my mind playing tricks. And yet… they just seem so real. You think I'm crazy, right?"

"No, Giancarlo. Like I said, you have witnessed a lot in your life. Maybe too much. You're like the men who came back from the War suffering from shell shock."

"You're probably right. Perhaps it will go away over time."

"Oh look, here comes our food," Devlin said, trying to change the subject. Once they'd been served, he said, "Tell me all about Sicily. I hear it's a beautiful place."

He smiled at Devlin and said, "Sicily is a place of great contrast. While it can be beautiful and magical, it is touched by poverty, crime, drought, and violence. It's a place I'm glad I left but that I miss at the same time."

Giancarlo went on to paint vivid scenes with his words,

describing the picturesque coastal towns, the rugged mountains, and the fertile valleys that adorned his beloved homeland. He spoke passionately about the warm Mediterranean climate, the azure waters that lapped against sandy beaches, and the aroma of citrus orchards filling the air.

The conversation naturally drifted towards Sicilian cuisine, a subject that sparked joy and nostalgia in Giancarlo. He reminisced about the flavors of arancini, cannoli, fresh seafood, and the comforting aroma of homemade pasta sauce simmering on the stove. The discussion evoked memories of meals shared with family and friends, the joy of gathering around a table laden with delicious dishes, and the sense of community that food brought to Sicilian culture.

Nothing else was said about spirits and visions.

THE LOUIS BESUMER TRIAL BEGAN ON APRIL 30TH AND WENT quickly downhill for the prosecution. Chief Mooney testified about the belief that the Axman was a single individual, and that he had committed the murders of Joseph Romano as well as Mary Cortimiglia. If one believed that the Axman was responsible for the attack on Mrs. Lowe, then Louis Besumer could not be the Axman, as he had been in jail at the time of the other two murders.

There was also much testimony about Mrs. Lowe's mental state. She had never accused her husband of the attack, until long after the attacks. Michael Devlin was called to testify, and he stated that she was completely lucid when she recanted her initial identification of the man who she thought had attacked her. The housekeeper put the nail in the coffin of the prosecution's case when she testified that it was only when Mrs. Lowe came home and became mentally unstable that she accused her husband.

The case went to the jury who quickly found Louis Besumer not guilty. When the verdict was read, Besumer yelled "Thank you," to the jurors, over and over again.

Now all eyes turned toward Gretna and the trial of the Jordanos. The trial was set to begin on May 19th. The defense had received a terrible blow in pre-trial hearings. The judge had ruled that any testimony regarding the Axman attacks in New Orleans was irrelevant and would not be allowed. That meant at the trial, any mention of the earlier attacks would be met by an objection by the prosecution, and an admonishment from the judge. The testimony of Chief Mooney and Michael Devlin for the defense would be subjected to that treatment, such that the jury was not allowed to hear one shred of evidence that the murder of Mary Cortimiglia might have been at the hands of the Axman.

The entire case, therefore, hinged on the testimony of Rosie Cortimiglia. At one point when she was on the stand, the defense attorney asked her, "If these men are convicted of murder, they will be hung by the State of Louisiana by the neck until they are dead, dead, dead. Do you realize that fact?" She agreed and stood by her testimony that Frank Jordano had killed her baby, and that he'd been assisted by his father.

Giancarlo was called for the defense. He testified about the end of the feud, and how the families were now friends. He identified a picture of Frank Jordano holding Mary

Cortimiglia and testified about how close Frank was to the child. He further testified that the child called Iorlando Jordano Grandpa, demonstrating the closeness between the two families.

Many other witnesses were called, and the defense tried to show that Rosie was bullied by the police to implicate the Jordanos. When the defense finally rested, the jury deliberated only a very short time. When they returned to the courtroom, they had reached their verdict. Iorlando Jordano was found guilty without capital punishment and would serve a lifelong sentence. Frank Jordano was found guilty with capital punishment and was sentenced to be hung.

As the Jordanos left the courtroom to go to jail and begin their appeals, they proclaimed their innocence, telling anyone who would listen that Rosie had lied.

Giancarlo, Chief Mooney, and Michael Devlin looked on in silent outrage as the Jordanos were handcuffed and removed from the courtroom. They all knew when the Axman heard of the verdict, he would be laughing at the ridiculous result.

Devlin stood with the Chief and Giancarlo. He said over and over again, "This is not right. This is wrong. So wrong." He quickly excused himself and ran toward the hallway where the guilty defendants were being taken to jail. He caught up with Frank. "I believe you, Frank," he said. "I'm going to do everything I can to get you out."

Frank's eyes welled with tears, as he hugged the reporter. Frank was then pushed by the officer from the back, making him move down the hallway, following his father to their fate.

MORE ATTACKS AND NO MORE VISIONS

Summer arrived in New Orleans. It was hot and rainy, which was normal for that time of year. The Axman had not been heard from since his letter to the *Times-Picayune*. There had been no attacks. Some people wondered if all that jazz playing around the city had quelled the killer's desire for violence.

Giancarlo's visions from his crime investigations had also apparently stopped. As a matter of fact, all of his visions ended. No Axman victims nor any sightings of the Axman himself. He had not seen Marguerite or Marie Laveau again. He began to wonder if his connection to the spirit world was closed. Unable to comprehend why, Giancarlo actually longed to see them again, and so he started paying visits to his friend in the French Quarter.

By July, Giancarlo was going to meet with Salvatore D'Antoni a few times a week. He used those visits to learn more and more about Voodoo and the spirit world. Giancarlo hoped that these visits would reawaken the spirits and make them appear to him again. And perhaps, some way, this would allow him to see his wife again.

Meanwhile, Salvatore spent these visits trying to convince him that the Axman was most likely a phantom. That's why he was never caught and never would be. Giancarlo debated that issue both with Salvatore and his own inner self.

Throughout his career, there were only a very few cases that he could not solve. But the Axman had tainted all these years, multiple attacks spanning his entire career, and Giancarlo had been unable to solve them. He had never believed spirits were real. But because of the Axman he was no longer certain.

It was in August when the shadow returned.

Steve Boca was an Italian grocer. It was 3 a.m. on August 10, 1919 when he was brutally attacked in his bedroom on Elysian Fields.

As the Axman struck, Boca attempted to protect himself, but failed, which quickly left him unconscious. When he awoke later, disoriented and in terrible pain, he ran outside to get a glimpse of the intruder, but he was gone. A bloodied axe was left at the crime scene and a conspicuously missing door panel were all that remained.

Bleeding profusely from his head wound, Boca ran to the home of his neighbor, Frank Genusa, where he collapsed on the front steps. Genusa came to the door and found his friend and immediately called for help. Boca would recover from his injuries, but like all the victims before him, could not remember any details of the incident, nor could he provide any information to assist with Mooney's investigation to determine the identity of the Axman.

As news spread across the city, all hope that the brutal attacks of the Axman had come to an end was extinguished. Instead, tension and fear gripped the citizens once again, their optimism shattered by the grim reality that the Axman's campaign of brutality persisted.

The citizens did not have long to wait for the next attack.

IT WAS LESS THAN A MONTH LATER AT 3:30 IN THE MORNING ON September 3rd. It happened to be one of the hottest nights of the year. The heat and daily afternoon rain made the mosquitoes thrive all across the city. The most important defense for the residents of New Orleans against the little pests was the netting they used to surround their bed at night.

The Lauman family lived at 2123 Second Street between South Saratoga Street and Loyola Avenue. The family's ancestors had arrived to Louisiana from Bavaria. The parents lived with their youngest daughter, nineteen-year-old Sarah.

The family was fast asleep when a dark figure hopped a fence in the backyard. He walked up to a shed in the yard, and when he opened the door, found an axe sitting atop firewood. He picked it up and proceeded to the home, humming the jazz tune *Baby Won't You Please Come Home*.

The mosquitos buzzed relentlessly, their chorus harmonizing with the figure's eerie hum. The heat pressed down on the city, intensifying the tension that hung in the air.

With each step, the dark figure's anticipation grew, hungry to unleash chaos and fear.

He smiled when he noticed an open window. He silently climbed into the home through the window, entering the dining room. He walked down the small hallway until he came to the first bedroom. It was Sarah Lauman's.

Sarah lay on her side, peacefully sleeping beneath the protective mosquito netting around her bed. The Axman loomed over her, his weapon raised high in the air. With a swift motion, he brought the axe down, but lucky for Sarah, it became entangled in the netting, causing him to miss his intended target and only graze the side of her head.

Sarah's eyes shot open, wide with fear and pain. With a primal instinct, she released a piercing scream that shattered the stillness of the night, jolting her parents from their slumber in an instant.

As the echoes of Sarah's cry filled the air, the intruder, realizing he had been exposed, swiftly turned and dashed towards the window through which he had entered. Clutching the axe tightly in his grip, he made a hasty escape, disappearing into the darkness outside.

Alarmed by the sound of their daughter's distress, Sarah's parents rushed to her room as fast as their legs could carry them. Bursting through the door, their hearts pounding with panic and concern, they found Sarah trembling on her bed, her eyes filled with terror.

Sarah's parents hugged her in a protective embrace, soothing her trembling body and ensuring her safety.

Later that morning, the old regulars were on the scene. Chief Mooney, along with Detectives Marullo and Bombay interviewed the entire family. Sarah had a slight cut by her ear, but she was otherwise fine. The physician called to the residence confirmed she had no other injuries. She had survived the attack of the Axman. For her mosquito netting, it was a different story. It was torn in places, and some parts were ripped from its anchors above. It was clear it had saved Sarah's life.

After listening to the story as put forth by Sarah, Chief Mooney knew the Axman had attacked once again. And like every survivor before her, she could provide no identifying characteristics of her attacker.

The next morning the headline of the *Times-Picayune* trumpeted:

Mysterious Axman Strikes Again

Devlin's accompanying article once again laid out all of the attacks by the Axman. His article left his readers on edge and yearning for answers.

Giancarlo learned of the latest attacks in the newspaper. Still, none of his visions had returned. Not even after all the time he spent with Salvatore. Salvatore kept assuring him that they would appear when the moment was right. After all, one cannot control the spirit world; he kept reminding him.

AUGUST SLIPPED INTO SEPTEMBER. AFTER THE ATTACK ON SARAH Lauman, the Axman once again returned to the shadows.

Giancarlo's heart condition had really flared up during the August heat. It was so bad by the end of the month he sought help from his doctor. The doctor used Southey's Tubes to remove some of the fluid around Giancarlo's heart. This did provide relief to him for a time. The doctor also prescribed some medication.

The recommended pharmacy was located at 514 Chartres Street. It held the prestige of being the first apothecary in the United States to have a licensed pharmacist, due to the fact that in the early 1800s, Louisiana became the first state in the union to require pharmacists to take an exam and become licensed in order to practice. At that time, Governor Claiborne established a board of reputable pharmacists and physicians to administer the three-hour oral examination given at the Cabildo in Jackson Square. Louis J. Dufilho, Jr. was the first to pass the licensing examination and he opened the pharmacy on Chartres Street soon after that.

Giancarlo stepped into the pharmacy over a hundred years later where he encountered Henry Lauve, the current proprietor and pharmacist, positioned behind the counter. Rows of shelves adorned with countless bottles lined the space, each containing the age-old "cures" and remedies relied upon to address the health concerns of New Orleans residents.

Giancarlo handed Henry his paper from his doctor prescribing what he needed. The pharmacist turned and grabbed three bottles and then placed them on the counter next to his mortar and pestle bowl.

As Henry began to compound the medicine, Giancarlo

looked around the old building. Medical gadgets, tools, instruments, and devices were scattered all around. He noticed a Victrola at the bottom of one of the shelves. Records were stacked on the side of it. They were jazz records.

Giancarlo commented, "You like jazz I see."

Henry lifted his head. "I do. I find the innovation inspiring," he replied, his tone dripping with mischief. He then added, "But don't tell anyone. The reformers will shut me down for listening to such vulgar music."

Giancarlo laughed. "Your secret is safe with me."

Above the Victrola were more bottles. Giancarlo began looking at some of them and was surprised to find that the entire shelf was dedicated to Voodoo medicine.

While Giancarlo was trying to read the labels on the bottles, Henry asked, "You have an interest in Voodoo?"

Giancarlo turned toward him, "Somewhat. My friend does. You may know him, Salvatore D'Antoni."

A wicked smile played on Henry's lips, and recognition danced in his eyes. "Sure, I know him. He comes in often to get cures and such from me. His mother was one of the best-known priestesses this city has ever seen, second only to the Voodoo Queen herself."

"I'm surprised your pharmacy would sell Voodoo medicines."

"Well, if you knew our history, you would not be. Our first proprietor, a Mr. Dufilho, was the first licensed pharmacist in America. After his death, Dr. Joseph Dupas took over. He not only ran the pharmacy, but he had a medical office upstairs. Dr. Dupas was a believer in Voodoo, but his interest had a darker side. It is said that upstairs he did more than treat patients. He also performed horrific experiments on slaves, particularly pregnant slaves. When an experiment went poorly, he would drop the body from a trap door in his office floor, into a carriage in the backyard. He would then take the body out to the swamps, never to be seen again. Dr. Dupas was also known to engage in Voodoo rites right here inside the pharmacy and out in the courtyard late at night. It was during those rites when spirits would supposedly appear to him."

"He would see spirits?" Giancarlo inquired.

"Supposedly. It was said that through his rituals, he was able to stir them from their world to enter ours."

"Do you believe it? Do you believe spirits came to him?"

"Let me answer your question this way. I believe he still haunts this place."

"What do you mean? Have you seen him?"

"Once. A middle-aged, mustached man with a brown suit and matching brown hat. I only saw him very briefly. Others have seen him more often. He disrupts stuff around the pharmacy. Many times, books are thrown on the ground or bottles smashed on the floor. We all know who the culprit is."

"Do you believe in the spirit world?" asked Giancarlo.

The pharmacist smiled before saying, "I can create medicines to cure people. Yet even I cannot save everyone. My own wife became very ill during her pregnancy. When all looked bleak, I went to the Voodoo Queen's tomb and asked her to cure my wife. I now have a beautiful baby girl, and my wife and I are expecting our second. So, do I believe in the spirit world? I do. After my wife's cure, I made sure to go back to the tomb to circle my X marks and thank the Queen for all that she had done."

Giancarlo raised his hands to face. "The circles on the tomb," he mumbled.

The pharmacist asked in return, "What did you say?"

"Nothing," Giancarlo declared. "There's just something I need to do."

Henry poured the contents he had been mixing into a bottle, wrote down instructions on the label, and handed it to Giancarlo.

"Here you go. I hope you feel better soon."

Giancarlo paid him for the medicine, stuck the bottle into his jacket pocket, left the pharmacy, and headed straight to St. Louis Cemetery No. 1.

It was dusk when he arrived. He went directly to the tomb of Marie Laveau. He stared at the X marks on the tomb. Some were circled, others were not. He wondered which of the circled X marks were those of the pharmacist. He looked on the ground and found a piece of stone. He walked up to the tomb, remembering where his X marks were placed.

As he placed the stone above his X marks, he said, "I'm so sorry for not thanking you for fulfilling my wish… my wish to enter the spirit world. Please, if you blocked me from reentering because of my ingratitude, with this act, let me back in. Let me find the Axman. And if possible, let me see my wife again. Just once."

Giancarlo's trembling hand circled his X marks on the tomb. All was silent. He dropped the stone on the ground and took a step back.

He had never been a believer in the world of spirits. Such

notions ran contrary to his Catholic upbringing and contradicted the very core of his beliefs. Yet, after tirelessly pursuing the enigma of the Axman for so long, he had grown desperate enough to grasp at any straw, no matter how outlandish. He still harbored doubts about the source of his visions, but he could no longer deny that something extraordinary had occurred. He was certain of that much.

Now, all he could do was wait. Wait to see if his actions that evening would catapult him into the realm of the spirit world, and perhaps, if fate would allow it, into a face-to-face encounter with the Axman himself.

Before leaving the cemetery, he stopped at his wife's tomb. He sat down and spoke to her, telling her how much he loved and missed her. He also told her of his request to the Voodoo Queen herself to see her again. As usual, before leaving her tomb, he ran his fingers across her name on the door.

He then departed the cemetery.

THE PEPITONE MURDER

September transitioned into October, and Giancarlo found himself still devoid of the visions that had once haunted him. His meetings with Salvatore became a constant in his life, offering solace and a shared interest in exploring the spirit world. They delved deeper into the mysteries that surrounded them, discussing ancient rituals, esoteric knowledge, and the interconnectedness of the physical and spiritual realms.

Salvatore also tried to assist with Giancarlo's lingering heart condition with old remedies. He crafted a special concoction, a "cure" of sorts, tailored to address Giancarlo's ailment. Giancarlo hesitated at first, uncertain of trusting such a remedy. But his belief in Salvatore and his longing for a return to normalcy compelled him to give it a chance.

With cautious optimism, Giancarlo began taking the elixir, following Salvatore's instructions meticulously. It tasted bitter, an amalgamation of herbs and ingredients hinting at its potent properties. He hoped that this concoction would not only heal his physical heart but also rekindle the connection with the spiritual realm he so desperately sought.

He also perfected his novel. The last case of his that he wrote about concerned the murder of an Italian jazz musician known as *"Maestro del Sassofono"* who was found dead in a smoky speakeasy with his saxophone resting beside him. Rumors of a rival musician's jealousy and a missing songbook led to a tangled murder investigation.

With that story written, Giancarlo believed his book was complete. But he would not seek out a publisher just yet. He pulled out one sheet of paper, which would be the last chapter in the book. He wrote the title of that chapter on the top of the page: *The End of the Axman*. The rest of the page he left blank.

Giancarlo understood that the resolution of his narrative hinged upon the Axman's capture and punishment. The empty space beneath the title represented the void that remained until that moment came to pass. It symbolized the unfinished business, the unanswered questions, and the yearning for justice that burned within him.

As October drew to a close, the Sells-Foto Circus descended upon New Orleans, bringing with it a sense of excitement and wonder. For two exhilarating days, crowds thronged to Tulane Avenue, eager to experience the spectacle under the circus tent.

Around the corner from the circus sat the grocery store of Esther and Mike Pepitone, Italian immigrants. Their grocery store was in the area known as Mid-City. The small grocery, with the couple's living quarters behind it, was located on the corner of Ulloa and South Scott Streets. The couple had been busy all that weekend, with people stopping in to buy drinks on their way to the circus.

The Pepitones name carried with it a complex history that extended beyond the realm of a simple grocery store. Known within the Sicilian community and even by the police, the family had deep connections with the Black Hand. Their ties to this shadowy underworld stretched back many years, implicating their lives within the intricate web of vendettas and power struggles that haunted the Sicilian community.

Giancarlo himself had surveilled the actions of the Pepitone family, conducting investigations that sought to unravel the complexities of their connections and activities. His encounters with the family provided a unique insight into the dynamics of vendettas and the intersecting loyalties within the tightly knit Sicilian community of New Orleans.

IN THE YEAR 1910, THE STREETS OF NEW ORLEANS BORE WITNESS to a series of violent events connected to the Black Hand. Vincent Moreci, an employee of the United Fruit Company, became a target of the organization and was shot, but had miraculously survived. The alleged perpetrators behind the attack were George Di Martini and Paul Di Christina.

Retaliation for the attack was swift. Vincent Moreci, driven by a thirst for justice, took matters into his own hands. He confronted George Di Martini, shooting and killing him as an act of retribution. Soon thereafter, Peter Pepitone, a close friend of Vincent Moreci and the father of Mike Pepitone, found himself face to face with Paul Di Christina, the other alleged assailant. In a fateful encounter, Peter Pepitone shot and killed Di Christina, further escalating the cycle of violence.

Giancarlo was intimately involved in the investigations surrounding both murders. He undertook the arduous task of seeking the truth behind these acts of violence. His relentless pursuit of justice led to the arrest of Vincent Moreci and Peter Pepitone. Moreci faced trial, but despite the evidence against him, he was found not guilty. On the other hand, Peter Pepitone stood trial and received a twenty-year prison sentence for his role in Paul Di Christina's death.

Throughout the course of the investigation, Giancarlo harbored suspicions that Mike Pepitone, Peter's son, may have had knowledge of his father's plan to target Di Christina. He also had reason to believe that Mike himself could have even been the actual shooter. However, the lack of concrete evidence prevented him from proving these suspicions beyond a reasonable doubt. Peter vehemently denied his son's involvement, insisting that his son had no part in the attack on Di Christina.

After his father's trial, Mike Pepitone feared retribution and moved out of New Orleans to Plaquemines Parish. In 1915, Peter Pepitone was paroled. Mike moved back to New Orleans to be with his father, and they purchased the grocery store on Ulloa Street, where they lived together along with Mike's wife and their six children.

On November 19, 1915, Vincent Moreci, a central figure in the vendetta that had been unfolding since 1910, was attacked for a second time. This time, however, the assailant proved successful, and Moreci succumbed to his injuries. Giancarlo, assuming the role of investigator once again, found himself on the frontlines of the case.

Believing that Moreci's death marked a continuation of the vendetta that had marred the city with violence for nearly a decade, his investigation ultimately led to the arrest of individuals connected to the crime. But there was one man whom Giancarlo believed was involved but could never get the required evidence to prove his theory to a reasonable certainty. That man was Joseph "Doc" Mumfre.

A pharmacist by trade, Mumfre was also a small-time thug and longstanding member of the Black Hand. His association with the notorious organization made him a prime suspect in the eyes of the detective. Giancarlo had also investigated Mumfre during the investigation of the abduction and killing of Walter Lamana, but no arrest could be made at that time either.

Giancarlo delved into Mumfre's background, meticulously piecing together the fragments of information that could link the pharmacist to Moreci's murder. The investigation took him down a treacherous path, where the shadows of the Black Hand loomed ominously. Giancarlo knew that he would have to navigate the intricate network of alliances and vendettas that defined the criminal underworld to unravel the truth.

Back in 1909, Mumfre had been convicted and sent to Angola for his involvement in the bombing of an Italian grocery store in New Orleans, an act attributed to the Black Hand. Giancarlo, as the investigating detective in that case, too, had played a crucial role in Mumfre's arrest and subsequent incarceration.

However, in June 1915, Mumfre was paroled, regaining his freedom and resurfacing in the city. His release coincided with the murder of Vincent Moreci, thrusting him under the spotlight once again. The police turned their attention to Mumfre as a prime suspect in Moreci's killing, suspecting that it was another act of retribution orchestrated by the Black Hand.

Giancarlo, driven by his determination to bring justice to the victims and their families, embarked on a relentless pursuit of evidence against Mumfre. He interviewed Mumfre repeatedly, hoping to uncover the truth and gather enough evidence to make an arrest. However, despite his efforts, the killer eluded him.

Mumfre was released from custody. Although never serving time for the Moreci murder, he would end up in jail for different crimes over the next few years until he finally moved out to Los Angeles. He was never seen in New Orleans again.

Mike Pepitone, along with his father, continued to run the grocery store, though, always with an eye looking over their shoulders, watching for an attempt against them for retribution.

ON THE NIGHT OF OCTOBER 26TH, ESTHER AND MIKE PEPITONE went to bed late after their long day in the grocery. The nearby circus certainly was a boon to their small store. They fell asleep a little past midnight.

Ben Corcoran was a deputy sheriff in Jefferson Parish but lived on South Scott Street, very close to the grocery store. He knew the Pepitones very well. He was returning home late that night when he heard the screams of a young girl. He ran to the corner where he found Mike Pepitone's eleven-year-old daughter yelling that her father was covered in blood.

He ran inside the home where he found Mrs. Pepitone in hysterics, saying that the Axman had come and injured her husband. When Corcoran looked at Mike Pepitone, he gasped. He was lying in bed, terribly beaten. Blood poured from the many skull fractures he had received. His face was completely caved in on the left side, a gruesome sight that made Corcoran's stomach churn. Blood was splattered up the walls of the room, nearly ten feet high. The murder weapon sat on a chair in the bedroom, but it was not an axe. The Pepitone's did not own an axe. Instead, the weapon was an iron bar with a large iron nut screwed on the end, its surface gleaming with fresh blood in the dim light of the room.

Corcoran called for an ambulance, but it was useless. Within the hour, Mike Pepitone would be dead. His wife and father and all of the children were inconsolable.

Chief Mooney and Detective Bombay came to the scene early that morning. Soon after, Michael Devlin arrived and stood outside the home. His sources within the police department told him that the police chief was blaming the attack on a vendetta, an overdue act of retribution against the family. He quickly placed a phone call and advised the person on the other end of the events. He asked that person to come to the crime scene. That man was Giancarlo Rabito.

Shortly thereafter, Giancarlo arrived at the scene where he was met by Devlin.

"They are still here?" he asked the reporter.

"Yes. Mooney is speaking with Mike Pepitone's wife and father as we speak."

"How did the killer get in?"

Devlin walked Giancarlo over to a window where the glass had been broken. The intruder must have broken the glass and then unlocked the window.

"Let me go in."

Giancarlo walked through the backdoor of the home and into the kitchen.

Both Mooney and Detective Bombay were surprised by his entrance. Mooney told Bombay to continue the interview, and he walked over to Giancarlo.

"I'm glad to see you. I was told by Bombay of your involvement in the sordid Pepitone matter way back when. You want to see where it happened?"

"Yes."

They walked to the bedroom.

The blood-soaked bed reflected the savage beating that had taken place. Giancarlo's heart began to beat faster and faster. His breathing became erratic. He should never have come.

Mooney, unaware of his companion's panic, said, "They finally retaliated against the family. Mike Pepitone has paid the ultimate price. I think we know who did this."

Trying to calm his nerves, Giancarlo took a deep breath and said, "Who?"

"You know who. This was a vendetta execution. If I had to venture a guess, based on what Bombay advises, Doc Mumfre was involved."

"Chief, I have followed his criminal career for a long time. He left New Orleans some time ago now and moved to

California to be with his daughter. I do not believe this attack is the result of a vendetta. I think this is the work of the Axman."

"The Axman? But it does not fit his crimes. No axe. No door panels."

"Chief, look at the room. This was a horrific beating. And yet, all six children, his wife, and his father heard nothing?" Giancarlo queried, perplexed.

"That's correct. None of them heard anything. His wife only heard Mike moaning next to her after the attack, which woke her up," the Chief confirmed.

Giancarlo looked at the blood on the walls. "And she never heard the beating?"

"No," the Chief replied tersely.

"This attack was vicious. How could no one hear it?" Giancarlo pressed, his confusion deepening.

"He was hit over 18 times, we think," the Chief revealed.

Giancarlo closed his eyes momentarily before responding, "Chief Mooney, he is back. He has attacked Steve Boca, Sarah Laumann, and now Mike Pepitone."

"This was a hit on Mike Pepitone. A result of a Sicilian vendetta," the Chief repeated obstinately.

"Believe what you want. But the Axman walks the streets once again."

"Let me go back and do my job. It was good seeing you again, Giancarlo."

Giancarlo nodded and left the house.

Most of the newspapers that afternoon chalked up the murder to one of those Italian murders, the work of the remerging Black Hand. Only the *Times-Picayune* connected it to the Axman. Devlin's article meticulously listed each and every one of the Axman's victims dating all the way back to the Cruttis. The citizens sided with Devlin.

Yet again, the Sicilian citizens of New Orleans slept uneasily as many believed the Axman was on his killing spree once again.

2 6

THE OPERA SEASON

It was at the end of October that the first public call for the firing of Frank Mooney was made by a newspaper. *The Times Democrat* said the inability to track down the Axman was a blemish on the entire police department, and they laid the blame squarely at the feet of its chief, Frank Mooney.

Mooney was incensed but privately, he was not surprised. His own frustration in failing to stop the killings and attacks had only increased with each new episode. He had spared no expense or effort in trying to bring the killer to justice. Still, his best detectives working the case had unearthed nothing. The detective from the Pinkerton Agency he had consulted with had thrown up his hands after the Pepitone murder. He too believed it to be the work of the Axman, but had been unable to provide any answers to the Chief. Even the person who was most directly involved with all of the Axman attacks, the retired detective Giancarlo Rabito, who had been studying the attacks at length, could provide no clue as to the Axman's identity.

Mooney was disgusted with it all. He slowly came to believe that perhaps Giancarlo was correct. The Pepitone murder was committed by the Axman, but this time the killer had used a new, brutal instrument of death. With no solution as to how to stop the culprit, all Mooney felt he could do was wait for news of the next Axman attack. The residents of New Orleans did the same. But for a time, no more attacks occurred.

In the weeks following the harrowing Pepitone murder, the city's focus gradually shifted away from the gruesome crime and back to music, the soul of its vibrant culture. Jazz, a quintessential part of New Orleans' identity, stood at a crossroads. The question of whether it would endure in the very place of its birth now hung heavily in the air, casting a shadow of uncertainty over the city's artistic heartbeat.

AFTER THE RELEASE OF THE FIRST JAZZ RECORDING IN 1917 BY the Original Dixieland Jazz Band, jazz was quickly becoming popular across the country. But in New Orleans, with the closing of Storyville followed by the flu epidemic and coupled with a desire to get out of the racial south, many Black jazz musicians began to look for employment opportunities outside of the city.

Louis Armstrong took jobs on riverboats that travelled up and down the Mississippi River. Clarinetist Sidney Bechet had left for Chicago and cornetist Joe "King" Oliver soon followed him, along with many of the other jazz greats. The landscape of jazz in the city was changing.

Meanwhile, opera was on the verge of a renaissance. The French Opera House was just about to begin its 1919-1920 season. With the opera house shut down for the second half of the 1917-1918 season and the entire 1918-1919 season, there was much anticipation in the city to see the house open once again.

The newly ordained leaders of the opera house, manager H.B Loeb and impresario Louis Verande, enthusiastically promoted the upcoming season in the newspapers.

The French Opera House calendar of performances had the citizens of New Orleans excited. Opening night, set for November 1st, was the opera *La Navarraise* by Jules Massenet. Also on the calendar were *Pagliacci* by Leoncavallo, and *Manon*, another Massenet opera. December would see two much-anticipated events. One of the New Orleans crowd's most favorite operas would be staged the first week of December: *Les Huguenots* by Giacomo Meyerbeer. It was the epitome of grand opera. And then there was *Carmen* by Bizet, another local favorite.

GIANCARLO MISSED OPENING NIGHT BECAUSE HE FELT UNWELL. But in mid-November, he went to his beloved opera house to hear the Vatican Choirs. That night, 70 singers from the choirs of the Sistine Chapel, St. John Lateran, and St. Peter's Basilica in Rome, performed from the stage of the French Opera House. The show was magnificent, with mostly religious music being sung. Giancarlo was moved to tears by a few of the pieces.

After leaving the concert, he met Michael Devlin at the Little Gem Saloon. They sat at a back table as a jazz performer on the stage near the front door completed his set. The next performer was why most of the patrons had come that night; Jelly Roll Morton would be entertaining everyone.

Jelly Roll, a Creole, was born in New Orleans in 1890 as Ferdinand Joseph LaMothe. When he was fourteen, he started playing piano at a brothel in Storyville where he picked up the nickname Jelly Roll, slang for female genitalia. Jelly Roll owned the nickname, and his music soon became staples in the jazz repertoire. He was the first to write down his jazz arrangements.

As Giancarlo and Devlin waited for his performance to start, the duo discussed the Axman case at length. When they got to the Pepitone murder, Devlin asked, "But no axe was used. The weapon of choice was perhaps the most destructive used by our villain yet."

"Yes. It was designed to do maximum damage. It was designed to kill," Giancarlo affirmed.

"And you believe, without question, Mike Pepitone was killed by the Axman?"

"All of us have tried to understand the actions of this fiend. Some of our beliefs don't match the reality, but we have put them on the side, and continue to believe what we should know is impossible,"Giancarlo explained cryptically.

"I'm not sure I understand," Devlin admitted.

"Let me put it this way. The Axman attacks Italian grocery store owners. That's a fact, but it's not the whole story. He is not limited to just Italians. The Besumers, Mary Schneidier, Sarah Laumann, none of them were. And none of them were grocery store owners. And yet, the talk of so many is that the Axman attacks only Italians. But that is not the true pattern, which then makes finding him even more difficult. Nearsightedness makes all of the citizens of New Orleans possible victims. Next, let's look at his axe. We know this is the same man who committed the attacks in '10 and '11. Back then, it was a meat cleaver. Then he moved to an axe. And for his last attack, a horrific weapon of death. Our killer *evolves* over time."

Devlin shook his head. "Like some of the other newspapers, my editors have begun discussing calling for the firing of Mooney."

Giancarlo laughed. "And they think the next chief would find the Axman and bring him to justice, just like that? I think Mooney has made mistakes in following some of his leads. But I'm not sure he could have found the Axman, even if he hadn't made those missteps. It could have kept innocent people from being investigated though, that's true."

"There are many who believe he is a phantom. As that might explain how he can fit through holes in doors. They say he can shrink his body, slip through the chiseled-out door panel, and then grows again once inside."

Giancarlo asked, "And what do you think?"

"I think he is a killer. A cold-blooded killer. But that he is a man. A breathing, living, human being. You agree, right?"

Giancarlo simply replied, "The murderer is just as real as the murdered."

Just then, Jelly Roll Morton took his seat behind the piano and began banging out the notes to his hit song *Jelly Roll*

Blues. His mastery of the piano and the interplay of the notes made everyone in the crowd move to the music.

It was when he played *The Crave,* however, when a listener realized that this was more than a master of the piano. It was more like he and the piano were one. He made the piano sound as if he were being accompanied by an entire jazz band. Giancarlo knew he was hearing the sounds of one of the greatest musicians alive. He looked around the Little Gem Saloon at all of the patrons mesmerized by the music. And then it dawned on him.

With perhaps one of the greatest jazz greats playing right here, right now on the stage in front of him, if you had any love of jazz and happened to be in New Orleans, there was no place on earth you would rather be. And there was one New Orleanian who loved jazz: the Axman.

Giancarlo began looking at the patrons one by one, but this time through the eyes of an investigator. He was looking for something, anything that would catch his interest in an individual. Based on the descriptions of the Axman from those who had been attacked, and from his own vision of him on Bourbon Street, he had an idea of the build of a man he was looking for. His eyes darted to and fro across the room.

He went from middle-aged man to middle-aged man, but none of them matched the image he had in his mind. Just as Jelly Roll tinkled the keys on the piano with an almost Spanish tinge of the piece, Giancarlo's eyes locked on the back of one individual. The man had the same build from the back as he imagined the Axman had. He strained to see the man's face. Just then, the man turned toward Giancarlo. They locked eyes. The man smiled and waved. It was the pharmacist, Henry Lauve. Giancarlo waved back, disappointed.

Giancarlo continued scanning the crowd. The crowd was cheering as Jelly Roll pounded out the last notes of *The Crave.*

Devlin made him momentarily turn toward him when the newspaper man said, "I have never heard anything like this in my life."

"That's the New Orleans sound. That glorious New Orleans sound that is taking the world by storm."

Jelly Roll then began to play *The Dirty Dozen,* a raunchy song he used to delight crowds with back in his brothel days. It was a song meant for the men in the parlor before they took their women upstairs.

As Jelly sang the lyrics, Giancarlo saw another gentleman in the corner of the saloon. He wore a dark shirt with a dark hat pulled low over his eyes. His back was up against the wall. Giancarlo eyed the man more closely. Middle-aged and stocky build, the man was there but not there, his outfit and the lighting of the saloon revealed nothing of his appearance.

Giancarlo stood up and told Devlin he would be right back. He walked toward the man, and when he got near him, he turned and pretended to be listening to the music, standing next to the shadowy figure in the corner.

When Jelly Roll finished his song, the crowd cheered.

Giancarlo turned toward the man. The man slightly lifted his head toward Giancarlo.

Giancarlo said to him, "What a gift."

The man said not a word, but merely nodded in agreement. Giancarlo looked down and saw that the man had strong, powerful hands. Just as he was about to say something else, a woman breezed past him, and walked into the now open arms of the man. He hugged and kissed her, as she turned her body, placing her back against his chest, as his arms enveloped her in an embrace. It was then when Giancarlo noticed the wedding ring on the man's left hand. The woman had a wedding ring on her hand as well.

The man looked back toward Giancarlo and nodded, before burying his lips into the neck of the woman, whom Giancarlo now guessed was the man's wife.

Giancarlo made his way back to the table where Devlin was sitting. As Jelly Roll ended his next selection, Giancarlo asked, "Do you think the Axman is married?"

"Married? I guess I've never thought about it. I think of him as a loner, so, I would say no. Why?"

"No reason. I guess like you, I've thought that as well."

For the rest of the evening, Giancarlo and Devlin listened to the music of Jelly Roll Morton, and Giancarlo continued staring at all of the patrons, hoping he might lay eyes on a killer.

27

MAMAN BRIGITTE

After attending the performance of Jelly Roll Morton, Giancarlo began to attend jazz performances around the city. He would eye each and every one of the men in attendance, trying to pick out any of them that resembled the supposed build of the Axman. If he found one, he would venture over and engage in a brief conversation. He was uncertain as to what he was expecting those conversations to reveal, but he was hoping that with his years as a detective spent interviewing hundreds of criminals, he could pick up on something, anything, that would spark his intuition.

To date, however, his jazz excursions had only increased his frustration. The Axman had to be stopped, yet, with no leads and no suspects, it seemed an impossible task. The only encouraging news was that there had been no further Axman attacks since the Pepitone murder. Giancarlo knew that would change soon though. The closest he had come to the Axman was when he had opened his mind to the spirit world. But his visions had stopped, and now he had nothing to go on. He longed to reenter that world.

On December 1st he visited Salvatore D'Antoni at his home on Pirate's Alley. Ever since his conversation with the pharmacist, he had wanted to ask Salvatore about connecting to the spirit world through a Voodoo ritual. He explained to Salvatore his desire and asked him to help in any way that he could.

"Spirits act on their own time," Salvatore said. "You have already visited the Voodoo Queen. She knows your desires. It would be best to wait for her rather than force the issue."

"Salvatore, I'm willing to try anything. Please help me. I did not believe that world existed. I now know it does. I now believe. I beg you."

Salvatore cocked his head. "I guess we can try."

Giancarlo smiled.

Salvatore continued, "But you must promise you will do everything that I tell you to do."

"I promise."

"I will use a Voodoo ritual to call upon the spirits to enter our world and take you into theirs. We will do it right here. Out on the patio. Pirate's Alley is a place where more spirits reside in our city than any place else, it's as good as anywhere. Come, help me set up."

Salvatore proceeded to take items from the table in the front of his home to a table on his patio. Candles, incense, bones, a small pot, and a picture of St. Joseph were all carried out. The candles were lit, and the incense burned. The entire patio became filled with their aromas. As the smoke curled and danced, the candlelight created a flickering, murky glow, casting intricate shadow patterns on the surrounding space.

Having created an atmosphere that felt both sacred and mysterious, Salvatore excused himself and withdrew into the house, leaving Giancarlo alone to be captivated by the patio's newfound enchantment.

Salvatore returned to the patio carrying a platter of fruit and a glass filled with rum and a pepper hanging over the rim. He placed the items on the table and excused himself again as he ducked inside once more.

Giancarlo stood by the table and coughed from the smell of the burning incense. He looked down at the bones scattered on the table. A sense of excitement grew inside him; he was about to experience a true Voodoo ritual for the first time.

When Salvatore returned to the patio, he was dressed entirely in white. In his hand, he held an empty, dried gourd covered in beads and snake vertebra. A bell was attached to it with a cord.

Giancarlo asked, "What is that?"

"This, my friend, is an ason rattle. This was my mother's. This is how we call upon the Lwa, the spirits who will hopefully agree to assist with your deepest desires."

"The Lwa?"

"Yes. Lwa. They are a sort of intermediary between the human and divine. They can speak directly to the Creator. We will call upon the Lwa to assist us. Papa Legba is always saluted first. He will open the way for the others. If he grants our wish, we will then call upon him to allow us to speak directly with a spirit. A spirit of my choosing. A spirit who I think can help us. A spirit whom my mother often called upon."

"What spirit?" asked Giancarlo.

"Maman Brigitte."

"Who is she?"

"She is a spirit associated with life and death and the underworld. Her roots can be traced back to the Emerald Isle of Ireland. She is associated with Saint Brigid of Kildare. She is a member of the Ghede family, known as a powerful force of both death and fertility. This family loves to have a good time. They are jolly, sexual, rude, and crude. Her husband is Baron Samedi, the god of death and the keeper of cemeteries.

"She drinks pepper infused rum, too spicy for any mortal. The oldest grave in any New Orleans cemetery is hers. Maman Brigitte is a powerful healer and protector, particularly of women. Your Axman has been attacking women. I can't think of a better person to help us. Her reputation for wrathful punishment of wrongdoers is legendary. I can't think of anyone better to call upon when the wicked need to be punished. She appears as a sultry, sexy woman, who loves to dance, party, and curse. Her Irish background is seen in the way she looks. She is milky skinned with red hair. Her eyes are a piercing green. She dresses provocatively and exudes a sexuality that is both powerful and terrifying."

"You've seen her yourself?"

"One time, when my mother called upon her."

"And you think she will help us?"

"Indeed. That is *if* she comes. Come, let us begin."

Salvatore placed the ason on the table and proceeded to put the bones into the pot. Picking up the picture of St. Joseph, he said, "And so we begin with prayers."

The ceremony began with the two men making a few Catholic prayers, including the Our Father and the Hail Mary.

Once completed, Salvatore walked over to the table and grabbed the ason. He began to shake the rattle so as to awaken the Lwa. Then in a deep, low voice, Salvatore began to sing an old Creole song.

Then, Salvatore saluted each of the main Lwa, beginning with Papa Legba. As he called each one, he sang a brief song dedicated to that specific Lwa. After Papa Legba, came Erzulie, Ogun, Damballah, Oshun, and culminated with the veneration of Baron Samedi.

As the song to Baron Samedi came to an end, Salvatore said to Giancarlo, "And now we dance."

Salvatore began to chant a new song and started swaying back and forth. Giancarlo tried to follow. Salvatore's rhythmic chant picked up in pace, and their dance matched the beat. Salvatore reached over to the table and picked up a bunch of grapes off the vegetable tray along with the glass of rum. He lifted them above his head as he called out the name of Maman Brigitte. He placed them back on the table and began to spin around, as he signaled Giancarlo to do the same.

Giancarlo began to spin. Salvatore continued chanting. The incense smoke covered the entire patio. Giancarlo began to feel his chest tighten. He slowly began to stop his spinning. As he did so, he looked at Salvatore who seemed to be in a trance. Giancarlo's hand instinctively clutched his chest, his heart racing in an unsettling arrhythmia.

In that very moment, a blinding flash of light erupted at the center of the patio, searing through the smoky veil. The intensity of the radiance was overwhelming, and it struck both Giancarlo and Salvatore like a bolt from the heavens. With a resounding thud, they collapsed, unconscious, their connection to the mystical forces momentarily severed. The patio fell into a hushed stillness.

Moments later, as Giancarlo gradually regained awareness, he found himself lying on his side. Groggily, he rolled over and discovered Salvatore close by, his eyes firmly shut. Giancarlo's own faculties began to return as he sat up cautiously.

And then, a gasp escaped his lips as his eyes fell upon a figure standing by the table. The glass filled with rum was cradled in the figure's hand. A woman, her presence both ethereal and bewitching, had materialized before him.

Her appearance was a vision of equal parts beauty and intrigue. Her skin was milky-white, her hair flaming red. But it was her crystal clear emerald eyes where her true mesmerizing beauty lay.

Her attire was a tapestry of contradictions, blending the sumptuous with the audacious. She wore a full-length silk brocade, its green threads woven with such finesse that it shimmered with an otherworldly radiance. The skirt boasted a daring high slit, offering a tantalizing glimpse of her fair skin, while a top layer of regal purple silk draped like a beguiling bustle on one side.

Around her waist, a skull hung from a chain belt like a talisman. This skull, a mysterious artifact, had been cut in half so as to lay flat against the skirt, a symbol of both the mortal and the supernatural. Her skirt, slung low on her hip, defied convention by forgoing the traditional full bodice in favor of a daring bandeau top, leaving little to the imagination. This provocative top was adorned with a smaller metallic skull and feathers, nestled between her breasts.

Perched atop her head she wore a stovepipe black top hat, its brim pulled low, haloed by tendrils of her fiery red hair that flowed like living flames. Feathers were nestled into the hatband.

Adorning her wrists and arms, metal bands glistened in the dim light, lending her an air of mystique that was impossible to ignore. She was a vision unlike any other, a captivating embodiment of both beauty and the arcane, a sight that Giancarlo knew very few men had ever beheld before.

Giancarlo quickly stood up, as the woman slowly sipped from her glass of rum, eyeing him under the rim of her hat.

"Maman Brigitte?" Giancarlo hesitantly asked.

"Aye," she said in a lilting Irish accent. "Who are ye?

"I'm Giancarlo Rabito. I was with…"

She waved her hand and said, "I know Salvatore. His mahther was a very powerfoehl priestess. 'E is an imbecile," she said with a laugh. "But I do like 'im. I know who disturbed me frahm me gatherin I was attendin."

Looking at Salvatore, Giancarlo asked, "Is he ok?"

"Aye. He'll wake soon. Dat boy needs to find a woman. 'E needs a good fuck. Now, why ded 'e call me?"

"He called you at my behest."

She walked over to where Giancarlo was standing. She moved as if she was dancing on air. Giancarlo couldn't help but look at her ample cleavage spilling from her halter top. Her whole demeanor exuded a commanding sexuality. His eyes left her chest as he focused on her beautiful face and those emerald eyes. She was even more beautiful up close. Stunning was more like it. An enchantress who seemed to hold the mysteries of the cosmos in her captivating gaze.

She reached out and dragged the back of her right hand along his face, saying, "Dere is a sadness about you, me child."

"A sadness?"

"Aye. You too need to get laid."

Giancarlo laughed.

"I can 'elp you, if dat's yooehr desire."

"No. I don't need your help with that, thank you."

She reached down and grabbed his crotch, saying, "It's been a while, asn't it?"

He awkwardly moved a step back, as she removed her hand. He said, "Not since my wife died."

"You loved 'er. I can feel it."

"With my entire being."

"Aye, lost love br'ks de 'eart."

Then in a lilting manner, she proceeded to sing a beautiful sea shanty song about lost love. Giancarlo stood spellbound as her voice filled the patio.

I dreamed a dream the other night
Lowlands, lowlands away me John
I dreamt I saw me own true love
lowlands away

I dreamed my love came in my sleep
Lowlands, lowlands away me John
Her cheeks were wet, her eyes did weep
Lowlands away

She came to me at my bedside
Lowlands, lowlands away me John

All dressed in white, like some fair bride
Lowlands away

And bravely in her bosom fair
Lowlands, lowlands away me John
Her red, red rose, my love did wear
Lowlands away

She made no sound, no word she said
Lowlands, lowlands away me John
And then I knew my love was dead
Lowlands away

Then I awoke to hear the cry
Lowlands, Lowlands away me John
Oh, watch on deck
Oh watch, ahoy
Lowlands away

Giancarlo wiped tears from his eyes, moved by the haunting beauty of her song as the final note faded into the night.

She said, "You loved 'er deeply. Da loss of 'er is de root of your sadness. But dere is more to you dan joehst sadness at a lost love. You 'ave an aura, I can feel it, deep wethin me sooehl."

"What do you mean? An aura of what?"

She leaned over and whispered into his ear. "I am de lady o'sexuality and death."

Giancarlo could smell the pepper infused rum on her breath.

She then whispered, "Yooehr aura is death."

Giancarlo instinctively pulled back; his wide-eyed gaze locked onto hers.

She laughed. "What I tell ye, ye already know. You are ill. You are on de edge o'death." She raised her hand and cupped it over his heart. She closed her eyes. Giancarlo could feel his heart beating inside his chest. When she opened her eyes, she said, "Yooehr 'eart is damaged."

Giancarlo said not a word but raised his hand to his chest.

"Did ye call me to save ye? Fahr I'm a powerful 'ealer."

"I do not need a healer, Maman Brigitte. I know what my destiny is."

She laughed even harder. "Italians and deir *'destino.'* Destiny can be changed ye know."

"If one wants it to change. I want you to help me in another way."

"Alright den, what is dat?"

"I want to enter the spirit world. I want to enter the spirit world and find an agent of the devil."

"Who?"

"I don't know his actual name. Here, he is called the Axman of New Orleans. He has brutally murdered and injured many people, including women, and even a child. You are of the spirit world. Can you confirm for me that this murderer is not human, but part of that world? I need to know."

She laughed. "Ye are a chivalrous romantic, wan'ten to protect wahmen."

"He needs to be punished. But to do so, I need to find him. I beg you, please tell me, is he of this world… or yours?"

"I would love nahthin more than to get me 'ands on

dis man's balls and squeeze before I killin' 'im meself. Men who 'oehrt wahmen are de lowest scum on de earth."

"I agree. So, if he is of the spirit world, let me in, and I will find him and make him suffer the consequences for his actions."

She pointed directly at Giancarlo, and then said, "Dis Axman ye seek. He is a spirit. I can con'frm dat. He's an evil monster, that prowls ye city, kill'ng when he desires. O dat, I'm certain."

Giancarlo sighed. "I knew he was not of this world. I knew it. That's why I could never capture him. Help me find him. I beg you."

"You want to enter de spirit wahrld. My friend, you 'ave already been allowed in. I sense it. You've visited 'er tomb, no?"

Taken aback, Giancarlo asked, "Madame Laveau's? Yes."

"She already petitioned the Lwa on yooehr behalf to enter de spirit wahrld. Dey agreed to let you in. De spirit wahrld is in ye."

"I used to see things. But the visions stopped."

"When dere is sahmethin to see, you will see. You see me now, no?"

Giancarlo slumped his shoulders. "I do. I was hoping to reconnect with that world. But you're telling me I have never left it."

"You 'ave a kind soul, although yooehr eyes 'ave seen much dat men are naht supposed to see. I'm goin to tell ye what is buried in the deepest crevasses of o' yooehr bahdy. No one knows it."

"And what is that? What do you think it is?"

"You dahn't want to be 'ealed. You are ready fahr death. You want to be wit 'er, fahr eternity."

Tears began to well up in his eyes for the second time that night. "I miss her with all of my heart. Can I see her again? Just once. How long I have left on this earth is unknown. I'm ready to see her now."

"When ye see me agin, ye will know dat death is callin. But you don't want to wait fahr dat to 'appen befahre you see 'er, no?"

"No, I want to see her."

"Me 'oehsband, Baron Samedi, is called The Master of the Dead. Only 'e could allow dat to 'appen. It's beyahnd me powers. 'll ask 'im on yooehr behalf. Me 'oehsband can be charmin, but 'e can also be joehst as rude. 'E loves me, but he also chases mortal women. E's naht a devoted romantic like you. So, what I'm saying is, when it comes to love, one never knows how he will respond. If it 'appens, it 'appens. Boeht I promise, I'll speak to 'im. Provided you do one thing."

"What is that?"

She pointed toward Salvatore still lying quietly on the ground. "Do naht tell 'im I came to ye. 'E'll never leave me alahne if 'e knows I can be cahled."

Before Giancarlo could respond, there was a flash of light, causing him to fall to the ground again. When his eyes opened, he found himself lying in the patio on his side, in the exact same position as after that first flash of light. He rolled over and saw Salvatore laying in the same spot. He looked towards the table, and then around the patio, but there was no sign or trace of Maman Brigitte.

He set up and rubbed his temples. The incense smoke had dissipated from the patio. He wondered if what had just occurred was a dream or if Maman Brigitte really been with him. He stood up and walked over to Salvatore. He bent down and began to shake him. Salvatore began to rouse.

"What happened?" Salvatore asked groggily.

"You passed out."

Salvatore slowly set up. "Passed out? I must have not eaten enough today. How long was I out."

"Just a few seconds. Are you ok?"

"Yes. I'm sorry I couldn't help you."

"C'mon, let me help you pick up."

Giancarlo offered his hand and assisted Salvatore in standing up.

Standing, Salvatore said again, "I wish I could have helped."

"It's fine," Giancarlo replied as he picked up a few items from the table and brought them inside.

Salvatore picked up the pot with the bones inside. He also picked up the glass with the rum. "Strange," he said under his breath, as he noticed there was less rum in the cup then he had put in it. He shrugged his shoulders. Maybe he was mistaken. He carried the items inside his residence.

28

THE LAST PERFORMANCE

Giancarlo awoke early the next day. He laid in bed thinking about the events of the night before. It had to be real. He really did converse with Maman Brigitte. At least that is what he kept telling himself.

He got out of bed and thought about the day in front of him. He would be meeting Devlin that afternoon to discuss the Axman case, and then that night he would be attending *Les Huguenots* at the French Opera House.

He ate a quick breakfast, got dressed, and went downstairs to the grocery store. Augustino was standing outside, smoking a cigar.

"*Buongiorno*, Augustino."

"*Ciao*, Giancarlo. No news on the Axman?"

"None. At least no more attacks. Are you still taking precautions?"

"Yes. Every night we put crates in front of the doors which will come crashing down if someone enters. I pray he is caught soon. I pray that justice is paid for the death of Charlie's child. I have some sad news to tell you. I heard Charlie filed for divorce from Rosie. He can't believe she still stands by her story that the Jordanos were the culprits."

Giancarlo shook his head in disgust and said, "Oh no. Really? The Axman has ruined so many lives throughout the entire city. I too pray that he is stopped." Giancarlo's gaze softened, and he managed to give a small smile. He asked, "On a happier note, are you going to the opera tonight?"

"Yes, we are. *Les Huguenots* is one of our favorites. We are also going to see *Carmen* in a few days. The opera house has seen a resurgence. Opera is once again king in this city. The magic of the French Opera House is back."

"Well, I'll see you there tonight. Have a great day."

***

Later that afternoon, Giancarlo met Devlin at the newspaper office. Devlin was visibly upset when he learned of the Cortimiglia's divorce.

"I'm still working on proving the Jordanos' innocence," Devlin said. "It would be just awful if Frank Jordano is hanged for something I *know* he did not do."

"It would. I hope you are successful or that Rosie finally comes to her senses and retracts her testimony."

"I'm trying to get approval to go speak to her. Perhaps she will, one day. Hopefully, before they hang Frank."

"You said you wanted to meet to go over some stuff regarding the Axman. What do you want to discuss?"

Devlin said, "I thought we could go to the addresses of all of his attacks, one after the other. To see if we missed anything. To see why those businesses stand out for some reason. I thought it was worth a try to see."

"I'm game. At the very least, it will help put the final touches on the completed parts of my novel."

"How is the novel, by the way?"

"Done, except for the last chapter."

"Reserved for the death of the Axman."

Giancarlo scoffed. "Either his or mine."

"C'mon, let's go take a look at the crime scenes."

As the day wore on, Giancarlo and Devlin combed through the crime scenes. The results of their expedition were as expected. Nothing. No new leads and no new insights. Who the Axman was and what motivated his choice of victim remained a mystery, a frustrating puzzle that refused to be solved.

Disappointment settled upon Giancarlo as he returned home in the late afternoon. However, he refused to let despair consume him. He ate a light dinner, knowing that the evening held a different kind of escape for him, an escape to the world of opera.

Bourbon Street was alight with excitement that evening. Giacomo Meyerbeer's *Les Huguenots*, a spectacular example of grand opera, was a sellout. In five acts, the opera has majestic music, lavish staging, and a dramatic storyline. Long a fan favorite of the New Orleans crowd, the opera was first performed in America on April 29, 1839. Since the premiere, it had been performed over 200 times.

The club room was filled with the high society of New

Orleans having their pre-performance drinks and mingling with one another. Some of the patrons spilled out onto the balcony, taking in the sights and sounds of Bourbon Street.

When Giancarlo arrived at the opera house, he could sense the excitement among the crowd. Without a doubt, opera had returned to its place of prominence in the musical life of the city of New Orleans.

The new management of the opera house had brought in an entire group of highly trained singers from France. They were set to perform not only the *Les Huguenots* performances but the upcoming *Carmen* performances as well.

Giancarlo met Augustino and his wife inside the lobby where they spoke about the opera. Giancarlo mentioned that the last time he had seen this opera performed here, the then-President of the United States, Howard Taft, had been in attendance.

Soon, Giancarlo made his way to his seat. If the atmosphere outside the theater gave an indication of the excitement of the patrons, the interior of the theater pulsated with anticipation. When the Conductor came into the orchestra pit, the audience clapped wildly. The Conductor bowed to the crowd, turned to the orchestra, and the opening notes of the prelude to the opera began. Giancarlo settled into his chair and got lost in the majestic, sweeping music.

In the enchanting spell of the performance, Giancarlo found himself captivated by the artistry and talent of the performers. He traced their graceful, delicate movements on stage, awe-struck by the resonant and magnificent sounds emanating from their throats.

As the acts unfolded, Giancarlo didn't merely witness the drama of the opera; he submerged himself in its depths, caught in the ebb and flow of emotions that cascaded from the stage. It was more than a spectacle; it was a journey into the heart of shared human experience between the singers and the audience. The performance that night reaffirmed for him that the magic of opera transcends the confines of time and space.

When the final notes were played, the audience stood as one and rained down applause upon the performers. It had been a stunning performance, one that showed what grand opera was all about. And without a doubt, based on the enthusiastic response of the audience, the French Opera House had returned to its glory and stature in the city.

Giancarlo walked down Bourbon Street afterwards, humming a few of the tunes from the opera. For the rest of the night, his thoughts were all centered on music. No visions. No memories. No Axman. Just the thread of opera, and the importance that music played in the fabric of New Orleans life.

2 9

AN ANNIVERSARY READING

The next morning, December 3rd, every newspaper trumpeted the return to glory of the French Opera House. The performance and the performers all received the highest of praise. Mention was even made in the *Times-Picayune* that with the emigration of the great jazz players away from the city, opera and the French Opera House were once again on top of the musical world of New Orleans, and that the performances of *Carmen*, which were beginning rehearsals later that day, were already sold out.

Giancarlo slept in late that morning. When he awoke, he still had the music from *Les Huguenots* in his head. It had been a late night, with the performance ending well past midnight. He only had two items on his agenda today. First, he would go to the French Market and buy a dozen red roses. Then, he would take those roses to his wife's tomb. For December 3rd was their wedding anniversary.

Around 3 p.m., he was walking amid the different tables

set up in the open-air French Market, and the booth owners were selling their wares. He held a bag in one hand.

The market stretched from Café du Monde - home of the famous beignets and chicory coffee - near Jackson Square to Esplanade Avenue. Dating back to 1791, the French Market originated in this same location where a Native American trading post used to stand along the Mississippi River. It didn't take long before both the French and the Spanish developed the area as they opened it to ships and traders from all over the world. By the turn of the 19th century, the market was turned into its bazaar type structure with people selling all sorts of different items. Then, with the surge of the Sicilians to New Orleans by the mid-century, produce became the staple up and down the six blocks of the market.

Giancarlo walked down the main walkway of the market. The air was alive with a mix of commerce and culture. Crates of produce piled high and brimming with nature's bounty caught his eye at every turn. Juicy, ripe tomatoes in shades of red and orange, plump grapes dangling from vines, and an assortment of leafy greens created a kaleidoscope of colors that burst with vitality. The scent of earthy mushrooms and the sweet aroma of ripe fruits intermingled, creating a heady perfume that wafted through the market.

Amidst this cornucopia of fresh produce, other tables displayed an array of goods, each one telling a unique story. Cups and plates adorned with intricate patterns enticed people passing by to stop and take a look. Exquisite leather goods, crafted with care, beckoned passersby to touch them and appreciate their artistry. Religious items, ranging from delicate rosaries to ornate crucifixes, offered a glimpse into the spiritual tapestry of New Orleans.

The lively chatter of sellers and buyers added a vibrant layer of conversation to the scene. Sellers passionately extolled the virtues of their products, while buyers bargained and haggled with equal fervor.

Giancarlo's presence didn't go unnoticed. Workers recognized him and greeted him with enthusiastic cries of "Detective Rabito!" Their genuine warmth made him feel like a treasured friend.

But it was when he reached the table adorned with an array of flowers that Giancarlo's senses were truly enraptured. The colors of the blossoms painted a vivid palette against the backdrop of the market's hustle and bustle. Scarlet poppies and azure irises, golden sunflowers and delicate lilies, they all stood proudly, their fragrances competing for his attention.

"Giancarlo. Good to see you. Can I help you?" the younger man from behind the table asked.

Giancarlo extended his hand toward the man. "Your flowers are as gorgeous as ever, Pasquale. I'm looking for a dozen red roses."

"You're in luck. I sold a bunch just a bit ago. But I have two bouquets left."

The young man turned and went to another table off to the side that had vase after vase lined up in long rows. Most of the vases were empty except the last two, each held a bouquet of roses. He picked up one of the bouquets and brought it to Giancarlo.

"I think she will like this one. They are beautiful. Must be for a special lady?"

"That's an understatement," he replied, as he pulled his money from his wallet and paid for the flowers. *"Buona giornata,* Pasquale," he said, as he turned and walked down the aisle from where he had come, carrying the roses in front of him in one hand and the bag he had brought with him in the other.

GIANCARLO WENT DIRECTLY TO ST. LOUIS CEMETERY No. 1. He entered the front gates and made his way toward his wife's tomb. He did look down the aisle at Laveau's tomb when he passed. Since his visit from Maman Brigitte, he'd had no other visions. He turned his head away from the aisle and continued his walk.

He arrived at his wife's tomb. He removed some old, dead flowers that were in a concrete vase in front of her tomb and placed his bouquet of roses there instead.

"Here you go, Piccolina. Happy Anniversary. I remember our wedding day like it was yesterday. You were so beautiful. You took my breath away.

"And our wedding night," he continued, his voice trembling with emotion, "the nervousness we shared, the uncertainty, but oh, the love that bound us together. Every day I spent with you was a treasure, my only regret being that I couldn't see you as a mother, a role I am sure you were born to embrace.

"I miss you so much. You are the light that once illuminated my days. Without you, my life has lost its purpose. Without you, my life has lost its passion. Without you, my life has lost its joy. I love you, Piccolina. I love you with my entire being. Happy anniversary, *mio amore.*"

With that, he sat next to the tomb and reached into the bag

he had been carrying. He pulled out the manuscript of his novel.

He said, "It's done, except for the last chapter. I wanted to read some parts of it to you. It not only covers my years as a policeman, but also talks about my marriage to you. I hope you like it."

He began reading from the first page. During the course of the reading, he would laugh at the funny parts and emphasize the dramatic parts. He even interjected comments that had not been written into the story, for Piccolina's ears only.

Time seemed to pause as he continued to read, his love for his wife infusing every word, every sentence, and every page. The sun dipped lower in the sky, casting long shadows across the cemetery, but he read on, undeterred. For hours, he sat there, by the side of his beloved's tomb, reading from his novel. However, it was the side comments to his wife, as if he was speaking directly to her, which acted as a testament to the enduring love he felt for her, a love that transcended the boundaries of life and death.

In that quiet and sacred space, his love regained its voice and resonated with the serenity of the cemetery. It was a love story that continued to unfold, even in the afterlife.

HE LEFT THE CEMETERY AROUND 10 P.M. THAT NIGHT. HE carried the manuscript with him in the bag. On his way home, he passed a saloon at the corner of Rampart and St. Peter. He needed a drink. Just one drink, an anniversary drink.

He entered the saloon and took his seat at the bar. He knew the bartender who was also the owner of the saloon, Dominick Terranova.

Dominick smiled as Giancarlo sat down. "Giancarlo Rabito, it has been a while since you have come inside my saloon."

"Yes, it has. Good to see you. How goes everything?"

"Well, the Axman hasn't gotten me yet. At least I can say that."

Giancarlo smiled and said, "Hopefully he will be brought to justice soon."

"Did you go to the opera last night?"

"I did. Did you?"

"Yes. I had two free tickets. The new managers come here after rehearsals often. They treated me. I thought the performance was spectacular."

"I agree."

"The French Opera House has returned to its days of glory."

"A much-needed thing for our city."

"What are you drinking?"

"Rum, please."

"Rum it is."

Dominick turned and grabbed a glass and pulled the bottle of rum from the shelf. He poured it into the glass and handed it over to Giancarlo.

"*Salute*, my friend."

"*Salute*," replied Giancarlo, as he took a sip.

Dominick and Giancarlo began discussing the opera performance until some other patrons came in. Dominick whirled away to fix their drinks. Two other men then walked into the bar. Giancarlo immediately recognized them as H.B Loeb, the manager, and Louis Verande, the Impresario of the French Opera House. The two men sat down at a table before Loeb came to the bar and stood next to Giancarlo to place their order.

Dominick came over and said, "Monsieur Loeb, my friend and I were just discussing *Les Huguenots*. What a night of music."

Giancarlo added, "Spectacular."

"I'm glad the both of you enjoyed it." He then extended his hand to Giancarlo saying, "I don't think we have met. I'm Monsieur Loeb," and pointing to the other gentleman at the table, he said, "And that is Monsieur Verande."

"It is a pleasure. My name is Giancarlo Rabito. I have been a long-time opera fan."

Dominick added, "He's also one of the greatest detectives to ever roam our streets."

"Retired now," Giancarlo added.

"Dominick, how about another drink for my friend here. Giancarlo, come join us at our table. We have had a full day of rehearsals for *Carmen* and could use the fresh company."

"I would be honored."

Dominick made the drinks, and then Giancarlo and Loeb met Verande at the table. They only sat for a second, as Loeb stood up, his glass raised in a toast. The other two men joined him.

Loeb said, "To the French Opera House, long may she stand."

Verande and Giancarlo repeated, "Long may she stand."

They all took a deep drink, then they sat back at the table and began talking.

Loeb and Verande spoke at length about the rehearsal of *Carmen*. It seemed the Escamillo at one time had dated the singer playing Carmen, but the relationship hadn't lasted. It had made for some awkward moments at rehearsal.

They then moved to discussing the opera itself. And it was here where Giancarlo surprised the both of them. His knowledge of the opera was impressive, and his attention to detail of the story took their breath away. Loeb and Verande became more and more mesmerized by his knowledge, so much so that they began to ask him about aspects of the staging of certain scenes.

Dominick brought another round to the table, as they continued speaking about the opera. Giancarlo loved every minute of it.

At one point, Loeb said, "You know at the end of the opera during the bullfight. While Escamillo is inside the arena killing the bull, Carmen is killed by Don Jose outside. As he admits to the murder, we hear the crowd inside the arena praising Escamillo, as red roses fill the scene, raining down upon Don Jose and the dead body of Carmen. Well, we want to make the scene even more magical. We want the stage covered completely with roses."

Verande interjected, "I think we bought all of the roses in the French Market."

Giancarlo nodded his head. "Almost all of them. I bought one of the last bouquets after you nearly cleaned him out."

They all laughed, as they continued discussing the opera late into the night. Thanks to Dominick, they never saw the bottom of their glasses.

THE FIRE

It was well after midnight when Giancarlo left the saloon and walked down Bourbon Street toward his home. The street was empty. He held the bag with his manuscript in his hand. There was a stillness in the air.

It was when he was about a half block away from the French Opera House when he first smelled the whiff of smoke. As he got closer to the theater, the smell grew stronger.

He walked over to the front door, but it was locked. He then went around the corner on Toulouse Street where the stage door was located. The smell of smoke was even stronger on this side of the building. As he approached the door, he felt a sudden knot in his stomach as he looked with dread upon the gaping hole at the bottom of the stage door. The left panel had been chiseled out. The chisel was lying off to the side along with the removed panel.

Giancarlo placed the bag with his manuscript on the

sidewalk. It fell over into the street, lying against the curb, but Giancarlo paid no heed, as his intention was focused on the door and its missing panel. He lifted his leg, and with one powerful kick, he kicked in the door.

Upon entering the back area of the theater, he found himself amidst numerous props and costumes for the upcoming performance of *Carmen*. There was a strong smell of smoke throughout the back of the theater. He wished at that moment that Benjamin Gill had not taken his revolver from him.

Giancarlo made his way toward the stage to see if he could find the cause of the smoke. Once he confirmed it was from the theater, he would run to get help. But the chisel and removed panel were in the forefront of his mind. That had to mean one thing: The Axman was here.

As he walked onto the stage, he noticed a haze of smoke in the theater. Giancarlo looked around but still did not see any fire. He sighed in relief as he speculated that the fire wasn't coming from the opera house but from a neighboring building.

As he was just about to turn and leave to head back through the stage door, he heard a noise in the orchestra pit. He walked to the edge of the stage and peered down. There he saw a man with his back to him standing near the conductor's stand. In one hand he held a torch while in the other, he held an axe. The flames from the torch cast eerie shadows across the man's face, concealing his identity.

Just then, Giancarlo looked up toward the second balcony, and his heart sank. Through the open doors, he could see flames in the second-story lobby. He had been wrong. The French Opera House was on fire. He then looked back down at the man in the orchestra pit. "What the hell are you doing?" Giancarlo yelled out.

Startled, the man quickly turned around, revealing his face. In an instant, Giancarlo recognized the man, the revelation striking him like a thunderbolt. All his years wondering who the Axman was, all the years chasing a mystery, how could it be that the embodiment of evil he'd pursued all these years was someone he knew.

Overwhelmed by disbelief, Giancarlo sputtered, "You? You are the Axman?"

"Yes, it's me," the Axman replied, his voice laced with a bitter tone. "The reign of the French Opera House is over. Jazz will take its rightful place of honor in New Orleans."

Giancarlo's eyes darted back to the flames seen through the balcony doors. There still might be time to save the theater, he thought, but he needed to get help. Meanwhile, the Axman stepped onto a chair in the orchestra pit and pulled himself up on the stage, his axe in one hand and the torch in the other. Giancarlo was about to run for help, but he froze in place as the Axman stood on the stage, holding the torch inches from the curtain that was pulled back near the wing.

"One step," the Axman snarled. "Take one step and I'll light it."

Giancarlo pleaded, "Please listen to me. Don't do this. Let me go get help. There is still time to save this place."

The Axman gripped the torch tighter as he held it even closer to the delicate fabric of the curtain, threatening to unleash an inferno that would surely consume everything in its path. If the curtain caught flame, the whole theater would follow.

"You don't understand," the Axman retorted. "The city needs to remember its roots and forever embrace jazz. That will only happen when this place is destroyed."

Anger and disgust coursed through Giancarlo's veins, fueling his words. "Your twisted actions have nothing to do with music. You are nothing more than a killer, plain and simple. Why do you have such hate festering in your soul? Why did you hurt so many innocent people? How could you? You even killed a child."

Before the Axman could respond, the flames from the second-story lobby burst onto the balcony. The entire area quickly became consumed with fire in a blazing inferno.

The Axman and Giancarlo both glanced up at the fiery spectacle. The Axman laughed triumphantly, proclaiming, "It's too late. It's all gone." With a flick of his wrist, he flung the torch toward the curtain as the flames began devouring the fabric with an insatiable hunger, catching the side buttresses of the stage on fire as well.

A surge of unrestrained rage grew inside Giancarlo, overpowering his very being. Without a second thought, he took three steps across the stage and lunged at the Axman, who caught the movement out of the corner of his eye. Reacting swiftly, the Axman extended the handle of his axe, striking Giancarlo squarely in the chest. Helplessly, Giancarlo tumbled headfirst into the orchestra pit, crashing onto music stands and chairs. He hit the ground with a thud, his breath short, and his chest wracked with pain.

Giancarlo tried to stand, but the shortness of breath and chest pain made it very difficult. Pressing his hand hard against his chest, he sat up and then got to his feet. The smoke became overbearing. The ceiling rafter above the orchestra pit had begun to burn.

Knowing that he was too weak to pull himself onto the stage, Giancarlo staggered toward the railing leading out into the theater. Just as he reached the railing, he saw the Axman jump from the stage down into the orchestra pit. He now held only his axe. Giancarlo bent down, trying to breathe while holding his chest. The Axman came toward him.

"They won't even find your body," the Axman hissed, his voice laden with sadistic satisfaction. "There will be nothing left. Not even your charred remains. The fire is raging and cannot be stopped. I could just let you burn. But I'll grant you the mercy of death first. After all, I am compassionate. My axe will be the end of you."

Still bending down, Giancarlo saw the Axman's sinuous shadow dancing along the orchestra pit's floor. He then looked up and, with an air of defiance, looked directly into the eyes of the Axman and said, "Go to Hell."

The Axman smiled. He was just a few steps away. Giancarlo fell to his knees, his strength fading.

The Axman lifted his axe high above his shoulders. "I am the worst spirit that has ever existed. I am a demon from hell. They will never catch me. They never have and they never will."

Just then, there was a loud shriek. A sound no human could ever make. The Axman paused for a moment and looked out into the theater. As he turned back, Giancarlo suddenly became aware of the presence of someone behind him. He turned and saw a woman in a tattered white dress and long white hair. Her red flaming eyes gleamed like the fire. She held a music stand in her hands and plunged it into the back of the Axman, making him go sprawling across the chairs and music stands in front of him. His axe fell to the floor.

Giancarlo, on his knees, looked upon the image of Marguerite. In her right hand, she held a red rose. She shrieked at the Axman, "You have destroyed my house. You have destroyed this magical place. You will suffer my revenge."

As the Axman began to try to stand, Marguerite looked up at the ceiling rafter above the orchestra pit, now fully engulfed in flames. With a wave of her hand, it came crashing down from the ceiling upon the Axman who was directly below it. It fell directly on the Axman's legs, crushing them and pinning him underneath the burning rafter. He released a blood-curdling scream as the flames burned his skin.

Marguerite quickly moved and picked up the axe. Holding the axe, she stood on top of the rafter as she yelled to Giancarlo, "Leave. Leave now."

The fire began to engulf the orchestra pit. Giancarlo, coughing, got to his feet and struggled to make his way to the back entrance of the orchestra pit. His last image was Marguerite standing on top of the rafter, axe in one hand and the red rose in the other, all the while staring down at the Axman, who was pinned. His screams of pain were drowned out by the ear-splitting, maniacal laughter of Marguerite.

Giancarlo got to the back of the theater. The props and costumes were now on fire. He fell to his knees and began to crawl toward the stage door. He found the strength to stand when he was just a few feet away. He did so and then ran out onto Toulouse Street. Once outside, he collapsed into the street.

The bag with his manuscript was still leaning up against the curb. The sounds of the fire wagons' bells, as well as people screaming for help, filled the nighttime sky as the flames and smoke bellowed out of the French Opera House. Giancarlo, lying on the street on his back, reached over for the bag with his manuscript. He grabbed it and pulled it on top of his chest. His shortness of breath was even worse now. The pain in his chest grew.

Suddenly, two men were standing over him. They kept asking him if he was alright. One of the men started yelling for someone to come help.

Giancarlo felt like he was going to lose consciousness. A man answered the call and came over to help. The man looked down and realized immediately who it was lying before him. He ripped off his jacket, placing it under Giancarlo's head. He then said, "Giancarlo, it's me. Michael Devlin. What happened? I was at a bar with friends and smelled the smoke from the fire."

Giancarlo tried to focus his eyes on the face of his friend. With a raspy voice and almost in a whisper, he said, "It's gone. The opera house is gone." He then groaned and pressed his manuscript against his chest even tighter.

The other man standing over him asked Devlin, "What's wrong with him?"

"It's his heart. This place was his heart and soul. It must have been too much for him to take to see it burn. Go get help! He needs to get to a hospital."

The man sprinted toward Bourbon Street as Giancarlo began to convulse.

Devlin's voice trembled with urgency as he called out, "Stay with me, Giancarlo. Stay with me."

Giancarlo's eyelids fluttered as he weakly extended the manuscript toward Devlin. "Finish it," Giancarlo whispered, his voice barely audible.

Devlin took the manuscript from his friend's hands.

Giancarlo then reached up and grabbed Devlin by his shirt, pulling him down toward him. His breaths were labored as he struggled to speak. "Michael… the Axman is…" Giancarlo's sentence trailed off.

Amid the chaos and the flames, Giancarlo's attention shifted abruptly. He strained to listen as the faint sound of a melody came into his ears. Someone was humming music. Not just any music, but *Lowlands Away*, the sea shanty that Maman Brigitte had sung to him.

Devlin asked, "What about the Axman?"

"Do you hear that?" Giancarlo asked, his gaze fixed over Devlin's shoulder, searching for the source of the haunting melody.

Devlin's own curiosity was piqued as he turned and looked over his own shoulder where the chaotic scene of the burning of the opera house, the frantic firemen, and the distressed onlookers. Confused, Devlin turned back toward Giancarlo and asked, "Hear what?"

Giancarlo remained silent as the melody grew in volume. And then, suddenly, his eyes widened with a mix of awe and fear, for at that moment, he saw a woman coming up from behind Devlin, humming the melody.

Devlin turned once again, desperately searching for the presence that had drawn his friend's attention but saw nothing.

Giancarlo's gasp broke the silence. The woman, clad in a black hat with her fiery red hair sticking out, peered down at him. The emerald green of her eyes met Giancarlo's gaze, and at that moment, he knew who it was before him. Maman Brigitte had come, and he knew she brought death with her.

"I'm ready," Giancarlo whispered.

Devlin, with tears in his eyes, was perplexed. "Ready for what? Giancarlo stay with me. Help is coming."

Maman Brigitte's smile grew wide. She then pointed her finger toward her left, drawing Giancarlo's attention. Giancarlo turned his head with a strained effort, desperate to see what she was pointing at.

From the shadows emerged a woman carrying a baby. Giancarlo's eyes welled with tears and his voice choked with emotion as he uttered a single word, "Piccolina." His hands stretched out, reaching for his wife and child.

His wife approached, positioning their daughter so Giancarlo could see the face of his sleeping child. A smile broke through his tears.

Devlin started shaking Giancarlo's shoulder. "Giancarlo. Giancarlo, stay with us. Come back to us."

Giancarlo's eyes flashed wide open for a moment, and he focused on his friend. He then simply said, "Spirits… live."

He turned back toward his wife and child. A final smile graced his lips as he gently closed his eyes. His arms fell to his side.

Devlin yelled out "No. Please, no!"

He then picked up the manuscript and held it close to his chest, bursting into tears. He looked toward the opera house, which was now entirely in flames. Clutching the manuscript, he looked into the face of Giancarlo.

His friend had died with a smile.

THE END OF THE WATCH

The charred remains of the opera house were all that stood the next morning. A pall sat over the entire city as word spread of the catastrophic fire. Men wept.

Firemen still were pouring water into the shell of the building to put out hotspots. The *Times-Picayune* summed up the feelings of an entire city. The article stated, *"The heart of the old French Quarter has stopped beating. Our French Opera was the one institution of the city above all which gave to New Orleans a note of distinction and lifted it out of the ranks of merely provincial cities. It was in a way the anchor of the old-world character of our municipality, and without it there will be the gravest danger of our drifting into Middle-Western commonplaceness."*

The fire was so hot that there was nothing to salvage from inside the theater. The stage door, with its missing panel, had succumbed to the flames. Strangely, the only thing to have survived was a red rose that was found where the orchestra pit was located. Luckily, there were no reported injuries from inside the theater. Loeb and Verande confirmed that they were the last ones inside the building after the rehearsal of *Carmen*. The cause of the fire was not known. The death of Giancarlo Rabito was marked down as just a tragic result of his heart giving out due to the stress of watching his beloved opera house burn.

Giancarlo's funeral was three days later. It was held at St. Mary's Italian Church. Almost all of the residents of Little Palermo were in attendance, as well as a strong showing by members of the New Orleans police force.

Devlin was asked to say a few words at the service. He spent the day before the funeral reading his friend's manuscript. He decided then and there that those in attendance would hear the words of Giancarlo Rabito.

At the funeral, he approached the altar and walked to the lectern. He placed a few pages in front of him. He took a deep breath and then said, "I had the pleasure of knowing Giancarlo, both when he was working as a detective and in retirement. This wonderful man was my friend. His word was his bond. His faithfulness to his friends and his coworkers and to our entire city was admirable. His love for his wife, and the despair at her passing, he wore openly on his heart as a testament to their union. Very early in his retirement, my friend began working on a novel. I want to read a part of it for you today. These are the words of Giancarlo."

He picked up the pages and began to read.

He always loved the city he now called home. It was an arduous journey coming from Sicily, but the belief that a better life could be had here spurred him on. It was in this city where he found a purpose, first working along the Riverfront, and then later as a detective on the police force. And it was in this city where he had found love. There is a magic to New Orleans. An old-world charm which shines through in the passions that the people exhibit while living their lives. From festivals, such as Mardi Gras, to religious days, like All Saints Day, the people here love and celebrate life. They relish being with each other and coming together as a community. And speaking of communities, there is not a stronger community than the Sicilians who live in the cramped conditions of Little Palermo. These people love each other, they love God, and they love their Sicilian heritage. They fought to preserve that heritage, even as forces rose up again and again against them. They persevered through it all. He loved these people, and that was why he dedicated his life to protecting them. He owed it to them and to the city he called home, the city of New Orleans.

Devlin placed the pages down. There was not a dry eye out in the church. He said, "My friend is dead. My friend is now at peace. My friend is now in the arms of his wife, and he is able to look upon and hold his daughter. His years of service to our community, even in his retirement, are over. Giancarlo Rabito, your watch is over. Thank you for all that you did in service to our city."

Devlin began to cry. "Music was in this man's soul. He never bought into the supposed war between opera and jazz. He loved them both. However, it is fair to say, opera had the place of prestige in his heart. And the French Opera House was his temple. Now both our grand opera house and Giancarlo are gone, and they both will be missed. Our lives must and will go on, but our friendship with Giancarlo will be in our memory for the rest of our days."

Devlin stepped down and made his way back to his seat. The priest continued with the rest of the funeral mass.

At the end of the funeral, Michael Devlin, Augustino Giorlando, Salvatore D'Antoni, Charlie Cortimiglia, Sebastian Mandina, and Frank Mooney carried the casket out of St. Mary's Italian Church.

Giancarlo was buried in the tomb with his wife in St. Louis Cemetery No. 1.

EPILOGUE

o this day, the cause of the French Opera House fire remains unknown. The Pepitone murder was the last known attack of the Axman. He vanished and was never heard from again around the city. Who he was and what happened to him remain a mystery.

As time passed, one thing became certain for the citizens of the city of New Orleans. The man who at one time held the city in a panic, soon became nothing more than a legend.

The last victim of the Axman was Frank Mooney, who less than a year later, was fired as the police chief. The inability to bring the Axman to justice was the impetus behind the firing. He returned to a railroad job, working for the Vaccaro brothers and their Standard Fruit Company. He was put in charge of their railroad lines in Honduras. He died there of a heart attack on August 22, 1923. His body was returned to New Orleans, where, accompanied by a full police honor guard, he was buried in Metairie Cemetery.

There was much talk among the leaders of the city to rebuild the French Opera House. But those plans never came to fruition. The remaining skeleton of the building was torn down and for the next forty years the area would sit vacant, until 1965, when developers erected the five-story Downtowner Motor Inn. Today, the Four Points by Sheraton occupies the location. A walk down Bourbon Street will allow one to see where the street widens out right in front of the hotel, the remnant of the old carriage lane in front of the French Opera House.

As for The Witch of the Opera House, even after the fire, people still claimed every now and again to see her haunting the area, her pastry shop, her apartment, and the apartment of her lover. Sometime in the 1950s, the new owner of the apartment where the murder occurred was renovating it. A worker found a letter stuck between the bricks on the side of the fireplace, which he'd lit to keep warm. He removed the letter and began to read it. It was a love letter from Marguerite to Pierre, expressing her undying love and asking him to come back to her. She begged him to leave Lisette and make love to her again, as they once had.

Just as the worker finished reading the letter, he pitched it into the fire. He heard a shrill shriek and then saw a woman dressed in a tattered white dress with flaming red eyes rush toward the flames. She tried to retrieve the letter, but it was too late. She gave one final shriek and then disappeared. With the letter being her only tie to Pierre, many locals believed that would be the end of the witch. She is no longer seen walking the streets of New Orleans. But even to this day, tenants who live in the apartment of her lover say they hear and see unexplained things, but only when women are present. And every now and then, after a night of lovemaking, a red rose is often found in the bed next to the lovers. For some, Marguerite is real. For others, she is just one of the many ghost stories of an old city like New Orleans.

That's the problem with spirits. Are they real, or are they just made-up images from one's mind? Did Giancarlo see his beloved opera house engulfed in flames and the scene too much for his weakened heart? Did he really encounter the Axman, or did this final showdown exist solely in the confines of his mind? Had the Axman died in the fire as a result of bad luck, being pinned by a falling rafter, or had Marguerite brought down the building as an act of revenge? Did Giancarlo actually see her, or was it just a memory from his past? Had he finally connected to the spirit world again?

We will never know.

Michael Devlin continued working for the *Times-Picayune*. He continually reached out to Rosie Cortimiglia to have her recant her testimony which he knew was to be false against the Jordanos. He wanted to fulfill the promise he had made to Frank Jordano at the trial. On February 2, 1920, that persistence paid off. Rosie, as she told the story, was visited by a vision of St. Joseph, who told her she could not die with that boy's life and the old man's liberty on her conscience. The next day she met with Michael Devlin and gave an interview in which she recanted her entire testimony. The Jordano family read the article the next day with elation. They had prayed to St. Joseph, and soon they were reunited with Iorlando and Frank when they were released from jail.

It was soon after these events that Devlin left the *Times-Picayune* and went to law school. He became a lawyer and then a district attorney to bring justice to his community. He married and had a son, whom he named John Charles, the English version of Giancarlo's name. He worked until his death in 1950.

For ten years after Giancarlo's death, his friend's manuscript sat on the desk in Devlin's study at his home. He finally decided he had to do something. So, he wrote a forward, explaining his friendship with Giancarlo and his friend's career. Mention was made why the book ended with a chapter named *"The End of the Axman"* but with nothing written for that chapter. He got the novel published in 1930. The simple title was *The Tales of a New Orleans Detective*. It became a best-selling novel.

In December 1921, the memory of the Axman came to the forefront of the citizens of New Orleans. All eyes turned to the bizarre newspaper reports out of Los Angeles, California. A woman by the name of Esther Albano had shot and killed a man in her Los Angeles home. That man was Joseph "Doc" Mumfre. Police identified Esther Albano as the former Mrs. Mike Pepitone, whose husband was the last victim of the Axman. Sometime after the murder of Mike Pepitone, she moved to California, where she met Angelo Albano, who was also originally from New Orleans. They wed, and she set up her life in California. However, soon thereafter, her husband disappeared without a trace. One day, Joseph Mumfre, the same Joseph Mumfre who was involved with the Walter Lamana abduction as well as the Di Christini-Moreci affair back in New Orleans in 1909, showed up at Esther's home and demanded money. He told Esther he had killed Angelo as a retaliation for a running feud the two had from their days back in New Orleans when they were both involved with the Black Hand. He told her if she did not pay up, she would suffer the same fate. Pretending to grab money from her dresser, she instead pulled out her revolver. She pointed it at Mumfre and unloaded the entire chamber into him. Mumfre died on the scene.

While the connection of these people to New Orleans ordinarily would have caught the attention of New Orleanians, it was Esther's statement to the police that really sent the city into a frenzy. She claimed that not only had Joseph Mumfre killed Angelo Albano, but he had also murdered her first husband, Mike Pepitone. If that was true, and Mike Pepitone was killed by the Axman, then it would lead to the conclusion that Mumfre was the Axman. The fact that Esther had said at the time of Pepitone's murder that she did not know who killed him was glossed over. However, Joseph Mumfre was not the Axman, as certain attacks in New Orleans that without a doubt were the actions of the Axman had occurred at a time when Joseph Mumfre was sitting in a New Orleans jail. The Axman remained a nameless phantom.

Salvatore D'Antoni continued living on Pirate's Alley until 1950. He then moved out to Metairie, a nearby suburb of New Orleans. Many of the residents of Little Palermo did the same, as they had finally fully assimilated into New Orleans society. Salvatore kept his house on the alley. As tourism became the staple of the New Orleans economy, he turned his old house into a Voodoo shop, and it made him a small fortune. Among his items for sale within the store was a novel, the novel by his friend, Giancarlo Rabito. Salvatore died in 1965.

With assimilation and the Sicilians moving out to the suburbs, Little Palermo soon became a footnote in history. Some locals and most visitors have no idea that at one time so many Sicilians lived in that part of the French Quarter. Tour guides speak about the French and Spanish influence without one mention that at one time, the heartbeat of the Quarter was Sicilian. The Sicilian community had stuck together and had persevered through hard times and discrimination. They had also survived the attacks of a madman, an agent of the devil himself.

The panic and hysteria that had been brought upon their community was soon just a distant memory of their past. The Axman of New Orleans now only existed in their dreams.

AUTHOR'S NOTE

Around 1900, my great-grandfather, Castranzio LoCoco, made the trip from his hometown of Monreale, a town near the Metropolitan city of Palermo, Sicily, to New Orleans. Upon arrival, he moved in with a cousin on his mother's side of the family, Pietro Giacona, who resided at the now called Beauregard-Keyes house across from the Old Ursuline Convent.

It was while living in that home that Castranzio wed his wife, Julia Lima, who had come to New Orleans from the capital city of Palermo, Sicily. They would eventually move to a house on Esplanade Avenue, very close to the French Market and "Little Palermo." They would bring into this world 6 sons and 2 daughters. A few years later, Castranzio purchased a 400 acre sugarcane farm in Lockport, Louisiana, and moved his family down to the Bayou.

One of his children, Vincent "Mustache" LoCoco, was my grandfather. As a young man, he left the sugar plantation and settled in New Orleans, working on the riverfront, and eventually for a produce company. A few years later, he married my grandmother, Mamie "Sugar" Tumminello, whose family had arrived in New Orleans from the small Sicilian town of Cefalù.

Our Sundays were always spent at my grandparents' home on Wilson Drive in Mid-City New Orleans, which they shared with some of their other relatives. (A tradition found in many families.) Pasta dishes and other Italian foods dashed with olive oil were always on the menu, as well as homemade desserts, or, for a special occasion, a pastry or some sort of treat from Brocato's.

As a child, I still remember vestiges of the Sicilian experience of New Orleans when I would go to the French Quarter with my grandfather and father, who was also a Vincent. (It's true that once Italians like a name, they stick with it.) I vividly remember the produce stands still run by Sicilians, and the Central and Progress grocery stores, where everyone still punctuated their conversations with Sicilian words or phrases. And then eating lunch at the Napoleon House, run by the Impastato family back then, where we would eat a muffuletta, and end with a Cassata dessert (which came from Brocato's) and a delicious, creamy cappuccino.

Regrettably, in today's New Orleans, the once vibrant "Little Palermo" enclave has vanished. A stroll down Royal Street or Chartres Street might not hint at the once erstwhile bustling Sicilian community - unless you know where to look.

St. Mary's Italian Church remains a steadfast witness to the passage of time. Though its doors are closed for regular Sunday services, the church still echoes with the joyous union of couples who choose its sacred space for their weddings. A poignant contrast unfolds just across the street at the Beauregard-Keyes house, where tours unveil the dramatic tale of Pietro Giacona's confrontation with the Black Hand members on the back porch, a narrative that still captivates visitors to this day.

The Monteleone Hotel built by an Italian immigrant stands near Canal Street. Visitors flock to sit at its iconic Carousel Bar, where they take in the sights and sounds of New Orleans Jazz singers, including Louis Prima's daughter, Lena, who treats her listeners to her father's greatest hits.

Central Grocery remains a beloved destination, drawing both locals and tourists alike who seek to indulge in the renowned experience of savoring their iconic muffulettas.

Brocato's moved out of the French Quarter in 1979 to mid-city. Its Ursuline Street roots are still visible as evidenced by the enduring name etched on the sidewalk outside its original location. Stepping into their current store is akin to a delightful journey through time, with a vintage cappuccino machine gracing the back counter and glass-enclosed shelves showcasing the delectable pastries and renowned gelato they're celebrated for. A visit is incomplete without witnessing the skilled hands of the workers, who tirelessly craft each individual cannoli by hand, ensuring a truly authentic and unforgettable treat for patrons.

Mandina's on Canal Street was turned into a restaurant in 1932. Now run by Sebastian Mandina's grandson, Tommy, and his daughter, Cindy, the restaurant is known for its Creole and Italian dishes. And twice a year, an Italian Night is held at the establishment, where the patrons are treated to a four-course meal and are entertained by the Italian-American music of Frank Sinatra and Dean Martin sung by a local lounge singer, the music of Puccini sung by a local soprano, and tales of the Sicilian experience of New Orleans being told to the attentive crowd by me.

And of course, you can still find the true Sicilian experience on St. Joseph's Day, where throughout the city you can find St. Joseph Altars, festivals, and parades.

I cherish the memories of my youth, and am truly grateful that I was able to grow up at a time when one could still see the strong Sicilian presence in the city.

And now we get to the Axman story.

His identity remains shrouded in mystery. According to some accounts, he might have been affiliated with the Black Hand, while others propose the possibility of the Axman being numerous copycats employing a similar *modus operandi*. Additionally, there are those who speculate that he was a phantom, which they argue explains his elusive nature and the inability to capture him.

When one reads the old newspaper articles from that time, you can feel the fear and tension that ratcheted the city. I hope I've been able to capture a little bit of that in the novel to give my readers a sense of what it was like living in the city.

For fictional reasons, I changed the names of our two leading characters, Giancarlo Rabito and Michael Devlin.

Giancarlo Rabito is based on a real detective from that time period. His name was John D'Antonio. He was a nationally known expert on the Black Hand. He investigated the earlier crimes of the Cleaver. At the time of the Axman attacks in 1918-1919, he was retired. He provided an interview to Jim Coulton, a reporter with the *Times-Picayune* in which he provided to the public what he believed they were facing—a cold-bloodied killer.

Michael Devlin was based on Jim Coulton, a real news reporter for the *Times-Picayune* back then. When researching the Axman murders, Coulton's reporting covers almost all of the attacks. He was relentless in trying to free the Jordanos from jail and having Rosie Cortimiglia change her story.

All the attacks discussed in the novel are based on the true crimes that occurred. The letter to the *Times-Picayune* is published verbatim as it appeared in the newspaper. Some scholars believe it was not written by the Axman. Others disagree. There is no doubt that the letter caused panic in the city, and the citizens did indeed listen to jazz all night long. For a city that always looks for a reason to throw a party, they gladly took part to avoid any attacks.

Upon my inspecting the original newspaper on microfilm during the research for this novel, a discovery emerged that appears to have eluded scholarly attention. The editors at the *Times-Picayune*, in recounting their reception of the letter, mentioned, *"The letter received by the Times-Picayune came in Friday's mail. It was posted in New Orleans, is written in a clear, easily read hand, <u>and is similar in some respects to letters that have been sent to Superintendent of Police Mooney from time to time while police were investigating the ax murder mysteries</u>."* (Emphasis added) Notably, there is no record in my findings or even mentions of other letters addressed to Chief Mooney. It raises the possibility that within overlooked or misplaced case files lie these letters, presenting an opportunity, given today's technological advancements, to determine if they share the same handwriting as the letter pertaining to the night of jazz.

Some investigators think that killings after 1919 in the Northern part of the State of Louisiana were the actions of the Axman. Others disagree. What ultimately happened to the Axman remains unknown. His fate, a mystery, as he continues to be an elusive puzzle, with his identity and actions shrouded in uncertainty.

There have been many books, both nonfiction and fiction, written on the Axman of New Orleans, who like Jack the Ripper, has captivated people over all these years.

I will not mention all those books but would like to name four which were instrumental in assisting me with the writing of this book. Some of the books listed cover a range of topics on New Orleans, but provide great details on the Axman's crimes.

The definitive nonfiction work is *The Axeman of New Orleans, A True Story* by Miriam C. Davis, published by Chicago Review Press. Through meticulous research, Davis presents a compelling argument against Joseph "Doc" Mumfre being the Axeman, highlighting his incarceration during some of the attacks as a key factor that contradicts the theory of his involvement.

A great nonfiction story of this time period is *The Empire of Sin, A Story of Sex, Jazz, Murder and the Battle of Modern New Orleans*, by Gary Krist, published by Broadway Books.

A fictional short story, *Mussolini and the Axeman's Jazz*, by Poppy Z. Brite, published by Open Road Media, provides a wonderful description of the time period.

And lastly, *Italian Louisiana, History, Heritage & Tradition* by Alan G. Gauthreaux, published by The History Press, gives a compelling sense of what life was like in Little Palermo.

Crafting a novel is a peculiar journey, a solitary endeavor where the act of writing unfolds in isolation. However, the realization of the final project involves the collective effort of numerous hands, transforming the solitary process into a collaborative project. Like all of my earlier novels, *The Devil's Jazz* is a testament to that teamwork, and I find myself indebted to the many individuals who played crucial roles in bringing this story to fruition. Their contributions have left an indelible mark on the pages, and I extend my heartfelt gratitude to each one who contributed to seeing the manuscript cross the finish line.

I extend my deepest gratitude to my friend, Kathy Schott, as she embodies the indispensable ally every writer requires. Kathy graciously devotes her time to reading chapters or even individual paragraphs throughout my writing journey, ensuring the narrative coherence, the alignment of characters' actions with the storyline, and the overall structural integrity of the tale. Kathy has consistently played this crucial role for me, and every one of my novels has benefited significantly from her involvement. I owe her a profound debt of thanks for transforming my aspiration of becoming a writer into a tangible reality.

To my aunt, Janet Foret LoCoco, I thank you for your ability to assist me in developing my stories. Your own writing provided to me the determination and confidence to become a writer myself. Janet married my uncle, Castranzio

"Teddy" LoCoco. They lived in Lockport, Louisiana on the same sugarcane plantation bought by my great grandfather, Castranzio. Janet's discussions about my own family history was instrumental in bringing this story to life. After the death of her husband in 2017, the sugar plantation was finally sold. It had been in my family for over 80 years. Janet still lives by Bayou Lafourche, where she is a writer of Cajun love stories.

The next person I cannot thank enough. Her name is Ana Grigoriu-Voicu. She is a talented artist from Stuttgart, Germany. She has designed every one of my book covers from my second novel on. All it takes is a conversation with her as to what the novel is about, and what I envision as the perfect cover, and within no time at all, her magical creation finds its way to my inbox. Ana, I cherish the opportunity we have had to working together and to your expert touch on each and everyone of my creations.

Cassidy Sachs is a professional editor. She edited my manuscript, and helped transform the book into what you are reading. She fell in love with the story, which I could tell in the care with which she offered her advice, making sure to keep my voice throughout the entire process. It was a joy working with her, and I thank her for all of her assistance. Of course, any errors in the text, both grammatically and structurally fall at the feet of me as the author.

This book is dedicated to the Sicilian immigrants who settled in New Orleans. I extend my heartfelt thanks to Franco Alessandrini, an Italian immigrant to the Crescent City, for generously allowing me to feature an image of his magnificent sculpture, *The Monument to the Immigrant*, in the dedication of this book. Positioned along the banks of the Mississippi River, the statue stands at the very site where numerous Sicilian immigrants initially landed. Crafted from white Carrara marble, the sculpture portrays an immigrant family on one side and, on the other, a woman resembling the figurehead of an old sailing ship - a poignant reminder of both the immigrants' arrival and a respectful acknowledgment of the significance of the Port of New Orleans.

To my mother, Lynda Goodier LoCoco (An *Americana* as referred to by my Italian Great-Grandmother) and my two sisters, Pamela LoCoco Montz and Elizabeth LoCoco Doody, I thank each of you for your support and the time spent reading countless versions of the manuscript.

To my late father, Vincent T. LoCoco, I thank him for passing down to me his love for and respect for the Sicilian culture of New Orleans. One of the greatest gifts a parent can give a child is the passing down of the invaluable treasure of family heritage. His teachings have enriched my life in countless ways, and I carry forward his legacy with pride and reverence.

Growing up, my father transformed New Orleans into a playground for my sisters and me, where every weekend was an adventure filled with historical revelations and fantastical stories, both told with equal abandon, sparking our imaginations and nurturing our understanding of the captivating blend of reality and myth that defines our city. His passionate storytelling not only entertained us but instilled in us a profound appreciation and love for our city and our heritage, which I know we passed down to our own children. I often think that in today's world of instant news and nothing but the facts, the children of today are denied the legacy of legend and lore, robbing them of the magic and wonder that shaped our cultural identity and fosters creativity.

I extend my heartfelt thanks to my good friend, Cinda Dimaggio who expertly helped me craft into words my vision of Maman Brigitte, from her hair sticking out of her top hat down to her skirt with the skull belt.

Two readers of the manuscript must get special acknowledgement for their contributions, Brian Morgan and Elisa Speranza.

Brian Morgan is a former cloistered monk, former Artistic Director of Opera Quotannis (New York) and former Programme Annotator of the New Orleans Opera. His writings on æsthetics have appeared in various publications, including *Opera News* and he is the author of the definitive book on the life of Norman Treigle. His input into my novel and his encouragement are greatly appreciated.

I met Elisa Speranza, a yankee transplant to New Orleans, just a few years ago upon the completion of her novel, *The Italian Prisoner*. Since meeting her, we have commiserated together on the world of writing and publishing. We have also given talks together to groups on our writings. When I first mentioned to Elisa that I wanted to write a story about the Axman of New Orleans, her encouragement gave me the drive to tell this story, and for that I am eternally grateful.

Fr. Patrick Williams serves as the Vicar General of the Archdiocese of New Orleans and holds the esteemed position of the current rector of the St. Louis Cathedral. However, our connection runs deeper than ecclesiastical titles - he was once my parish priest at St. Pius X Catholic Church in New Orleans and, beyond that, a cherished friend. In 1998, he presided at my wedding. He currently resides on the serene grounds of the Old Ursuline Convent in the French Quarter.

On a beautiful, cold Thursday December morning, Fr. Pat took me, along with my wife, daughter, my sister Beth, and nephew, Ian, on a tour of Ursuline Convent and St. Mary's Italian Church. This church truly was the heartbeat of the Sicilian community of Little Palermo. Its intimate interior, remarkably beautiful, resonates with the echoes of history, each wall whispering tales of a vibrant past. I could not help but conjure up images of my own family attending church, praying with the other Sicilian immigrants to the city. Perhaps, even praying to remain safe from the terrible deeds of the Axman.

We also toured the Beauregard-Keyes house across the street, and then ended our morning with a fabulous lunch at The Napoleon House, a setting that offered the perfect occasion to immerse ourselves in the captivating stories of New Orleans' past.

I extend my deepest gratitude to my wife, Wendy, and my children, Matthew and Ellie. Their encouragement has been an invaluable force, not only shaping my creative endeavors but also enriching our shared experiences. Many a novel has been completed on the balcony of a Florida beach house overlooking the Gulf of Mexico on a quick get away with my family so dad could finish his novel, drawing inspiration from both the views and the love of family. To Wendy, Matthew, and Ellie - your unwavering support and the moments we've shared have been the driving force behind my literary pursuits. I am profoundly grateful for the encouragement, inspiration, and love that each of you brings into my life. Thank you.

This is my first novel that takes place wholly in the city of New Orleans, a city in which I was born, raised, attended school, met and married my wife, and raised our two children. A city for which my wife and I fought back to return to after the loss of our home in Hurricane Katrina.

Despite all its imperfections, it's a city that continues to hold on to its culture and spirit. It's a war worth fighting. It's what makes New Orleans what it is.

Music is a vital ingredient of that culture and spirit. New Orleans really does have a love affair with music. It punctuates each and every celebration, from weddings and funerals, to sporting events and Mardi Gras. Music is the pulse of the city.

Sadly, the French Opera House was never rebuilt after the devastating fire of 1919. The cause of the fire to this day in unknown. Photos of the exterior and the interior show us of today what a magnificent structure it was and how attending a performance there must have been a spectacular event.

I am often asked if the great opera tenor, Enrico Caruso, ever sang at the house. He did not, although in 1920 he did sing in New Orleans at the Athenaeum Theater, an event witnessed by my grandfather.

Exploring the narratives of New Orleans' bygone landmarks within the pages of the novel, such as the enchanting French Opera House, now relegated to the realm of memory, has been a source of immense joy for me. Among these evocative spots, Spanish Fort holds a special place with a deep connection to me.

I recall stories from my mother's grandmother, Rose,

about how she and her husband, Ben Gill, would dine and dance at Spanish Fort during weekend getaways. Today at the site, all that remains are the weathered remnants of Fort St. John and a gated-off, unnamed burial spot with headstone. It was at Fort St. John that as a child I played "key to the fort" with my dad and my sisters, and then as a father myself, played the same game there with my own kids.

Residing in a historical city intertwines your life with eras long gone; every step you take echoes with the resonance of those who preceded you. In this graceful dance between the past and present, New Orleans emerges as a profound teacher. Through the echoes of history, the city imparts invaluable lessons, urging its inhabitants to savor the sweetness of good times and hold dear the precious moments that transcend the sands of time. It teaches us to look beyond adversities and the mundane, eagerly anticipating the end of a workweek to embrace free time and spread joy.

In New Orleans, these lessons aren't just words; they are a way of life. We don't just weather the storms; we dance in the rain. We celebrate in the face of challenges. We even bring our passion for joy to our cuisine. Ultimately, we let the good times roll, echoing the resilience of those who came before us.

For over 35 years, I have ridden with the Krewe of Thoth on the Sunday before Mardi Gras. Perhaps nothing better sums up the New Orleans spirit then the annual Mardi Gras season. It's a time where celebration becomes a remedy for the soul, and where the pulse of the city beats to the rhythm of joy.

It is true. Once New Orleans touches your soul, she never lets go.

At the heart of my novel lies the indomitable spirit of

those who found a home in New Orleans, particularly the Sicilian community. Against the backdrop of prejudices, the shadows of the Black Hand, and the haunting presence of the Axman, they not only survived but thrived.

Their story is a testament to the resilience embedded in the very soul of this city.

Chip LoCoco
New Orleans, Louisiana
March 19, 2024 - St. Joseph's Day

ABOUT THE AUTHOR

Chip LoCoco's love of music, stories, and of his Sicilian-American heritage shines in all of his novels. His novels have won awards and have been ranked on Amazon as Bestsellers and Top Rated novels.

His first novel was *Tempesta's Dream - A Story of Love, Friendship and Opera*. *Tempesta's Dream* was awarded the Pinnacle Award in Historical Fiction.

Chip's next novel, *A Song for Bellafortuna*, forms Book 1 of his much beloved Bellafortuna Series. That novel won the B.R.A.G Medallion Award in Historical Fiction.

Book 2 of the Bellafortuna series is *Saving the Music*. It has been listed as a Top Rated novel on Amazon and as a Bestseller in Italian Historical Fiction. It was selected as the Winner of the 2022 American Fiction Award in Historical

Fiction. It was also named as a Finalist in the 2022 International Book Awards in the Historical Fiction Category and Best Fiction Cover Design, and awarded the Gold Medal in Historical Fiction in the Global Book Awards. It was also selected by Kirkus Reviews as one of the Great Indie Books Worth Discovering. In 2025, it was optioned for a film.

Sicilian Melody is Book 3 of the Bellafortuna Series, and is the final chapter of the Series. It was named a Finalist in the Best Book Awards in Historical Fiction.

The Devil's Jazz is his first novel set entirely in his hometown of New Orleans. The manuscript was selected as a finalist in the prestigious William Faulkner Literary Contest.

A true son of New Orleans, Chip attended Jesuit High School, Loyola University, and Loyola Law School. Chip is an estate planning attorney in New Orleans, where he lives with his wife, Wendy, and two children, Matthew and Ellie. He is a member of the Italian American Writers Association and has been awarded the Buddy D Media Award for his contributions to the Italian-American community of New Orleans. Chip has given extensive talks to book clubs, organizations, and has appeared on WWL Radio in New Orleans and The Catholic Channel on Sirius Radio.

For more information, visit his website at www.vincentlococo.com.

facebook.com/Authorchiplococo

x.com/VincentBLoCoco

instagram.com/chiplococo_author

amazon.com/author/vincentlococo

youtube.com/@VincentBChipLoCoco98

THE MUSIC OF THE DEVIL'S JAZZ

We have put together a Spotify Playlist with music from the novel along with some music from New Orleans to give the reader a flavor of this magical city. Be sure to follow it to get updates.

The Spotify Playlist can be found as:

THE MUSIC OF THE DEVIL'S JAZZ

MORE INFORMATION

If you would like to let others know about this novel, please consider leaving a review on Amazon.

If your group or book club is interested in inviting Mr. LoCoco to discuss his novels or the writing process in person or by Zoom, please use the contact form on his website at www.vincentlococo.com.

Also, please subscribe to Mr. LoCoco's Blog on his website to receive updates, news, and discussions on all things Italian.